MRV

LOVE IS A GAMBLER

Roxanne Haldane, the daughter of an English newspaper baron, was officially in Lac to cover the forthcoming speedboat race between Adam Douglas of Great Britain and Gil Rogers of America. Unofficially, she had come because she was madly in love with Adam, who was scarcely aware of her existence. When she discovered there was another woman in Adam's life, she tried to ease her troubled heart by turning to the attractive Gil Rogers . . .

Books by Maysie Greig
Published by The House of Ulverscroft:

DOCTOR IN EXILE

MAYSIE GREIG

LOVE IS A GAMBLER

Complete and Unabridged

ULVERSCROFT
Leicester

First published in Great Britain in 1974 by
Robert Hale and Company
London

First Large Print Edition
published 1999
by arrangement with
Robert Hale Limited
London

British Library CIP Data

Greig, Maysie, *1902 –*
Love is a gambler.—Large print ed.—
Ulverscroft large print series: romance
1. Love stories
2. Large type books
I. Title
823.9'12 [F]

ISBN 0–7089–4122–2

Published by
F. A. Thorpe (Publishing) Ltd.
Anstey, Leicestershire
Set by Words & Graphics Ltd.
Anstey, Leicestershire
Printed and bound in Great Britain by
T. J. International Ltd., Padstow, Cornwall

This book is printed on acid-free paper

For my son Robert Murray,
who wrote the words of the song
Love is a Gambler
for me.

1

'Excuse me,' said the young man, crossing his long thin legs in order to lean forward more comfortably, 'but this is your first assignment, isn't it?'

The pretty fair-haired girl facing him looked at him in some annoyance. All the same a faint flush rose to her temples. She had been very conscious for some time of his rather intense and faintly disturbing scrutiny ever since he had entered the train at Basle. She was fairly used to men admiring her for she was certainly pretty. Her windswept blonde hair was like dull beaten gold, her eyes, not blue but almost purple, were wide and inquiring. Often they were amused but sometimes in their depths was the look of a hurt child. The pencilled brows above them were just a shade darker than her hair. The face was small and quite lovely — disturbingly so.

Martin Cheswick had been trying for the past hour to resist making her acquaintance. She looked rather too intent for his liking. He'd learned during the past few years of travelling about from one place to another, from one country to another, doing publicity work for the European Publicity Bureau, that intent-looking young girls as attractive as she was can get you into one heck of a lot of trouble. They didn't take their love affairs like sportswomen. They looked beaten and crushed when the affair came to an end and a fellow felt an awful brute. Martin Cheswick didn't like feeling a brute, and it usually took him at least a month to escape the sense of guilt he felt. He preferred the snappy sophisticated pieces who were just as liable to hurt *you*. That was fair . . . it was all in the game — the comic or tragic game of love — and Martin liked to think of his love affairs on a comic, rather than a tragic basis. But now he was waiting for the girl to answer his question.

'How did you know this was my first assignment?' she challenged him finally. She had a low, sweet, rather husky voice.

He grinned across at her, a pleasant engaging grin. It had got him out of many a difficult corner in the past. 'You've been looking out of the window taking notes with such a desperate concentration. No old hand would be so determined. They'd lie back and relax, smoke a cigarette and later, if they had to write about it at all, draw most of it from their imagination.'

2

'But that would be cheating the public,' the fair-haired girl said angrily, then added, 'How did you know I was a journalist?'

'Those sheets of paper. They're used in newspaper offices. I'm not wholly unacquainted with the Press.' He tried not to let his last remark sound smug.

'You're a journalist yourself?'

'Not a journalist — a publicity man. It's not quite the same thing, though very nearly. I have to sell *you* publicity.' He grinned again and added: 'Almost throttle you with it, if I can. *Your* job is to see through the welter of lies I give you and decide what is worth printing and what isn't.'

'But need they be lies?'

He felt uncomfortable and angry. Even though this might be her first assignment, she must know something about the publicity racket. He ran a hand over his thin rather battered-looking face. He heard himself mumble, 'Maybe they're not all lies, but sometimes you've precious little to build a good story upon.'

'I see.' She nodded slowly. 'You have to help facts along with your imagination. Well, all good journalists do that, don't they?'

He laughed. 'Certainly, but they mustn't be found out. Readers expect a journalist to tell the truth.'

'Then I shouldn't like being in publicity.' She lowered her eyes to her notes rather determinedly.

'Look here!' he said irritably. 'How long have you been working on a newspaper?'

She kept her head bent. 'A few months.'

'A few months!' He repeated it almost grimly. 'And before that you were at school?'

'Finishing school, here in Switzerland, near Vitry-sur-Lac.'

He didn't comment that working girl journalists didn't usually come out of finishing schools in Switzerland. But then he had known from the first that she wasn't an ordinary working journalist. She wasn't tough enough.

'It's going to be some jamboree,' he commented. 'The little town of Vitry will be like Rip Van Winkle, waking up after a hundred years' sleep, and it's slept pretty soundly since the war. But now all the hotels will be crowded, guests billeted in every available room in every available cottage, all the restaurants and the Casino packed every night. The streets of Vitry will be paved with gold for its inhabitants for the next few weeks.'

'It's an awfully pretty little place,' she said, and glancing up she suddenly smiled at him. She was very excited about this first assignment even though she would only write her impressions in the form of gossip paragraphs. Her press baron father had already sent over an experienced reporter to cover the speedboat race and the week of preparation. She aimed at giving short and vivid sketches of the notable people who had come from all over Europe to watch the speed trials and race — not only speedboat enthusiasts but that mysterious and charmed group known as the international set. She was determined not to fall down on this job. She had stormed her father into allowing her to come. Her father controlled all the newspapers and magazines of the great Oxenham Group.

'Baby, you wouldn't know what to do with the job of a gossip writer,' Lord Oxenham had said wearily, when she had been trying to talk him into giving her the assignment. She had got mad and had told him she knew quite well what she should write about — what would interest the public.

She had been persuading him into doing anything she wanted to do since her mother had died when she was seven years old, and Lord Oxenham wasn't an easily persuaded man. In the huge Press building over which he ruled — Oxenham House, off Fleet Street — no one would have dared to try to persuade him into doing anything on which he didn't immediately give a snort of approval. But Roxanne took no notice of whether his snort was approval or disapproval, she just kept sweetly, determinedly on until she had her own way. She had been like that since a child, quite determined in the sweetest and most reasonable way. She was probably the only living soul of whom Lord Oxenham was afraid.

'I wonder if either Douglas or Rogers will set up a new speed record,' Martin Cheswick now remarked. 'They're both out to try for it. Gosh! I wish I knew which one of them to put my money on!'

'You'd put it on Adam Douglas, surely?' Her voice was half scandalised, half angry.

'You mean because he's English, and incidentally, a great friend of mine? But I thought in sport you were supposed to keep an open mind: let the best man win, no false patriotism, all that sort of thing.'

'I know,' she agreed soberly and seriously. 'But Adam Douglas isn't just an *ordinary* man who is out for a world speed record, is he?'

'No?' he asked in a faintly amused voice. 'Just what do you mean by saying he's not just an ordinary man?'

'Well,' she frowned slightly, nibbling her

lower lip as though trying to think out what she meant. 'Speedboat racing is almost a religion with him, isn't it?'

'Because of his father?'

'Of course. Motor-boat racing, breaking one record after another, was his father's *whole life*. It wasn't just a sport. And his son Adam must feel the same way. Look how he's been setting up one record after another and then trying desperately to break it ever since his father died. It's only recently he's been unfortunate.' She broke off as though afraid she had let her emotions run away with her.

Martin Cheswick, who had few illusions, if any, smiled across at her tolerantly. 'You're quite sure that personal vanity doesn't come into it? It comes into most things we do, you know.'

'I'm sure personal vanity has nothing to do with Adam Douglas's love of racing boats. I met him once.' She looked away from him through the carriage window on to the landscape. The train was winding its way through mountain ranges. She looked up to distant snow-clad peaks, then to huge boulders and lower down to a colourful carpet of Alpine wild flowers. It was beautiful. There was so much that was sordid and uncertain in life to-day that out here on these mountain

7

slopes with the clean fresh air she felt in a completely different world.

She had met Adam Douglas at a house party two years ago. She had been over from Switzerland on a vacation. She had thought him wonderful, not only for the fact that he had just broken the latest speedboat record in his famous boat *Scotsman III*, though that in itself would have made him a hero in any young girl's eyes. But he was pleasant and modest, a young man about six foot two, with broad shoulders, lightish brown hair and grey-brown eyes. He had talked to her as an equal, not attempting to laugh at her schoolgirlish enthusiasm, *making her feel that her conversation was helping him,* even inspiring him. She had adored him ever since, and soon she would meet him again. She hadn't seen much of him that week-end. There had been many others in the house party. Marlene Farrar for one, the movie star, who was supremely lovely with her rich auburn hair and the figure of a wood-nymph.

Marlene had been very much in the news at that time. She had been making two pictures simultaneously. But lately she had seemed to drop out of things. No one seemed to know what had become of her.

One evening during the house-party Marlene

had come over and said, as they had all stood on the wide veranda drinking cocktails, 'You have rather a crush on Adam, haven't you, my dear? But need you make it so obvious?'

Roxie had felt confused and embarrassed, but the grit and determination which had built up the Oxenham fortune had stood her in good stead. 'Even at my age, I think I know what I want,' she had replied.

Marlene had merely looked at her, amusement on her lovely heart-shaped face. 'You're a queer kid. How old *are* you, by the way?'

'Seventeen,' Roxie had returned.

Marlene had shrugged her thin shoulders — she was almost painfully thin, even for a movie star. Her smile this time had been warm and pleasant. 'Well, good luck. As things are, I should be the last person wishing you that, but although I suspect you're a brat I like a brat who speaks up for herself.'

She had moved away and a moment later Roxie had seen her over by Adam's side. He had one hand in his pocket and her hand was slipped carelessly through his arm. It was an oddly possessive gesture and it had disturbed Roxie. She was too much infatuated with him to be able to accept it easily. She would have liked to have gone across the balcony and snatched Marlene's hand away from his arm. Probably Adam himself would have been most startled. Roxie knew only too well that the interest he had shown in her had been mainly prompted by kindness. But it won't always be like that, she'd promised herself. In a year she'd be grown up. She would make him notice her then.

2

The train was slowing down. They were arriving at Vitry-sur-Lac, circling the shores of the lake which was sparkling in the glowing sunset that lighted the whole countryside, drenching it and the surrounding mountains in shades of purple and gold. The lake was so still you could see all the colours of the sunset reflected in it as though it were a mirror.

The town itself nestled at one end of the lake, the buildings caught the dying sun's glow; the church steeple looked as though it had been made out of pure gold.

Roxie leaned forward, staring towards it eagerly. It was a gem of a small Swiss town, but how on earth was it going to hold all the people who would flock to it for the race? She spoke the query aloud.

Martin chuckled. 'Trust the Swiss. They're not only born hoteliers, but they'd take bricks out of their very walls to fit in another tourist — at least if he or she were gilded with American dollars. The town may split at the seams, but we'll all be fitted in, don't worry! Where are you staying?'

'At the Excelsior Palace.'

He grinned across at her impishly. 'Your paper *must* think a hell of a lot of your work! Not many sob-sisters will be staying at the Excelsior Palace.'

She flushed. 'But surely it's the *logical* place to stay? I'm sure to meet people there, and meeting them and writing about them is my job. I understand that both Mr. Rogers and Mr. Douglas are staying there.'

'Naturally. The hotel would put them up free for the publicity value even if they couldn't afford to meet the bills. Their respective teams will stay at more modest hotels.'

'But surely they're both rich — they must be to go in for a sport like speedboat racing?'

He chuckled. 'Who said it was a sport for them? When you get to the top rank in any sport, as they have, it ceases to be a sport; it becomes a darned hard taskmaster.'

'Then why do they keep on with it?'

He shrugged. 'Maybe they're afraid to give it up for their self-prestige, or maybe for financial reasons. It might also be they have no real job to turn to: anyhow, they'd be out of the limelight. The cruellest thing for anyone to face is to have been a celebrity and then to become a has-been. You can't live on the past. No ex-sportsman or even ex-royalty has ever been happy doing so. You've got to keep going — even if it kills you. And it may easily do that. The water barrier may hit one or other of them at any time.'

There was a slight pause. A little shiver ran through her.

He went on: 'All top-rate athletes' nerves go to pot at times, but it is especially true of men who race planes or cars or speedboats. They're under a terrific tension and that overflows into their ordinary lives — *if* they have any ordinary lives, which I doubt.'

'You don't think men like Gilbert Rogers or Adam Douglas lead ordinary lives?'

He laughed. 'I bet they're both as neurotic and highly-strung as any unbalanced society woman who lives on a psychiatrist's couch!'

Roxie didn't like that. She had built up her own image of Adam Douglas. She wasn't going to have it spoiled by this cynically minded young publicity man.

She changed the subject: 'Where are you going to stay?'

'Not anywhere as impressive as the Excelsior Palace, the Hotel de Suisse as a matter of fact, a modest little bistro at the far end of the town. Either my firm can't afford it or they don't consider me worthy of more expensive accommodation. You must be very worthy — or lucky,' he amended.

Again she had the feeling he was making fun of her. She concentrated on getting her hand luggage stacked together. He helped her down with her suit-cases and offered to carry them off the platform for her to the hotel bus. 'It will save you the porter's tip, if that's any consideration to you,' he said with a wry smile. 'Or maybe you'd like to give *me* the tip. I'm sure I could use it before the week is out.'

She said coldly, 'I feel certain your publicity agency doesn't keep you as short of cash as all that.'

He said seriously, 'We're a fairly new concern and all of us have to scrabble along on a shoe-string until the firm really gets going.'

'You've been with them long?' she asked as the train shuddered to a standstill.

'About two years. That's given me one trip to America and another to the Argentine. I met Gil Rogers in America.'

'Did you?' Her tone was faintly antagonistic. She wasn't prepared to like Gilbert Rogers since he was Adam's rival.

'He's a good chap, but in my view slightly insane. He inherited a whack of money from his father, but instead of loafing about like any sane normal person, he seems to spend all his time trying, as I said before, to kill

14

himself to prove he's something in his own right. Mad!' He said explosively.

'You think Adam Douglas is mad too for dedicating himself to speedboat racing as his father did?'

'Not mad in quite the same way. I think with Adam it may be mainly a commercial venture.'

She almost snatched her suit-cases out of his hand, but already he was handing the suit-cases out of the window. She saw that the platform was crowded, not only with passengers, but most of the local inhabitants had come to watch the arrival of the train.

Roxie adjusted her small green beret and followed Martin. As she stepped down on to the platform in the fading glow of the sunset, many eyes turned to stare at her — she was an extremely pretty girl. In most other countries she might have been given wolf whistles, but a Swiss peasant is a naturally good-mannered young man.

3

The suite reserved for Roxie at the Excelsior Palace had every luxury, but Roxie, having mainly travelled with her father, was used to luxury. The manager himself accompanied her to the suite, bowing her into it, showing her all its attractions — the balcony leading out of the sitting-room, hanging almost over the lake, the delightful tiled bathroom, the cocktail cabinet built into the wall which opened itself out when you pressed a button.

M. Henriot smiled: 'Mademoiselle will see that some invitations have already arrived and are on her mantelshelf. There is one here,' he extracted a square white envelope from his pocket, 'for Mademoiselle, with the management's compliments. We are giving a champagne cocktail party to-night before the Grand Ball. Our little party is in honour of M. Douglas and M. Rogers, both of whom are our guests. I venture to hope Mademoiselle will accept.'

'I shall be delighted,' Roxie smiled.

She stood a moment looking about her after the door had closed behind him. She felt taut with excitement. She was actually here and

Adam Douglas was in the same hotel. She would meet him again this evening. The invitation said 7.30 p.m.

She took off her green travelling beret, threw it down on the couch and stepped out on to the balcony. The sunset had faded, the lake was in shadow, but the stars had begun to come out and the sky was turning a brilliant blue-black; the slight wind which came up from the lake made the air clean and fresh. She breathed deeply as she ran her fingers through her hair, shaking it out, letting the breeze run through it.

'Hello, lady with the silver hair!' a man's voice said from the balcony which ran alongside her own. It was a laughing voice with a slight American accent.

She turned, and even in the deepening twilight she recognised Gilbert Rogers from the many newspaper photographs she'd seen of him. He was even better looking in the flesh with his very dark hair and his finely etched aquiline features. He was fairly tall and very slim. She found herself thinking he had the sort of face and figure you might associate with a gigolo, but he wasn't effeminate looking. Oddly, he didn't look the sporting type either. Adam looked the typical sportsman. Gil Rogers looked more like a dilettante in the field of arts.

'Hello!' she replied smiling. Gil Rogers wasn't as good copy for the English Press as Adam, but he was good enough copy to rate some notice.

He leaned further over his balcony. The rising moon played on his rather dark skin. 'Is your hair really silver?' he asked.

She shook her head and answered him quite seriously, 'No, but it's fair.'

'Hush!' he said, raising a finger and shaking it at her. 'You mustn't disillusion me: I like to think it's silver. Have you come out of fairyland to see the race?'

'I've come out of England to see the race.'

He straightened and smiled across at her. 'You're rather prosaic, aren't you? Can't you pretend you've just come out of fairyland?'

'I don't much like pretence. I think it is so horrible when you're disillusioned.'

'But isn't one usually disillusioned, and does it really matter if one is, so long as one has once *had* the illusion?'

'I don't agree, and I'm sure there are people in whom one could never be disillusioned.' She said it quite firmly.

He continued to smile. 'You're lucky if you think so, but be warned,' he shook his finger again at her, 'one is often disillusioned in one's friends and nearly always disillusioned when one falls in love.'

She looked out on to the lake. 'I don't think I could live if I were disillusioned in love,' she said finally.

He gave a half laugh of incredulity which he smothered quickly. 'Gosh! I believe you're serious. *Are* you serious?'

She turned back to face him. 'Is it a crime to be serious? I don't think life would be worth living if one wasn't serious about the important things.'

He asked lightly, a half mocking inflection in his voice: 'And you think falling in love so very serious and important?'

She looked at him unsmiling, her young pretty face whitened by the rising moonlight. 'I think love is the most serious and important thing in the whole world,' she said finally.

'H'm, H'm.' He made a noise in his throat. He felt suddenly out of his depth. He wasn't used to such intentness and momentarily he was irritated with it as Martin Cheswick had been that afternoon.

Gilbert Rogers had a happy attitude towards life. That he was the top American speedboat racer he took as a joke. He had grinned over the articles: 'Millionaire Playboy Turns Speedboat Racer,' and thoroughly approved their lightness of style. No one thought he'd make good, but oddly, he had made good. He held the American record and in the last trials had been only a few seconds behind the world record.

He had supervised the building of his latest and most beautiful boat, the *Virginia II*, but only — as he carefully explained to friends — because it gave him something to do between parties. Now he was to challenge Adam Douglas's *Scotsman III*. 'Gosh! I wonder I have the nerve!' he'd said to everyone, 'but anyhow it will be a nice little outing, especially for those who are standing on the shores of the lake!'

'Will you have supper with me to-night?' he asked Roxie. 'I mean after the champagne 'do' the management are giving us? And they darned well ought to give us this free champagne do after all the trade and custom we've brought them.'

He put his hand over hers on the balustrade. She drew hers away rather sharply. 'Will you?' His voice was so urgent that he himself was surprised. It seemed years since he had felt so eager that a girl should accept an invitation of his. Usually they accepted even when they already had another date.

'I might. I don't know what my own plans will be.' She backed away towards the french windows leading into her sitting-room.

'Thank you all the same. I'll let you know.'

He stood for a few moments after she'd disappeared and thought: 'Is she real? She seems out of this world, and she hasn't even a flirtatious line though she must know who I am. She'll let me know! That's one in the eye for you, you bum!' He laughed out loud.

Roxie had a bath and felt as fresh as though she'd never had the night crossing and then the long train journey from England. She shook the steam out of her hair, slipped into a blue silk dressing-gown and went into the bedroom to get an evening dress out of the wardrobe suit-case. She would wear the cream brocade to-night. From the moment Madame Renée had slipped the finished dress over her head, she had thought: 'I'll wear that dress when I meet Adam again.' Would he remember her from two years ago?

As she powdered her face and touched up her lips, she thought how queer it was she should have met Adam Douglas's opponent, Gil Rogers, to-night. She decided she didn't like him very much and it wasn't only because she had been prepared to dislike him as Adam's opponent. She felt there were few — if any — things in life he would take seriously, and yet he couldn't

21

have become America's ace speedboat racer if he hadn't taken *that* seriously. Maybe it was only women he didn't take seriously. She told herself she detested men who didn't take women seriously.

4

In the neighbouring suite Gil Rogers stood looking at his reflection pensively in the long mirror. Evening dress — tails and the stiff white shirt — suited his type of good looks. The narrowed eyes which looked back into his own were a deep blue. His dark hair showed his Irish heritage: his mother had been a Dublin girl; his father, from a southern U.S. state, had met her when he was visiting that city during a college vacation.

Gil straightened his white tie, made a half-grimace at himself in the mirror, left the suite, ran lightly down two flights of stairs to a suite at the back of the first floor and tapped a sharp rat-tat-tat on the door.

'Hello, there! Wait a mo' — I'm just finishing putting on the good old war-paint,' a girl's voice called. It, too, had a soft Southern drawl.

'Hurry,' Gil called back. 'If I keep the management waiting they'll expect me to pay for my own board and lodging. Adam and I are the attraction to-night.'

'You idiot, Gil!' Elizabeth Hamilton said,

laughing as she opened the door to him. 'As if you couldn't buy the hotel twice over for that matter!'

He smiled back into her attractive upturned face. 'Since I've become an international sporting guy, I've come to expect having things paid for me. *You're* my big expense. They don't expect me to tag a secretary along as well as all the members of my team.'

She threw the door wider open. 'Are you coming in? I've just arranged with great difficulty for some ice to be sent in. You wouldn't believe with all the ice and snow about on the mountains how difficult it is to get a few cubes of ice in this country.' She added, 'I still have a bottle of bourbon left, incidentally.'

'Well, that is an inducement.' He came into the room, smiling at her. Her features were rather flat, but the large grey eyes were lovely and the corners of her lips turned upwards in a suggestion of laughter. She had short, dark curling hair and a tallish, graceful body with lovely long limbs. She had the hips of a boy and now she rested her hands upon them, laughing across at him. 'I thought that would fetch you — the bourbon. You'll need it before you lash into the sweet champagne the management have lined up for us downstairs.' She turned sharply towards the cocktail cabinet, showing the arresting but rather angular curves of her body.

'Sorry I can't ask you to drink it on the balcony.' She added with a humorous grin hovering around her rather large mouth: 'You're a meanie. Why didn't you shout me to a suite with a balcony overlooking the lake? Why must I be pushed away here in a back suite like a poor relation? Blast you, Gil — don't I earn my money and decent accommodation?'

'Hold it, Liz! You'd have had the best accommodation in the hotel if I'd been able to get it, but you know when I booked you in the management protested they were already full.'

'A back office suite *and* on the first floor,' she grumbled, but still humorously. 'But then what else am I these days but an office rat?'

'A good-looking rat-ess in that dress.' He smiled and nodded his approval.

She wore the gown superbly. It was green taffeta and went well with her dark hair that had reddish tints. Her grey eyes fired. 'You like this dress, Gil?' But the way she said it sounded too casual.

'H'm, h'm, pretty good.'

'I wanted to look nice for you to-night.'

She spoke softly and lowered her eyes and half turned from him.

'You always look nice.' His voice was almost disinterested.

He poured out the whisky and handed her a glass.

'*You* think so, Gil?'

He laughed. 'Now who's fishing for compliments?'

Liz Hamilton and he had been friends for so long — almost as long as he could remember. Both their families had lived on Park Avenue and gone to the same summer resort in Cleveland for the long school vacation. Liz had been a tomboy as a child and there was still a great deal of the tomboy in her, even at the advanced age of twenty-three. He liked her, but he had never felt sentimental about her. He had an uneasy feeling that she might be coming to feel sentimental about him.

Liz's father, a Stock Exchange speculator, had died a bankrupt. She had had to do something, so she had taken a course in shorthand and typing, and it had seemed natural enough to Gil, when he found he needed a secretary, to offer her the job. She had accepted it eagerly and here she was at the moment with him at Vitry-sur-Lac.

'I want you to do something for me,' Gil

said finally. 'There's a girl staying in suite 211, a small fair-haired girl. She arrived earlier this evening. I want you to find out who she is and as much as you can about her. It shouldn't be difficult.'

'Why do you want to know about this girl, Gil?' But the moment she'd said it she bit her lower lip sharply. She knew by the slight stiffening of his body that she had over-stepped the mark.

'I just want to know.'

She took a quick swallow of her drink. 'Is this information you want so pressing?' She smiled. 'To-morrow I could see M. Henriot on some excuse.'

He finished his bourbon and put the glass down. 'I'd like the information to-night, within ten minutes as a matter of fact.'

She made him a mocking salaam. 'Certainly, since the master orders.'

As he walked back along the corridor towards the main lounge he felt a sense of uneasiness. Maybe it hadn't been such a smart idea to have taken Liz on as his secretary. Her obvious reluctance to find out about the fair-haired girl might only be a streak of possessiveness in her. Women were naturally possessive, he consoled himself, even when they weren't particularly interested in a man.

★ ★ ★

Roxie came timidly in to join the party, her note-book and pencil hidden in a rather large but attractive diamanté-studded evening bag. The party was going well judging by the chatter and laughter. The wide doors of the lounge opened out on to the lake, the electric chandeliers brilliantly lighted the assembly — the lovely and distinguished looking women in smart expensive evening gowns, and the men either in uniform or in full dress or dinner jackets. The shelves behind the imposing long bar were stacked with bottles of champagne, and every now and then you could hear the faint sound of a pop of a cork above the din.

Roxie felt somewhat at a loss. She recognised a great many of the guests by their faces. She couldn't see Adam but she was aware of Gil standing over by the bar. She tried to avoid him since he might repeat his invitation for supper and she didn't want to tie herself down. Adam might invite her to join his party on the strength of their previous meeting.

'Hello! Why are you trying to hide yourself behind that palm?' Martin Cheswick's voice made her turn sharply.

She forced a smile. 'I wasn't hiding. I was

28

trying to get my bearings and see whom I knew.'

'You looked as though you were hiding, anyhow,' he persisted. 'Surely you haven't met a big bad wolf in Vitry in such a short while? I've just seen one of the directors of the Casino. He, as well as all the other hotel managers in this town, is tearing his hair out in handfuls because the Excelsior Palace is getting too much publicity. Why didn't the directors of the Casino have the sense to put on a show like this to-night? Oh, well — ' He shrugged his thin shoulders in the rather ill-fitting jacket, 'they'll get all the publicity they're entitled to now I've arrived on the job. Have you ever worked for a town council? My advice is, don't. Stick to your nice little gossip paragraphs, they're much more rewarding.'

'Have you seen Adam Douglas?'

He looked over her head about the room. 'No, but come with me and we'll see if we can't locate him. There's a fair crowd in the next room. Here the bar is the attraction, and Adam always tries to keep out of the limelight, or he pretends he does,' he added cynically.

'You don't like Adam?'

He grinned down at her tolerantly. 'Of course I like him. He happens to be one of my best friends. That's why I feel at liberty to say what I like about him.'

They passed through an open doorway into the smaller adjoining room. It was full, but not so full as the room they had just left.

'I'm going to get you a drink from the waiter with the tray. A glass may relieve some of that tension you seem to be suffering from.'

'I don't really feel like a drink.'

'Don't ever refuse champagne. You never know where your next glass will come from.' He broke off to exclaim suddenly: 'There's Adam now!'

She turned slowly. This would be the first time she had seen Adam Douglas in person in two years. Would he have changed? But the moment she looked at him, she knew at once he had changed. He had been a good-looking young man of twenty-three at the time of the house-party; now he looked not two, but five or six years older. He was thinner, there was a network of crinkles under his grey-brown eyes, and a faint crease at the side of his jaw. He still looked a young man, but he looked, too, a man troubled by many responsibilities.

'He's changed.' She said it aloud.

He shrugged slightly. 'Men who flirt constantly with death do age prematurely.

Adam has plenty on his mind as well. I shouldn't be surprised if he didn't sprout some grey hairs overnight. Come along.' He took her by the shoulder and pushed her forward. 'You said you wanted to meet him again.'

5

Adam's attractive, rather blunt-looking face lit with pleasure when he saw them approaching. 'He *does* remember,' she thought, and her heart lifted under the tight-fitting bodice of the brocade gown.

But Adam's pleasure seemed entirely reserved for the man she was with. 'Gosh! but I *am* glad to see you, Martin! I've just been phoning your digs.'

Martin said pointedly: 'I think you've met Miss Haldane before.'

'Er — ' Adam gave her a quick smile but he still looked harassed. 'Of course, Miss Haldane.'

'It was a week-end at the Copenhowers' near Hailsham in Sussex,' she reminded him.

'Of course,' he said again, more heartily. He put a hand on Martin's shoulder. 'I've got to talk to you, old chap. Some dashed unpleasant things have turned up.'

'Always at your service, Adam.' Martin gave a faintly mocking subservient bow.

'Good — good! Supposing we slip up to my suite? There's plenty of time before dinner.' He was so preoccupied he turned on the word, to lead the way, completely ignoring Roxie.

'If Miss Haldane will excuse us?' Martin said, hesitating.

Adam swung back and smiled guiltily. 'I'm so frightfully sorry to rush away like this and take Martin with me, but one or two things have cropped up and I'd like his advice.' He winked and added: 'Martin's a damned knowledgeable chap. But perhaps you know that. Maybe I'll see you later, Miss Haldane,' he added conventionally.

'Of course.' She smiled. She forgave him. She sensed by the desperate urgency in his manner he was in need of advice from someone, though it didn't seem to her that Martin was exactly the one to turn to — he was far too cynical.

She reached out and took another glass of champagne off the tray the waiter presented to her. She drank it down quickly.

'Hey there, Miss Haldane! Don't go and get lit before our supper date,' Gil Rogers's voice came from behind her. She swung round and he laughed down at her, completely sure of himself and of his welcome.

★ ★ ★

33

In a third floor suite given Adam by the courtesy of the management of the Excelsior Palace, Adam and Martin stood facing one another. Martin was taller, but Adam more squarely built and better looking. Adam's attractive face was an open one. All the world could read the emotions through which he was passing, but Martin's rather battered-looking face was a screen.

'It's nothing new,' Adam said moodily. 'Rather the same old story that I suppose every speedboat racer faces. That is if he hasn't got a fortune of his own to back him up. You know I've been unfortunate in my last few attempts on the world speed record. The sponsors have been very slow in coming forward and very sticky.' He added with a bitter quirk to his lips: 'They seem to have lost confidence in me. I've put up every cent of my own money; I've even been forced to borrow heavily, and the debts I left behind me in England are nobody's business — including five years' accumulation of unpaid income tax. But I know I'm going to break the record this time, Martin, and then everything will be fine. The sponsors will all come haring back to me: I'll be able to take *Scotsman III* over to the States to try for a new world record — not that I'm not going to try

34

for it this time, with heaven's blessing and weather permitting, but all round, things are being pretty difficult. One thing that keeps up our morale and keeps me cheerful is our present team — they're a wonderful bunch of fellows and most of them are doing it for the sheer love of it, and they don't expect any payment.

'Our chief engineer — a Scotsman named McPherson — is doing this as a holiday job, and most of the others are connected with one or other of the universities of technology. But I'm worried about *Virginia II*. The Yanks have done a first rate job on her, and Gil Rogers has all the money to back the venture. Even if he lacked sponsors — which he doesn't. The present jet-turbine engine in *Scotsman III* is a year older. She is the one that failed me before, but now she's in first class condition, thanks mainly to McPherson.'

'But you're a more experienced driver than Gil Rogers,' Martin pointed out.

'I'm not all that much more experienced. And don't forget I've had several disappointments within the past year. Last time Gil raced *Virginia II* he topped the American speed record. He can afford to pay extra technicians to become members of his team, and they work together all the time. He isn't harassed continually by writing out letters to prominent firms asking for assistance as I have to do. I admit I love the life and wouldn't give it up for anything in this world, but,' he grinned wryly and added, 'there are times when I wish I was a book-keeper or clerk in some little out-of-the-world office. It's not all that much fun being an international racing figure, especially when others seem to lack confidence in you and debts are accumulating all the time. My expenses have soared terrifically during this past year. And then,' his face clouded, 'I have personal commitments — commitments I wouldn't get rid of but which at times I have found embarrassing.'

'But you'll win this race, Adam, and take a new world speed record back to England,' Martin said heartily.

'I'd better,' Adam said, grinning wryly. 'Otherwise it looks as though I'd put paid to speedboat racing. And that's just one thing I can't afford to do. It's not only finance and the confidence in myself as a racing driver, but I'd hate to let the team down. They have been simply magnificent. They've given up all their free time to the overhauling of *Scotsman III*. They've untiringly worked all day and every day, far into the night. No one ever thought of taking a Saturday or a Sunday off. They're all pretty nerved up. We've got to bring it off this time, not only win the Vitry Cup by beating Rogers, but we've got to set up a new world record.'

'You will do it, Adam,' Martin said confidently. 'And that's what's eating you up — the worry you're having about getting the sponsors for this race. Directly they know you're dead serious and you have an excellent chance of beating the world record, they'll come along. At least,' he amended, 'I hope they'll come along. But is that all?'

'No,' Adam said slowly. 'I'm damnably worried about Marlene. To-night I had some very serious news. I keep trying to get on to her doctor, but he isn't available. They said he won't be back at his house for a couple of hours. Oh, heavens, I hope it's going to be all right with her.' He spoke hoarsely and he looked thoroughly dejected.

Martin slapped him between the shoulder blades. 'You'd better put in an appearance at the party again, old man. Don't forget it's being given in your honour. By the way, that was a very pretty little girl I introduced you to. She's Lord Oxenham's daughter. She said something about having met you before.'

★ ★ ★

Gil had had drinks with various members of his team and it seemed that they were having a good party, and now he was free to dance with Roxie.

Since Adam and Martin had left her, she had been feeling rather alone and lost. So now she welcomed dancing with him. The champagne she so rarely drank — but she'd had two glasses to-night — gave wings to her feet.

Gil danced smoothly, effortlessly, as most Americans do, and she found rather to her surprise that she was enjoying immensely dancing with him. Lots of people spoke to him as they danced by, and every once in a while when they passed one or other member of his team, he waved vigorously.

But presently they found themselves dancing out on the patio. The noise from the reception rooms was softened, there was moonlight overhead. His gay mood turned to a sentimental one.

'I swear that your hair is silver in this light,' he said softly, bending down towards her so that momentarily his cheek touched hers.

She drew a little away but she laughed back at him. 'Of course it's silver. If you want to know the truth, it's a silver wig. I had it specially made up for me in Fairyland.'

'Auction the fairy wig for charity, and I'll

38

be the first bidder, Miss Haldane.' His lips touched the top of her hair lightly.

She didn't resent him. His easy flattery helped the ache of disappointment over Adam's abrupt departure and the fact that he hadn't recognised her as the girl he had known during that long week-end in Sussex. Her mind registered the fact he had called her Miss Haldane. 'But how did you know my name?' she asked.

He laughed and winked down at her. 'Another of your little fairy friends told me.'

But Liz hadn't looked very like a fairy when she'd come up to him swinging her flat boyish hips and glaring at him almost defiantly. 'The name is Haldane, since you want to know,' she had told him. 'Roxanne Haldane. She's a gossip writer on the *Clarion News* — one of the Oxenham Group of papers. But she must either have a very special line or be in the dough to rate a suite at the Excelsior Palace. I'll find out more about her in the morning, if you like.'

'Thanks, Liz, I'll be grateful. And have yourself a swell time to-night,' he had replied.

'You bet I shall have a swell time,' she had said. But he hadn't liked the way she had said it. Again he wondered if he had been wise in bringing Liz over here as a secretary. He could have brought a man secretary who would have been taken care of by the team and wouldn't have been continually on his hands, as Liz was. But his offering her the post had been an impulse, and one shouldn't, he knew, give way to impulses. 'But darn it all!' Gil thought, 'I'm always giving way to impulses, half the time regretting them, and yet some of the time they've turned out fine.'

Certainly he wasn't regretting his latest impulse in dancing with Roxie and taking her to supper afterwards.

'Can I call you by your first name, Roxanne? We Americans always call each other by our first names, as you probably know.'

She smiled. 'All my friends call me Roxie.'

'Roxie.' He repeated it. 'All my friends call me Gil. I hate Gilbert, and I think I'd murder anyone who called me Bert. Let's walk down by the lake, shall we?'

'But I must collect a few gossip paragraphs first,' she exclaimed, hesitating. 'I have to phone them through first thing in the morning.'

He smiled indulgently. 'Those can wait. I'll give you a few good paragraphs for your paper, I promise you.'

She looked at him uncertainly but she allowed herself to be led out into the night.

'What do you want me to tell you about myself?' he asked quietly as they walked together along the shores of the lake.

'Something personal, please; something you haven't given to any other paper. Why you became interested in speedboat racing for instance.'

'Our summer place was by a lake in Cleveland.' His voice was pleasantly low and reminiscent. 'It was so smooth that at times when I was a boy, I felt I wanted to run across it; I longed to drive a speedboat across it. Father had enough money and was indulgent enough to allow a young man with no fixed purpose to play about with speedboats. I began playing bigger and faster boats and having them built to my specifications.'

'Speedboat racing was always your hobby?'

'It's never been a hobby exactly. Call it an obsession. It's the one thing in this world I care about.'

She nodded slowly. 'I suppose you'd *have* to care about it in that way to have made such a big reputation for yourself. You care about it in the same way that Adam Douglas does.'

He smiled a little sourly. 'Last time we

met he wrested the laurels from me — only a matter of seconds, but seconds make history in our game. But next week I'll give him a run for his money. If I don't beat his record I'll swear I'll give up.'

'But you wouldn't.' She stopped walking and shook her head slowly. 'I don't think you'd ever give up, and neither would Adam.'

'You call him Adam?'

She flushed and laughed. 'Well, most people do. Isn't to be called by one's first name the wages of fame?'

'What else do you want to know about my misspent childhood?' he asked after a slight pause, and went on: 'At school I just scraped through the exams. The masters were pleasantly helpful. I have an uncomfortable feeling they were even helpful grading my papers. I was not only Benjamin Roger's son, but I was a good athlete. I won honours for the school at running and rowing. It was the same story when I went through college; tutors cramming me to get me through the exams so that I could continue to win athletic honours for the college. But every summer when we went back to the lake I thought of nothing but speedboats. I could never leave them alone — they've always tormented me. But maybe if I can beat Douglas and win the world record on Saturday week I'll be satisfied.'

She shook her head. 'You won't be.'

'No,' he agreed softly, 'you're right — I'll never be satisfied. I'm always seeking the unattainable — even in loving a woman, I'm never satisfied. But don't quote me, please!' He flung up a hand with mock horror and then added soberly, 'But you might make me change my mind, Roxie.

'You're very sweet, Roxie,' he went on gently, and took her quietly into his arms.

She was amazed. Until it happened she would have sworn she had no idea what he intended. She tried to break away from him, but if she'd stepped backwards she would have fallen into the lake.

He laughed at her protests and holding her closely he kissed her lips, kissed them with a possessive ardour, as no man had kissed her yet; kissed her in the way she had dreamed that one day Adam might kiss her.

He had a strong hard body. It pressed closely against hers. She couldn't move, but almost abruptly he released her. 'You're a sweet child, but I don't like kissing children. Damn it all, I want some response! I'd like to shake you or give you a good ducking.' He grinned towards the lake. 'When are you going to decide to grow up?'

His words coming on top of what she liked to think of as his presumption infuriated her. She had been kissed before, but those kisses had been nothing to the way Gil had kissed her to-night. She felt not only angry, but immeasurably older, and as well she felt a new self-confidence. Suddenly she laughed, and all her former anger left her.

Gil had expected some reaction from her, but not laughter. His manhood was affronted. 'What on earth are you laughing about, you little idiot?' he demanded.

Her laughter ceased abruptly and now she couldn't understand why she had laughed. But it was because his kisses and his close embrace had set something free in her. 'I don't know,' she said truthfully.

'You don't know?' he repeated after her roughly. 'You think it funny for a man to want to kiss you, to be crazy for you?'

'No, it's not funny,' she agreed soberly. 'It's . . . ' But she couldn't find the right words, or perhaps she didn't want to say them.

The uncertainty in her face, white and lovely in the moonlight, made her look very young and sweet. His compassion in that moment was stronger than his desire for her. He put out his hand towards her, a gentle friendly gesture. 'I should be grateful that

44

you can laugh, even at my expense. Laughter is life's most precious gift. It heals better than time.'

'I wasn't laughing at you, Gil,' she said quietly, and heard herself use his first name quite naturally, as though they were old friends.

'No matter what you were laughing at,' he said, 'it's enough that you *were* laughing. Come inside. We'll crack a bottle together and then I suppose you must go upstairs and write your wretched little gossip paragraphs.'

'Yes, but I haven't a great deal to write about yet.'

His attractive face twisted in a grin. 'Haven't I just given you the story of my boyhood exclusive?'

'I'm grateful, but I want to put in something about Adam too.'

'Damn Adam! All you need to write about him is that I'm going to beat him and regain the record for the good old U.S.'

'You're very sure!'

He nodded. 'I *am* sure — as sure as I am that some time soon I'm going to kiss you again.'

Towards the end of the evening, dancing with Gil, they passed another couple. Roxie particularly noticed the girl. She wasn't pretty but she was attractive, and the emerald taffeta gown was perfect on her. The girl spoke across her partner's shoulder to Gil: 'Do I rate a dance, Gil?' Her voice was light but there was an undercurrent.

'Sure, Liz. What about the next one?'

'I can scarcely wait for it.' She grimaced faintly, then her glance shifted from Gil to Roxie. 'I've earned it too, I think.' She laughed, waved gaily and danced away with her partner.

'That's my secretary, Liz Hamilton,' he explained rather uncomfortably. But even on that first night, Roxie knew that being Gil's secretary didn't explain Liz. She sensed from the girl's manner there was more to it than that — much more to it.

6

When Gil went to find Liz for the next
dance, Roxie decided to escape upstairs, and
anyhow it was well after midnight.

On her way through the ballroom and the
adjoining supper room she had looked for
Adam. She had a curious urgency to find
him. The excitement of the evening, the
unexpected thrill of Gil's kisses and her
new feeling of self-confidence had created
this urgency in her. She felt she had to
find him. She excused herself by thinking
she must get some paragraphs out of him
for her column. She hesitated, then went into
the foyer and over to the reception desk.

'Please, could I have the number of Mr.
Douglas's suite?'

The girl clerk looked at her curiously
and said with a faint foreign accent, 'You
want the number of M. Douglas's suite,
Mademoiselle?' Her plucked eyebrows rose;
her look was both humorous and cynical.

Roxie's violet shaded eyes looked straight
back at the girl. 'Please, I'd like the number
of Mr. Douglas's suite. I want to get a
paragraph from him to telephone through

to my paper in the morning.'

'Oh, yes, Mademoiselle,' said the girl, and smiled in complete disbelief. 'No. 301 on the third floor, Mademoiselle.'

'Thank you.' Roxie gathered up the folds of her long evening gown and ran across the foyer and up the stairs. She felt if she waited for the lift she might lose courage. She was breathless when she reached the third floor but she walked quickly down a passage where an arrow pointed to the numbers which included Adam's. The door of No. 301 was slightly ajar. She hesitated a moment before she knocked.

From inside the room suddenly she heard his voice speaking on the telephone, saying: 'Doctor, I'm sorry to have called you at this late hour, but you were out the three other times I called. Yes, I do understand and I apologise for troubling you now, but you must realise how much this means to me!' His voice broke with real anguish. There was a longish pause. When he spoke again his voice was under more restraint, as though he was determinedly holding himself in check. 'The operation is absolutely necessary, you think, Doctor? . . . I know you are doing everything you can and I'm very grateful. But everything possible *must* be done. I'll telephone you to-morrow. Good-night, Doctor.'

She heard him thrust the telephone back on to its cradle. She paused another moment before she finally knocked. She heard him walk across the room. He flung the door open wider. The light shone down on his blunt good-looking face. He had looked harassed and worried earlier in the evening, but now his face was almost ravaged.

She didn't know what had happened, but she felt a deep and genuine compassion for him. There was a feeling of crisis in the atmosphere. Not quite realising what she was doing, she pushed past him. 'Do you mind if I come inside? You see, I have to see you.' She was breathless with the intensity of her own emotions. She wasn't thinking of any gossip paragraphs at that moment.

'Well, you're here, aren't you?' He spoke almost rudely and slammed the door to sharply. 'You're here and you've seen me, so why don't you go?' But she forgave him his rudeness. She knew he was emotionally overwrought, as she was.

His grey-brown eyes looked her over dispassionately. A very pretty girl, his mind registered, but pretty girls didn't interest him. In fact pretty eager young girls irritated him at that moment almost unendurably. She moved easily and gracefully; it was such a contrast to *her*. This girl had so much to look forward to, the whole of her life.

His nerves had been ragged all day. First this mess he'd got himself into financially, then this news about *her*. He felt he hated the whole world and everyone in it, especially girls who pushed their way uninvited into celebrities' suites. What did she want from him anyhow?

'You don't really remember meeting me at the Copenhowers' at that week-end party, do you?' she asked quickly.

He stood looking down at her, his firm lips tightening. He *did* remember now. He had thought her a pretty kid, but no more than a kid, and her open adulation had flattered him. Maybe he'd played up to her a little and he might have continued doing so over the weekend if Marlene hadn't pointed out that he was making rather an ass of himself playing up to such a very young girl.

'Yes, I remember,' he said. 'I'm sorry I didn't recall you when we met earlier this evening. But all the same,' he went on, his voice roughening, 'I think it would be a good idea if you left now. Don't you agree?'

But she didn't want to go. She was secretly thrilled at being here with him in the cosy intimacy of the suite's sitting-room. The french doors leading out on to his balcony were open, the blue-black night like a starful drop-curtain outside, and in the distance the lake gleamed silver. She felt reckless with the champagne she had drunk; it was as though for two whole years she had been waiting for this moment.

'I've wanted so much to see you again, Adam.' The name slipped out without her realising it. 'Please don't send me away. There are so many things I want to ask you.'

Watching her move with apparent confidence about his sitting-room, an uninvited guest, the bitter angry mood swept over him again. He forgot their former meeting, the friendship, even warmth he'd once felt towards her, a friendship that might have continued but for what Marlene had said. He only thought of her as one of the female pests that every celebrity has to eradicate from time to time from his life.

'All right, you've asked for it,' he said furiously as he caught her to him.

He was so angry he didn't care whether he was hurting her or not. 'You don't want to ask me questions, do you? This is what you want, what all little girls like you want, isn't it?' He kissed her hard on the lips and then thrust her away from him and laughed. 'Do you want some fine romantic phrases to go with it? Sorry, but I don't feel in the mood

51

for fine romantic phrases to-night. I don't feel in the mood for any romantic nonsense, or even for signing autographs, if that idea was in your mind, which I doubt. Well, are you going or do you want me to kiss you again?'

'I'm going.' Her eyes blurred. She fumbled wretchedly in her bag for her handkerchief. Her note-book and pencil slid out to the floor, but she didn't notice them. She wiped her eyes hastily.

'Very pretty but not very convincing,' he said. But suddenly he was more angry with himself than he was with her.

She moved towards the door. He sprang forward and opened it for her. 'Good night,' he said bluntly, hating himself more than ever.

'Good-bye.' She spoke through stiff lips and walked unseeingly down the corridor.

He went back into his suite and saw her note-book on the floor, lying open at a certain page. He bent and picked it up and sprawled across it were the words: 'Gil Rogers spent his childhood . . . ' He closed the book, rang for the bellboy and asked him to take it to Miss Haldane's room. He was in too bitter a mood to admit that he might have made a grave mistake, but he felt uneasily that he had.

7

The lake at Vitry had never been more beautiful than it was in the full blaze of the morning sunlight. A slight breeze ruffled the surface of the lake, which was a deep clear blue. Roxie walked through the streets of the town from the hotel, looking up at the quaint old buildings with the weathered painted figures on the façades. She saw the old church with its clock tower and the figurines which came out at midday and midnight to chime the hours and the church where the townsfolk had worshipped for generations. She saw the gay little shops in the main street, the butcher, the baker, the grocer and those arty-crafty shops, their windows full of the small wooden carvings eagerly bought by tourists, the bears and the woodmen, the clocks built into the frame of minute Swiss chalets with the cuckoo that came out from under the roof to call the hour. Fascinating little shops. She could have spent the whole day wandering through them.

But she had no time this morning. She had to hurry down to the quay. She was going out with Gil. He had telephoned her that morning asking her to go for a run with him in one of the launches he had hired to carry members of his team when he went out on a trial run.

She had spent a restless night, sleeping only in broken snatches. But this morning she had made herself believe that part of last night's fiasco had been her own fault. She *had* thrust her way into Adam's sitting-room. She hadn't explained at once why she had come. Could he really be blamed for having mistaken the reason for her visit? After all, she had said nothing about her work. She blamed herself, the champagne, she tried to lay the blame anywhere but on him. She remembered the look on his face when he'd opened the door to her. Her heart went out to him. What was troubling him so much?

On the way down to the wharf she had to pass by the Casino. It was an attractive modern building set in a small park with a huge glass-enclosed balcony where you could dine and dance. This summer it was gay with fresh white paint and flowers. Two gardeners were rolling the lawns and another tending the flower-beds.

She stopped and thought what a charming little place it was for such a small town. As she was about to walk on, Martin ran down the steps, saw her, and waved.

She waited. Although at times his remarks distressed and annoyed her, she had a feeling that he could be a good friend, and uneasily and for no apparent reason she felt that in the near future she might need a good friend.

'Hello,' he said as he joined her. 'Where did you get to last night after you finished dancing with Gil? I had business to attend to and when I was finally free you'd disappeared and he was dancing with that secretary of his. I fear you'll have competition, Miss Haldane.'

'I haven't set my cap at him.'

He laughed easily. 'So it's still Adam? Oh, there's no need to blush. I knew it after our talk in the train.'

Since she didn't speak, he went on, 'Where are you going? Can I walk with you a while. I've finished my business for the moment. I've just had a pretty stormy interview with the director of the Casino. As I told you last night he's mad at the Excelsior Palace grabbing so much publicity, so I told him to put on a show equal to the one the Palace turned on last night. He nattered about his co-directors, but I told him outright that either he or they were too damned mean. They want all the celebrities, but they expect *them* to pay. I told M. Chevalier that he's got to wake up and realise what century and year he's living in and that any publicity he gets has to be paid for by himself. He didn't like it. He's a sour old puss, but he agreed to throw a gala ball, strictly invitation. You'll get an invitation, of course. I've arranged for that.'

'Thank you.'

'Hey! you're walking pretty fast. What's the hurry?' His eyes looked her over with pleasure. She was such a neat little person in her blue sleeveless linen dress. Her very fair hair caught the sunlight as she moved.

Last night on the balcony Gil had said her hair was silver. This morning it was a corn-coloured gold. For no reason to which he cared to give a name, Martin felt disturbed about her. She shouldn't be mixing with this hardbitten international set of world-famous sportsmen, the ultra rich and their hangers-on.

But he didn't want to feel depressed walking along beside Roxie in this brilliant sunshine. He would have given a great deal to feel as young and eager as she seemed, to have believed in something or anyone.

'You haven't told me where we're going,' he reminded her.

She half turned. 'I'm going down to the wharf to ride in one of his launches with Gil.'

'With Gil — not Adam?'

'No,' she answered quietly, 'not Adam.'

He grinned down at her. 'I gather the dance was a success last night; at least you're going for a ride with Gil.'

'Oh, yes, the whole evening was a great success,' she assured him quickly.

He didn't mistake the undercurrent and was puzzled. 'I'd like to ask Gil to take me along too,' he said, 'but I've an appointment up in the mountains. Anyhow, I don't think he'd be pleased if I offered my chaperonage.' He laughed, and added easily, 'He's a nice fellow. He wins most of the races in U.S., and whether he wins or loses he's a damn good sport about it — he just laughs.'

They were strolling down the narrow lane towards the wharf.

'Are you implying Adam isn't like that?' She didn't know why she should have read this implication into his remark.

'Adam is much more serious,' he said soberly, 'and whether he wins or loses means much more to him than it does to Gil. Speedboat racing isn't just an amusement with him. He has to keep on top or go completely under.'

'You mean his heart would break if he lost all hope of regaining the world speed record?' she asked seriously.

57

'He wouldn't like the prospect,' he said dryly, and added, 'Let's leave it at that.'

They had reached the wharf. Two motorboats were drawn up alongside the quay. Gil sprang out of the cockpit of one of them to meet her. 'Hello, hello!' He grasped both her hands. 'We're all set for a spin on the lake?'

'Yes.' She smiled at him. 'It's a lovely morning.'

'A wonderful morning — as wonderful as you look!'

'I thought I'd probably look pretty woebegone after last night,' she laughed back at him.

'Girls don't at your age. Late nights don't seem to matter to them. It's only when you feel old age creeping on, as I do, you look your age.'

Adam was walking down the wharf wearing stained slacks and a striped sports shirt. He had just come out of the shed where he'd been working with his team of enthusiasts on *Scotsman III*. He paused beside Gil and Roxie. He looked uncomfortably at Roxie, almost guiltily.

'Good morning, Miss Haldane. I sent your note-book back to your suite. I think we were rather at cross purposes last night.' He greeted the other two, and added, 'Perhaps you'll all lunch with me?'

'I'm afraid I've got a luncheon date,' Gil said.

'And I,' said Martin, glancing down at his watch. 'As a matter of fact I must be off at once.'

Adam shrugged slightly and smiled. 'Well, it's nice to see you all on deck after last night.' Again he glanced at Roxie, but she didn't meet his eyes; she turned her head rather pointedly aside.

'Come on, Roxie!' Gil called, as though suddenly impatient. 'Let's get aboard.'

It was thrilling skimming across the lake in the fast launch. She stood in the cockpit with Gil, the breeze blowing back her blonde hair, her eyes sparkling, her breath coming in short gasps. He drove the boat very fast; she had never experienced such speed in her life on water. It lifted her right out of herself.

Presently Gil slowed the boat down so that he could talk to her and seemingly carelessly he put his arm about her shoulders: 'Like it?' he asked.

She laughed. Even his arm was comforting. His open adoration was such a contrast to Adam's behaviour of last night. It helped rebuild her morale. 'It's wonderful!' she agreed.

'You must come out with me often. When

I'm not making speed tests in *Virginia II*, I like taking a social run in a launch. You must come out in one of the launches and watch one of my tests. Would you like that?'

'I'd enjoy that immensely,' she said.

She was thrilled with this glorious trip across the lake in the sunshine with the breeze striking her in the face almost as though it were a physical blow. The spray leapt up, sometimes wetting the trim linen dress she wore.

Gil turned his head again. 'You're the loveliest creature I've seen in years. I'm afraid I'm falling in love with you.'

She was suddenly a little afraid. This wasn't what she wanted. She wanted Adam. Adam had kissed her last night, but he hadn't made any pretence of being in love with her, yet the odd part of it was that she hadn't felt insulted.

'It's too early for you to say anything, I guess,' Gil laughed, and added: 'After all, we only met last night.'

'Yes, much too early,' she agreed quickly, bringing her thoughts back from Adam.

'But you like me?'

She smiled. He was really *very* likable. 'How could I help liking you?'

'Good!' he said with emphasis. 'We'll let it ride at that for the time being.'

The boat swung round and they sped back across the lake.

'You'll lunch with us, of course?' Gil said as he helped her out of the launch.

'I'd love to,' she said, 'but who is the 'us'?'

'My secretary, Liz Hamilton. She's a very good secretary. I don't know what I'd do without her.'

Roxie didn't reply. They had returned to the wharf. She looked for Adam, but he had disappeared.

8

Adam had an early lunch and then he was on his way up into the mountains, high above Vitry, where the Glink Memorial Hospital was. It was a large white modern building and the gardens at this season were full of Alpine flowers. He looked stern and worried as, having parked the car, he walked up the hospital steps. He had heard the final verdict from the doctor last night. He wondered if Marlene herself knew, and if she didn't know, how he was going to break it to her? And anyhow, where was she to find the money for this final expensive operation? It was her one chance, the doctor had said, and the only surgeon who could do it would have to be flown over from the United States. It would cost a considerable sum of money. He would have lent it to her gladly had he had it, but as things stood at the moment he could not help her.

But he smiled pleasantly at the nurse at the desk. He was still smiling as he walked up the stairs to Marlene's room on the first floor, which gave out on to a balcony. You had to smile when things were pretty bad. Marlene had been here two years and because of his old love for her, he had tried to do everything he could for her. He had already lent her all the money he could lay his hands on, and now apparently, she needed more. 'Oh, God!' he thought, 'there's Gil Rogers with all the money in the world, not knowing what to do with it, frittering it away.'

They had pushed her bed out on to the balcony into the sunshine. Her rich auburn hair framed her thin tired face; she looked so frail and ill the smile he had forced on to his face disappeared entirely.

'Hello, my dear.' She waved a thin hand. 'Come and sit close by me. I don't feel much like shouting to-day.'

He sat down by the bed, kissed her forehead and pressed her hand. 'How are you feeling — O.K.?'

'O.K.' She gave him a too-bright brittle smile. 'It must always be O.K., mustn't it?' she added, coughing.

'Not with me.' He squeezed her hand tighter. 'We've been friends too long for that.'

She looked at him in an odd way. 'It's strange that since we never became definitely engaged you're the only person who's stood by me all through this ghastly illness, Adam — bless you. And now the doctor tells me I must have this new operation if there is any hope of a cure.'

He asked sharply: 'They've told you of this new operation?'

She nodded. 'But my dear, I can't have it; it's out of the question for me to find all that much money.'

Suddenly he felt fiercely determined that in some way he must get hold of the necessary funds. She must have that operation, whatever it cost him. 'I'll find the money somehow.'

She smiled faintly in gratitude. 'But how *can* you, Adam? Things are becoming a bit difficult for you financially, I've gathered.'

'Who told you?' he asked quickly.

She shrugged slightly. 'Martin Cheswick was here a little earlier to-day. He mentioned something about your being in financial difficulties and being in need of sponsors.'

Adam said angrily, 'He's a damned busybody. I wish I hadn't confided in him now. Why can't he keep his nose out of other people's affairs and his mouth shut?'

She laid a thin hand on his arm. 'Don't talk like that, Adam. I think he's a very good friend to both of us. He admires you very much.'

'Why me, for heaven's sake!'

She answered seriously. 'I think you've always done the things he's wanted to do. You're a big figure in the world of international sport. He would like to have been like you. He's sort of imagined himself in your shoes and he *is* your good friend I think. Don't you feel that, Adam?'

'Maybe,' he said soberly. 'I don't suppose I would have burdened him with my financial troubles last night if I hadn't felt he was.'

She said carefully after a pause. 'Martin tells me that a young girl we met two years ago at the Copenhowers' place, Lord Oxenham's daughter, Roxanne Haldane, has arrived out here. She had a terrific crush on you, Adam, if I remember rightly. I was annoyed at the time, perhaps even jealous, and I ticked her off. I was ashamed of myself afterwards.'

'Well, what of it?' His voice rasped slightly. 'I understand she's out here doing some gossip paragraphs for one of her father's papers.'

She nodded. 'Martin tells me you've already met her again. She was all agog to meet you.' She laughed shortly. 'She would be a nice rich wife for you and that would solve all your money problems, wouldn't it?'

He looked really angry. 'You know I'd

never marry any girl for her money, however much I might need it, Marlene!'

She turned her large grey eyes upon him. 'You wouldn't marry any girl for her money, but if you're to carry on and keep breaking speed records you *need* money, Adam. You've got to get it somewhere, and if anything should happen to me, it might be a solution.' She laughed shortly again. 'You might even fall in love with the girl.'

'You're talking a lot of damn nonsense,' he returned irritably. 'I hate rich girls, anyhow; it makes them too darned cocksure of themselves.'

She raised herself and laid a hand on his arm. 'Please think over what I've said, Adam.'

He got to his feet and said furiously: 'You must be quite out of your mind, Marlene, to think of such a thing!'

9

Gil didn't consider it the most successful luncheon party he had ever given. In fact he didn't consider it successful at all. He took both girls to lunch on the wide sun-glassed balcony of the Casino. It was an ideal setting. There was even a softly playing orchestra.

Liz pulled a long face when he told her that Roxanne would be joining them at lunch. 'I never knew you were such a darned good hustler, Gil,' she said caustically. But she was pleasant enough to Roxanne when the three of them were sitting together at table, though most of her remarks were directed towards Gil.

He did his best to bring Roxie into the conversation and became more than a little annoyed with Liz for, so it seemed to him, deliberately excluding the younger girl. Liz laughed frequently, the corners of her rather large mouth turning upwards. She kept running her fingers through her short dark curling hair.

Roxie thought her very sophisticated and she admired her for that. But she couldn't like her a great deal. She felt, without quite knowing how it was happening, that Liz was putting her at a disadvantage. It was almost as though she was saying aloud to Gil, 'Here's your pretty little English girl. Let's see how well she can defend herself. Has she the wit or the brains to do so?'

Roxie wasn't a good fencer and she was too naturally serious minded to have a sharp and caustic tongue. She felt uncomfortable and wished the lunch would end quickly.

The director, M. Chevalier, had come across to their table and greeted them on their arrival. 'Such a pleasure to have you at one of my tables, M. Rogers. And you too, Mademoiselle Haldane and Mademoiselle Hamilton. I 'ope you are all coming to our big party to-morrow evening. But of course it would be no party without the great M. Gilbert Rogers.' He laughed and thumped Gil heartily between the shoulder blades.

Gil started laughing too, and they all laughed, and for a little while the tension at the table was eased, for even on that first day with the three of them together there was considerable tension.

Roxie was very conscious of it though she didn't understand the reason for it. Why should this American girl resent her, other than of course that she was in love with

Gil? Well, what of it? Did she think *she* was in love with Gil? The very idea made her want to laugh and then she remembered Gil's kisses of the night before. She felt uncomfortable and not like laughing. She hadn't responded but she'd accepted his kisses. She had even been a little thrilled and they had given her a renewed self-confidence. Enough self-confidence anyhow to walk up to Adam's suite . . . But she closed her mind down abruptly on that memory.

The Casino's orchestra was playing the new hit tune 'Love Is a Gambler.' The pianist was crooning softly in English:

'Love is not an endless romance
Or a crown to be worn for a day,
Nor a kiss that may follow a dance;
Love is a gambler's game.'

'I adore that song,' Liz said rather over-loudly. 'Love *is* a gambler's game. Don't you agree, Gil?'

'I suppose I do.' He nodded slowly. 'But then everything in life is a gambler's game — love, sport, fortune — your whole life is in the Great Gambler's hands. What do you think, Roxie?' He turned towards her rather deliberately.

'I hadn't thought of love as a gambler,'

she replied quietly. 'But of course you may be right, Mr. Rogers.'

'Gil, please.'

She smiled back at him. 'Very well, Gil. I suppose if you say everything in life is a gamble, love must be.' And she went on a little hoarsely: 'A good gambler doesn't mind whether he wins or loses, does he?'

'You bet he doesn't. He plays for the game with courage, with enthusiasm, and if he wins, good for him, but he's without regrets if he loses. If he wins — bravo! There's always another gamble ahead.' He looked straight into her violet shaded eyes, and said, 'I consider myself quite a gambler. Are you a gambler, Roxie?'

Her eyes fell in confusion beneath the ardency of his gaze. 'I've never thought of myself as a gambler,' she said quietly. 'And I have never thought of love as a gamble either.'

'You thought of it as just a wonderful experience that arrived between two people and stuck for ever and ever. Amen,' Liz's voice came mockingly across the table to them.

Roxie flushed faintly. 'Yes, I suppose I had thought of it like that. But I don't think I do any longer.'

'Don't tell me the short while you've been

70

in Vitry-sur-Lac has changed your mind?' Liz taunted.

'Yes, I think it has changed my mind,' Roxie said, and again Gil was conscious of that undercurrent.

He pushed back his chair. 'Well, girls, if you've finished I'm going to get into my funny little old costume and take *Virginia II* for a bit of a try-out. I'll have the lake to myself. I understand that Adam is out of town this afternoon. I'll walk you two girls back to the hotel.'

'You needn't bother,' Liz said. 'We can manage on our own, can't we, Miss Haldane?'

'Of course,' Roxie said quickly.

'All the same I'll walk you back,' Gil said determinedly. He wasn't going to have the two of them get into a huddle. Already he sensed that the situation was going to be difficult.

★ ★ ★

Roxie didn't see Adam until the following morning. She met him at the hotel's swimming pool. They had it to themselves. As yet it was too early for any of the other guests to emerge. It was a lovely clear crisp morning and the pool looked a brilliant

71

blue in the early morning sunshine. They stood for a few seconds looking at each other without speaking, without moving. He looked a splendid physical specimen in his bathing trunks. His broad shoulders were nicely sun-tanned and so were his well-built legs. He'd already been in for a swim and his lightish brown hair was wet and curled slightly. His face was more deeply tanned than any other part of his body. She saw the network of crinkles under his grey-brown eyes that half closed when he smiled.

He was smiling at her now in a diffident, embarrassed way. He reminded her suddenly of a great big awkward boy. 'Hello, Miss Haldane!' He spoke with a certain hesitation. 'I hope you're not going to bite my head off over what happened the other night. I am sorry. I apologise.'

'Please don't think any more about it and if anyone was to blame, I was, thrusting my way into your apartment uninvited. You'd no idea who I was or what I'd come for. You might easily have thought I was just one of your fans forcing myself upon you at an inopportune moment. I apologise too.'

He smiled more naturally. It was a very charming smile. 'It's nice of you to take it like that. I admit I was rather rattled that night. Certain things had happened . . . ' He broke off.

She said a little wildly, as though trying to put him further at his ease, 'Don't certain things always happen? And you must have felt very ragged after that big cocktail party and then the ball with all your admirers milling about you. But I did want to get a few exclusive pars that night cabled back to London. I must have explained myself very badly.'

'I don't think I gave you a chance to explain yourself. That's why I apologise,' he said quite quietly. Momentarily his grey-brown eyes met her dark violet ones — only momentarily and then they moved away.

'What a lovely day it's going to be,' he said finally.

'Yes,' she agreed. 'It's going to be a truly magnificent day.'

There was something in her voice that made him turn and look at her more closely and he thought despite his embarrassment at meeting her again that she was an uncommonly pretty girl. Her hair looked pure golden in the strong morning sunlight. Her figure was trim and alluring in the close fitting one-piece swimsuit. She was looking at him now in an almost amused way which disconcerted him.

'Darn it all,' he thought, 'why did Marlene have to suggest all that utter nonsense about this girl and I making a match of it? The very thought of it is making me feel a damned fool.'

'Shall we stop making polite conversation and go in for a swim?' she said presently.

He liked her low sweet husky voice. Thank heavens she wasn't one of those shrill talkative women. He liked a woman for her silences even more than for what she actually said. There can be something intimate, even close, in a silence.

'Yes, let's swim,' he agreed. 'I'll race you to the end of the pool and back again. You dive in first. I'll give you half-way up the pool before I dive in.'

She made a little mocking nod with her head. 'That's generous of you. All right, here goes.' She dived in and a few seconds later he dived in after her. She didn't wear a cap; she didn't need one since her hair was naturally curly and could easily be combed back into its waves.

She swam with swift sure strokes. She'd won the swimming prize at the finishing school she'd been to near here. But even with the advantage he'd given her, she never would have had a hope of beating Adam. He swam strongly, beautifully. His whole body

74

moved to the rhythm of each stroke. He finished ahead of her but not too far ahead to make her look foolish. And afterwards, breathless, laughing, they both clung to the side of the pool.

'You'd better give me the length of the pool next time,' she said. 'And even then I don't think I could beat you.'

'I swear you could.'

'It's a date then. Next time you'll give me the length of the pool as a start.'

But next time was vague. She wanted something more concrete. 'When?' she asked.

He looked faintly surprised, and again she saw that he was embarrassed. 'To-morrow morning down here at the same time. If the party at the Casino to-night is any good we'll need something like this to freshen us up.'

He climbed out of the pool and stretched out a hand to help her up. 'You're going, Miss Haldane?'

She clung to his hand a little longer than was necessary. 'Yes, I'm going. I want to send some paragraphs over to England.'

'I'll see if I can help you dig some up.'

'That's sweet of you, Mr. Douglas.'

But she didn't go. They both sat on the side of the swimming pool, smiling at each other.

'Couldn't it be Adam?' he suggested.

'Yes, of course it could be Adam,' she said. 'My name is Roxanne. I'm mostly called Roxie.'

'But I shall call you Roxanne,' he said. 'It's a very pretty name — unusual too.' He smiled again and the network of wrinkles showed under his deep-set eyes. 'Well,' he sprang to his feet, 'I must be off and get me some breakfast. I want to do some tinkering about with the team on the engine of *Scotsman III* this morning. If you come down to the wharf give me a shout; I'll show you over her.'

'I certainly will,' she said. 'I'll stay here for a few minutes. Maybe I'll take another dip.'

He grinned wryly. 'The enthusiasm of youth for cold water.'

'Yes, it is pretty cold,' she agreed, shivering a little. 'But you feel wonderful afterwards.'

'I wish you felt as wonderful after most unpleasant things as you do after a cold dip. Unpleasant things should be a stimulus, but they aren't always.'

'No,' she agreed soberly, 'they aren't always.'

He shook his head slightly as though shaking some thought from him. 'Well, I must be going,' he said abruptly and turned on the word.

She watched him go with a little confident smile. The first hurdle was over. She felt very happy with the result. She was calling him Adam and he had asked her to come down to the quay where *Scotsman III* lay on its cradle in a shed in between trial runs. He had also said he would see her that night at the Casino gala.

She spent a busy morning interviewing managers of the various hotels and finding out what celebrities were staying there. When she could track them down she got them to give her gossip paragraphs. Mostly they were nothing loath. They might live on caviar, pâté de fois gras and champagne, but juicy gossip paragraphs were the cream of their existence.

She also interviewed M. Chevalier, the director of the Casino, and he gave her the names of the most prominent people who would be at the gala this evening. 'But all the interest will centre around M. Douglas and M. Rogers and their rival teams, of course,' he ended. 'We are going to have dancing and supper and roulette. We must make on the roulette to pay for the entertainment we give. Is that not so?' M. Chevalier chuckled, and his fat good-natured face beamed at her.

'I've never played roulette,' she said.

'Then you must play to-night. But if

this is your first time, play cautiously, Mademoiselle. Back the red or black or one of the columns. You cannot lose too much that way. You might even win.'

'Thank you. I may try it.'

'But you will be too occupied with the dancing, I am sure, Mademoiselle,' he said, bowing gallantly. 'All the young men will want to dance with you.'

10

It was past noon when she got down to the small quay to remind Adam of his promise to show her over *Scotsman III*. But Adam, the launches and the boat were gone.

She shaded her eyes and looked across the dazzling surface of the lake. A speck in the distance travelling at a terrific speed might easily be Adam's boat. She sat on the end of the quay, dangling her legs down, looking quite absurdly young in the soft corn-coloured dress she wore. She heard footsteps on the quay. A man's tall shadow fell across her.

'Hello, Miss Sunshine. May I sit beside you for a while?' It was Martin Cheswick.

She didn't welcome him especially. She wanted only to enjoy the sunshine and the blue surface of the lake slightly rippled by a breeze. She wanted to think only of that meeting with Adam at the swimming pool this morning and wonder how long it would take him to come back and whether or not she ought to wait for him.

'Just resting or waiting for someone?' Martin asked.

He would ask that.

'Resting. I am worn down to the ankles running round from one hotel to another collecting gossip paragraphs.'

'Got any good ones?'

She nodded solemnly, importantly. 'Quite a few, I think. Some of the people were a bit stuffy, but most were extraordinarily communicative.'

'They probably knew you were Lord Oxenham's daughter. Most celebrities and members of the international set aren't very kind to gossip scribblers. But of course being Lord Oxenham's daughter you are one of them.'

'I hate you when you talk like that!' she said vehemently.

He turned on her equally vehemently. 'And I hate you when you're being so stupidly naïve. You're not really naïve at all, you've just got an obsession that you want to think the best of everyone.'

'Isn't it better than thinking the worst of everyone as you do?'

'I don't think it is. You don't let yourself in for so many heartaches.'

'But I'd rather have the heartaches than feel as you do about people,' she retorted with spirit.

'Hello! What are you two children

squabbling about?' a light voice with a soft American drawl said behind them. They both turned sharply to see Gilbert Rogers standing there, laughing down at them.

'You know each other?' Roxie asked.

'Yes. Cheswick and I met the other night,' Gil replied.

'I was trying to teach her that there's a worm in the heart of almost every rose,' Martin said.

'But there isn't. It isn't true at all,' Roxie returned hotly.

Gilbert smiled at them indulgently. His graceful body looked at its best in the short pants he was wearing and the open necked shirt. 'I came down to look for Adam,' he said. 'I thought we two rivals might have a friendly lunch together and dispel the ugly rumours of a hated rivalry between us and establish the fact that apart from being competitors in the race and trying to break the speed record we are the best of friends.'

'He's somewhere out on the lake, I believe,' Roxie said. 'At least some little time ago I saw something in the distance which looked like the *Scotsman III* going at a terrific speed.'

Gil shaded his eyes and peered across the surface of the lake. 'That might easily be him trying her out, and it may be ages before he gets back. What about you two coming along and having lunch with me?'

'Certainly, if you really want to include me,' Martin grinned and jumped to his feet with alacrity.

'Come along. I was out in *Virginia II* early this morning and we've been tinkering around with the engine ever since, and now I'm almost starving.'

They didn't lunch at the Casino, they lunched at the Excelsior Palace. Roxie enjoyed the lunch much more than she had on the previous day. They laughed and talked naturally, there were no undercurrents. Roxie told herself she didn't dislike Liz Hamilton but it was a great relief that she wasn't with them.

They lunched out on the terrace of the hotel that gave a lovely view of the glittering lake. The terrace was an exciting scene that noontime; glamorous women in linen costumes or sunsuits, men with multi-coloured linen slacks and gaily patterned sports shirts. The waiters, in white jackets, wove in between the closely packed tables. An orchestra was playing softly so as not to interrupt the conversation.

Roxie recognised the tune they had been playing at the Casino yesterday and which had caused that slight argument:

'Love is not an endless romance
Or a crown to be worn for a day,
Nor a kiss that may follow a dance;
Love is a gambler's game.'

The crooner sang the second verse:

'Love's like a star in the sky,
To shine in your heart or to die,
The feeling is great, but it's one you can't
    tame;
Love is a gambler's game.'

Gil grinned across at her. 'You liked
that tune yesterday, didn't you, Roxie? I
requested it.'

Her eyes fell before his, a faint colour rose
to her temples. 'That was nice of you. Yes,
I do like that tune.'

'It's damnably sentimental,' Martin growled.

'Is it?' Gil took up. 'I don't agree. What's
sentimental about being a gambler — whether
it's roulette or love? Listen to the verse they're
singing now:

'Love's like a roulette wheel's spin,
One turn and you may a fortune win,
Or lose your heart on the same;
Love is a gambler's game.'

'That's not sentiment; it's stark frightening reality,' he said laughing. 'A spin of the wheel and you win or lose. It may be on the spin of that wheel you've lost your whole life's future happiness.'

'It seems that you have to be a gambler in love to win anything at all.' Roxanne's voice was very quiet suddenly. 'I didn't understand that until,' she hesitated, 'recently. I believe I've grown up considerably since I've been here.'

'Don't grow up, my fairy princess,' Gil said. 'I like you too much as you are.' He was laughing affectionately across at her.

They had finished lunch. Martin pushed back his chair and got to his feet. 'That, I take it, is an invitation for me to go. I have to leave anyhow, I've got an appointment with the town council in just under ten minutes. I'm trying to make the old devils disgorge some of the wealth that's going to accumulate in the next week or so and spend it on decent publicity.'

'Too bad you have to go,' Gil said.

'Yes, it's too bad for you, isn't it?' Martin said with a cynical grin.

Gil's eyes followed Martin's lean figure out of the room. 'He's a queer chap, isn't he?'

'I don't know whether his cynicism is a pose or real. I think he mainly hurts himself,' she murmured. She was still thinking of the words of that song:

'Love's like a roulette wheel's spin,
One turn and you may a fortune win
Or lose your heart on the same;
Love is a gambler's game.'

She tightened her small hands resolutely under the table. Well, *she* would be a gambler. She might lose but she might win, and if she did lose she hoped she would be a good loser.

'It was decent of him to move on anyhow,' Gil murmured. 'I had visions of him sticking close to us all afternoon. I think he has an eye for you, my princess.'

Yesterday she might have laughed and denied it heartily. Now she merely answered calmly, 'Do you think he has?'

'I'm sure he has, but I don't think you'd find much happiness married to him, honeybunch. He'd always expect the worst of you.'

'I ought to go up to my room and type out those paragraphs.' She half rose to go but he caught her hand and drew her down on to her seat again. 'Don't go yet. I thought I'd take you down to the quay and introduce you to the team and show you *Virginia II* after lunch. I've a whole glorious afternoon free.'

'Aren't you usually free?'

He frowned ever so slightly. 'I am. Of course I am.' He hesitated. 'It's just that — well, you don't like hurting someone whom you're really fond of — but as a friend, if you know what I mean.'

She knew he was talking of Liz Hamilton.

'Yes,' she agreed soberly, 'it's hateful to feel you're hurting someone. You go to all lengths to avoid hurting them and half the time you hurt yourself in doing so. She's in love with you, isn't she?'

He made a little mocking sigh. 'I'm afraid she is. I didn't allow myself to think so until very recently. But ever since I did admit the fact to myself, I've been feeling self-conscious and embarrassed in her presence. I haven't felt I was complete master of myself any longer. I haven't liked feeling this way, Roxie,' he ended soberly.

'No. It wouldn't be a happy feeling, especially if you didn't love the person whom you didn't want to hurt,' she agreed quietly.

'I sent her on an errand for me to Geneva to-day so I could have this talk with you,' he said after the waiter had served them a fresh pot of coffee.

'You sent her in with a fake message?' Her

sweet rather husky voice reproved him.

'It wasn't altogether fake, but — ' He hesitated and grinned boyishly, 'it wasn't all that urgent either. It could have waited until to-morrow. It could even have waited until next week.'

'Do you think she knew there wasn't all that hurry for the message?'

He looked disconcerted. 'I've a feeling she guessed, but she didn't say anything. That worried me afterwards, that she hadn't said anything, for usually Liz is the first to speak out her mind. We're old friends, as you know. There's no employer-employee relationship between us.'

'But why did you specially want to get rid of her today?' Roxie asked.

'You're acting like a little goose,' he grinned at her. 'I told you I wanted to take you to lunch. I wanted you to spend the afternoon with me. There are things I want to say to you.'

'I'm afraid I can't spend the afternoon,' she said decisively. 'I have quite a lot of work to do. And then there's that big party at the Casino to-night, I don't want to be tired for that. But what was it you specially wanted to say to me?'

He reached for her hand under the table and took it, folding the fingers back gently in his, cupping the one folded hand in both his hands. 'I've said I was falling in love with you, Roxie. How do you feel about it? Do you like me at all?'

'Yes, of course I like you,' she said after a slight pause. 'I like you very much, Gil, but I'm not in love with you.'

'I didn't expect you to be in love with me so soon, though maybe I hoped you'd say something a little more encouraging,' he laughed. 'But I'll wait. I'll play a waiting game although its not much in my line. I've always done things quickly, impetuously, perhaps. But for you I'd wait until the cows come home, Roxie. At least,' he amended more truthfully, 'I think I would.'

She smiled back at him. 'I'm glad you added that last sentence. It makes it possible for us to go on being friends.'

'It wouldn't have been possible otherwise?'

She hesitated, then she shook her head slightly. 'No, I don't think it would have been.'

'You don't give a chap much encouragement, do you?' He grinned wryly. 'At least I know where I stand more or less. Come along down now and I'll show you *Virginia II*. Afterwards we could go for a spin in one of the launches.'

She hesitated. She liked him very much;

she didn't want to hurt him. She found herself thinking that if it hadn't been for Adam ... If she hadn't loved Adam so terribly much, she might have been more responsive to Gil's outspoken words. 'I'd love to see *Virginia II*, and if we go for a spin afterwards then it must only be a very short spin.'

He squeezed her hand tightly and let it go.

'Half an hour then, no more. I'll see you get back in time to type your wretched little paragraphs and rest up a bit before the big gala to-night.'

11

Gil escorted Roxie to the Casino. She had hoped that Adam would offer to escort her, but he had made no move. She hadn't even seen him since that swim early this morning. Music rushed out to meet them down the Casino steps, couples were already dancing in the large supper room. Others were sitting out drinking at tables on the patio. Through the big archways were the gaming rooms and as you approached them you could hear faintly the tinkle of little balls on the roulette wheels.

When Gil had knocked at the door of her suite and asked if he could take her round to the Casino, she had asked him where Liz Hamilton was.

He made a faint wry grimace. 'She hasn't got back from Geneva yet, so I left a note in her room asking her to put on her glad rags and to come on round to the Casino.' His grin turned more happy as he added, 'I see you're wearing my orchids.'

'Oh, they're yours. That's very sweet of you.' She had hoped against hope that they had been from Adam.

He booked a table for four for supper. 'We'll get Martin to join us. He's bound to be about somewhere.'

Martin turned up most opportunely after Gil and she had had the second dance, for it was just when Liz Hamilton arrived a little breathless and looking not a little annoyed.

'You are an old so-and-so,' she said to Gil. 'You might have waited at the hotel for me after the long tiring day I've had in Geneva attending to your wretched business.'

It was said humorously but there was a definite sting. A faint flush rose up under the tan on Gil's face. 'But dearest girl, isn't that what a secretary's for — to attend to her employer's business?'

'Is it? Then I'm not that sort of secretary,' she snapped back at him.

Roxie felt distressed and uncomfortable. She was glad when Martin said abruptly, 'Will you dance with me, Roxie? I'm not much of a dancer but I'll do my best.'

They danced away to the tune which seemed to have become her own:

'Love is like a gambler's heart,
Twisted and troubled from the start.
Love is a thing that two must play the
    same;
Love is a gambler's game.'

91

'On the subject of gambling,' he said, frowning, 'I wish someone would knock some sense into Adam's head. He's been in the roulette room all evening. The one thing he can't afford to do is gamble. He can't afford to lose, anyhow.'

'He may be playing for small stakes,' she demurred. 'Surely he can afford that?'

'He isn't playing for small stakes; he's doing some pretty hefty gambling. He's not playing a safe game at all.'

'Surely Adam himself knows what he can afford to stake,' she answered coolly.

'I told you he can't afford to stake anything. If he doesn't win and regain his speed record he's absolutely on the rocks,' he said bluntly. 'I suppose that's what the silly ass is trying to do — win a fortune to try and finance Marlene's operation.'

'Marlene Farrar?' she caught him up quickly.

He nodded, 'Yes.'

'But where does she come into it?'

'Another of Adam's damn quixotic gestures,' he rumbled. 'She has T.B. badly and is in the Glink Memorial Hospital near here. Adam has already done more than half the financing. She has to have a very expensive operation, with a surgeon flown over from New York, to save her life.'

'Adam's in love with her,' she said flatly. 'He must be to want to do all that, mustn't he?'

There was a note in her voice which made Martin look down at her sharply. 'I'm a silly fool talking through my hat like this, aren't I?' he said, angry with himself. 'But I don't think Adam is in love with her — not in that way any longer. They were almost engaged at one time two years ago, but it seems they decided to drop the love nonsense and become friends. He's certainly proved himself a wonderful friend to Marlene. I think he loves her very dearly without being in love with her, if you know what I mean.'

'Yes.' She caught her breath for a moment and held it. 'I think I know what you mean. But if he breaks the speed record, that should stave off his creditors, at least for a while.'

'But if he doesn't, I think it will be good night to him and to further speedboat racing. They'll probably put *Scotsman III* up for auction,' he said.

'But they couldn't! — they mustn't!' She raised her voice sharply.

'Creditors can do any darn thing; they have no heart at all.'

At the end of the dance she excused herself saying she wanted to go to the powder room. She did go in there for a few minutes to powder her nose and run a comb through her hair. She also looked in her handbag to see if she had her travellers' cheques. The importance of Lord Oxenham's paper allowed his staff very liberal currency allowances. Then she straightened her shoulders like a little soldier going into battle, showed her Press pass at the door of the gaming hall and went inside.

The fashionably dressed crowd was playing roulette in the front room, baccarat in the adjoining room. Large glass chandeliers shed glittering lights on the gaming tables, on the bare shoulders of the women gamblers, and on the sleek heads of the men.

Roxie walked round several of the roulette tables before she saw Adam. He was sitting on the edge of a chair, his eyes intent on the spin of the roulette wheel. His grey-brown eyes were both excited and agonised. He had one small pile of chips beside him for a hundred francs each — that was all.

Roxie went up to the cashier's desk and changed several thousands of francs into chips. There were so many chips they bulged out of her handbag. Then she went and stood beside Adam. He was so engrossed in the game he didn't notice she was there at first. It wasn't until he'd lost his final chip and turned round that he saw her.

She'd never seen defeat and despair written so clearly across any man's face. He looked beaten. 'Oh, it's you, Roxanne,' he said. 'Please excuse me. Would you like to take this seat?'

'No, I've never played roulette. I know nothing about it. I want you to play for me, Adam, and we'll go halves if we win anything. That's fair, isn't it?'

'It isn't fair, but we'll talk about that later. But if you want me to, I don't mind playing for you. Sure you wouldn't prefer to play for yourself?'

'Oh, no, I couldn't; I don't know the first thing about the game. I'd lose everything at once!'

'I've lost everything pretty smartly myself,' he said bitterly. 'How do I know I'll have any more luck with your money?'

'But you will; I know you will!' she said in a small breathless rush. 'Oh, Adam, please sit down again. I'll stand beside you. I just know these chips are going to bring you luck — to bring us both luck.'

He shrugged slightly. 'If you insist, Roxanne.'

'I do insist.'

He took his place again at the table.

'Roxanne, have you any preference as to

what number you want to play on?' he turned his head to ask her.

'Yes,' she whispered back, 'three. *Scotsman III*.'

He smiled a little sadly. He put a chip on the three.

The three won. It seemed almost incredible when the croupier's grating voice came 'Messieurs et Mesdames, faites vos jeux. Les jeux sont fait.' And then after the little ball had spun round it crept unobtrusively into number three.

'Oh, Adam!' she gasped. 'You see, I *have* brought you luck. You've won!'

'You mean you've won,' he said hoarsely.

'We're partners in this. What shall we do now?'

'We'll leave one chip on the three in case it turns up again. What's next, Roxanne? You seem to have the luck to-night.'

'We'll back on everything with a three in it,' she said decisively. 'Thirteen, twenty-three, thirty-three, thirty-six — six is twice three; that should be especially lucky.'

'Yes, three did us a good turn. What's the next number, thirty-three?'

Thirty-three it was and they won again.

After that they tried almost every combination with three. They didn't always win but they won enough. Gaily coloured chips, square and round, were piled up on either side of Adam. His sun-tanned face was flushed with excitement. Roxie was literally trembling with excitement. What fun it was to gamble, especially what fun it was to win!

When finally their luck began to turn, Roxie leant over and said quickly, huskily, 'Let's leave now, shall we, while we've got all those beautiful chips left? I've a feeling our luck has run out for the moment. We don't want to lose everything we've won.'

He nodded slowly as though coming out of a hypnotic trance. 'Just as you say, Roxanne. It's your money — you're the boss.'

'No, it isn't my money. You know you agreed we'd be partners.'

'We can't argue that out here,' he said almost roughly. 'Let's go over to the cashier and change these chips.'

The amount they had made was staggering in itself. Nearly £500. Roxie went straight over to a desk at one side of the room and counted the money out into two neat piles. She folded each one and thrust them into her handbag. Then she said to Adam, 'Come along now to the piazza and we'll have a drink to celebrate our mutual winnings.'

The piazza was fairly deserted at that hour of the evening. Most of the guests were either in the gaming rooms or were in at supper.

It was lit by lanterns and white moonlight. There was a view of the lake but it was sheltered from the breeze.

Roxie deliberately chose a table half-screened from the other tables by palms. She made straight for it, holding her small slight body very erect. But inside she was a tight ball of nerves. So much depended upon this talk she was determined to have with Adam. It was all planned feverishly in her mind. But had she the courage?

The waiter hovered about for their order.

'Let's have champagne,' Adam said. 'It's on the house.' He laughed and there was an excited note in his laughter.

She laughed too, tightly, nervously. 'Certainly champagne.' She thought: 'I'm getting used to champagne. Thank heavens I'm beginning to be sophisticated. What a little idiot I've been up till now — just living, not grasping life and making it as I want it to be.'

She laid her handbag on the table and unlatched the clasp. 'Now we're alone we divide the spoils,' she said with the mocking air of a conspirator.

'We do nothing of the sort,' Adam said harshly. 'I told you in the gaming room it's all yours — I was playing for you.'

'But you agreed we should be partners in

the winnings,' she insisted.

'I only did so to stop you shouting it out before the whole table.' He spoke angrily.

'Was I shouting?' she asked in a hurt voice.

He smiled at her in a more friendly way. 'Of course you weren't shouting, but even a whisper sounds like a shout at the roulette table. People hate you to speak at all.'

'I suppose they think it breaks their concentration and they think concentration has a lot to do with roulette.'

'You think so?' He shrugged. 'I tried to concentrate and I lost everything. You just followed your woman's intuition and won everything.'

'I didn't win — you won. You won on the three — just as you're going to win the race against *Virginia II. Scotsman III.*'

He glanced down at her in a still more kindly way. 'You've a great deal of confidence in me, Roxanne.'

She looked up at him steadily though her heart was thumping dangerously. 'I've all the confidence in the world in you, Adam,' she said quietly.

He reached for her hand which lay on the table, raised it to his lips and kissed it. In most men it might have seemed a theatrical gesture, but somehow with Adam it didn't.

It was a sincere gesture. 'I need people to have confidence in me. Confidence always helps. I like to feel you have confidence in me, Roxanne.'

'I have all the confidence in the world in you, Adam,' she said again, with even more sincerity.

'I feel you're going to bring me luck,' he said, then added with a short laugh. 'I'm even beginning to have confidence in myself.'

She moved her chair a little closer to his. 'But why shouldn't you have confidence in yourself, Adam? You've everything in this world to give you confidence. You've already held the world's speedboat record and you'll regain that record this time you race. You've done so much with your life. You're going to go on doing things — greater, almost impossible things. I know it.'

'You're very sweet, Roxanne.' His voice was a little unsteady. 'I like listening to you. It makes me feel better. I thought my luck was dead out to-night, especially when I lost much more than I can afford to on that crazy roulette game. I thought I'd not only lost all that money but I'd already lost the race and all hope of beating the record. I've been feeling that way for days.'

'I'm going to bring you luck, Adam,' Roxie

said decisively. 'I do believe that's what I came over here to do.'

'But I thought you came over to write your gossip paragraphs.' His voice was faintly teasing.

'Oh, yes, I did. But I wouldn't have insisted that Dad give me the assignment if I hadn't known you before, Adam, if I hadn't wanted to meet you again so much.'

'Hey, what's all this? You're turning my head.' He still tried to treat it as a joke.

'But it's true, Adam.' She kept her eyes fixed on his face. 'I wanted to meet you again very, very much. You see . . . ' She caught her breath sharply, then took her courage in both hands and plunged: 'I've been more than a little in love with you ever since I met you at that house party two years ago.'

Even in the moonlight she could see the colour creep up to his temples. 'Please, Roxanne, you'll probably be sorry to-morrow you said anything like this.'

'No, I shan't be sorry. Will you be sorry I said it, Adam?'

His knuckles were clenched in tight fists on the table. He felt in the grip of an emotional strain himself. 'No, I don't think I shall be sorry, Roxanne. I may even be glad.'

She let out her breath in a half-audible

101

sigh. 'Thank you, Adam.'

They didn't notice the waiter had brought the champagne. He was standing beside them, turning the bottle round in the ice bucket prior to opening it. The pop of the cork startled them both. It was probably the first time they had been aware of his presence. He poured a little of the liquid into Adam's glass. Adam raised it mechanically and tasted it. 'Very good, thank you.'

'Thank you, sir,' the man replied suavely in flawless English.

Roxie saw Adam's flush deepen. She knew he was wondering how much of the previous conversation the man had overheard. Roxie wondered too, but she didn't care. Her luck was holding, the luck she'd had backing three on the gaming table; the present luck she was having with Adam's responses.

When the waiter was gone she waved her glass: 'To our mutual winnings.'

'Your winnings,' he corrected, and again his voice was rough. 'You don't think I'd take any of that money, do you, Roxanne?'

She clenched her hand tightly about the stem of her champagne glass. 'But . . . forgive me, Adam. Please forgive me if I'm speaking out of turn. But you need the money, don't you?'

He half-pushed back his chair as though

he would rise from the table.

'Please don't go, Adam,' she said quickly, and suddenly there were tears in her eyes. They spilled down her cheeks.

He saw them shining whitely in the moonlight. His sudden sharp fit of anger evaporated. 'Who's been talking to you about me, Roxanne?' he asked quietly.

She didn't want to give Martin away. She knew that despite everything he had said, he was very fond of Adam. It was just his outright cynical way of speaking. 'Just gossip I've picked up here and there,' she evaded.

'Then the whole town must know that I'm practically broke,' he said, his face set in heavy angry lines.

'I don't suppose at all that everyone knows. But when you're doing the sort of job I am, you pick up things.'

'What else have you picked up about me apart from the fact that I'm very nearly broke?' he asked bluntly.

Again she had to take her courage in both hands before she spoke. 'There's talk of you and a girl — the ex-film star, Marlene Farrar. I've gathered she's in a T.B. sanitorium somewhere near here. That if she's to recover it's necessary for her to have an almost immediate operation, and that the only surgeon who can do it lives in

New York. Is that true, Adam?' And when he still looked angry and resentful, she went on, pleading with him: 'Please don't think I'm being unnecessarily nosy. I'm only trying to help.'

'But how could you help?' he asked deliberately, even rudely.

'I don't know. I might be able to help. I don't know. But is it true?'

He nodded jerkily. 'It's true enough. The doctors here say Marlene won't live unless she has this special operation. It's a toss of the dice anyhow, but it would give her a chance. But where's the finance to come from? You're right when you say you've heard I was broke. My personal finances are nil; everything I own has been swallowed up by *Scotsman III* — even sponsors are wary. I can't even get any personal credit. If I break the speed record on Saturday week, I might be able to get credit. I could sell the story to the newspapers and sponsors would appear. Even the builder of *Scotsman III* might feel disposed to be lenient. But in the meantime they're at my heels. I may not even get a chance to try for the record. They're threatening an extradition order.'

'But they can't do that!' she said sharply. 'You must try for the record on Saturday week. You must win it, Adam. I swear you will win it!'

He said almost in wonder, 'You've great confidence in me, Roxanne. Even Marlene has not had all that confidence.'

She might have said, 'Perhaps she has never loved you as I do, Adam,' but she bit the words back.

'I'll do my best, of course,' he said quietly. 'There's a great deal at stake. England must regain the speed record for motor-boat racing. It's vital to the speedboat building industry.'

'Then why don't they do something more substantial to help you?' she asked angrily.

'They've done a great deal in the past. I am greatly in their debt. The last few times I've tried to beat the record and failed, I lost heart; I went a bit wild and reckless. The rumours reached them. They clamped down on the money they were allowing me. They said something to the effect: 'Do something to prove you're really worth all this money we're pouring into you, Adam Douglas.' ' He added with a humorous, cynical quirk to his lips: 'I wish they had the faith in me you seem to have, Roxanne.'

'They will have. They'll have all the faith in the world in you after Saturday week, Adam.'

He took her hand again and pressed it. 'You say the nicest things, my dear.'

Again her heart missed a beat. She felt confused for a moment and then resolute again. 'I don't only want to say the nicest things; I want to do the nicest things.'

'But what could you do for me except encourage me?' he said as he might have to a child.

Again her small hand clasped fiercely the stem of her champagne glass. 'I could help you in other ways — financially, if you'd let me, Adam.'

He stared at her for a long moment and in that long moment she went hot and cold, wondering if she'd said too much; wondering if she'd lost him for ever.

'What sort of a heel do you take me for that I'd take money from a woman?' he asked hoarsely at last.

She laughed softly. 'You are a little old-fashioned, aren't you? Men do take money from women these days. That is if the woman has plenty of money and is eager to lend it to them. It's no stigma. And don't forget we are on equal terms with men. All those old-fashioned ideas such as not taking money from a woman have gone out. Can't you look upon me as your friend, Adam, not just as a woman? And I do want to help you.'

'I suppose I am old-fashioned,' he said. 'I find I still can't look at it like that.'

'If you won't take it from me, what about taking something from Dad?' she asked presently. 'Dad would advance you quite a bit if you wrote up the story of the race afterwards exclusively for our papers.'

'That would be different,' he said. He tried to keep the eagerness out of his voice.

She laughed lightly with a throbbing undercurrent. 'You are an old silly,' she said. 'I suppose it would be different. At least you'd think it would be different. But I know Dad would like the story and he'd hate like anything to have his rivals get it. I could drop him a hint that other papers were after your story. Would that help?'

He nodded slowly. He kept his face averted from hers. 'It might help a great deal.'

'It's a deal then,' she said. 'I'm over here as Dad's representative. I'll see they send you a cheque through at once.'

'I shouldn't take it,' he said. 'It's camouflage, of course. I'm not that much of an idiot. But . . . ' His voice shook suddenly with a hint of desperation, 'I have to take it, Roxanne.'

'Then that's settled,' she said gaily. 'Fill up my glass. I need another drink. The champagne baby — that's me. I find I adore champagne. It does something to you.'

'I wish you wouldn't talk like that,' he said angrily. 'It isn't like you at all, Roxanne.'

She asked curiously: 'How do you know what is like me?'

He didn't answer at once. He took a sip of his drink. 'I've been remembering how you were that first week-end we met. I admit I didn't recognise you at first but then you've changed in appearance. You look so much older. But you were a terribly sweet kid, sincere, maybe a little naïve. But I liked you all the better for that. Not the brassy young woman I was used to encountering. And then this morning in the swimming pool you were sweet and natural.' He added suddenly, and his words surprised even him, 'I don't want you to change, Roxanne.'

A thrill of sheer joy ran through her. She could have laughed with joy. 'I won't change, if you don't want me to, Adam.'

He took her hand and squeezed it tightly in both of his: 'Please don't, Roxanne.'

She said haltingly, 'We can be friends, can't we, Adam? Great friends. You'll take me about while I'm here?'

He almost made a bitter rejoinder, asking her if she thought she'd bought him as well as the exclusive articles for her father's press. But he found suddenly he didn't want to hurt her. Almost he couldn't bear to hurt her. It was a very strange feeling. 'If you want me to, Roxanne, of course.' The gentleness in his voice surprised even himself.

She opened her violet-blue eyes wide and looked up at him very steadily. 'Yes, I do want you to, Adam.'

Suddenly he found himself feeling confused and embarrassed, as though he were the young naïve one. It was quite a new feeling for him. Suddenly he was almost a little scared of her — she was really too intent. He was flattered, perhaps more touched than flattered. And curiously, he was feeling rather happy.

'Let's start our new friendship with a dance,' he suggested.

12

She got to her feet with alacrity. She had always dreamt of dancing with Adam. Now she was going to dance with him.

They went into the main hall where the dancing was, with the supper tables packed closely around the walls. The orchestra was playing on a raised dais. She held her breath for a moment as she gave herself into his arms.

They started dancing and Adam danced just as she'd known he would dance — in a straightforward manly style, not in the loose intricate way that Gil danced. Not so well, perhaps, but in a more aggressive masculine way, which pleased her. But then everything about Adam pleased her to-night. She had never been so happy.

Adam didn't talk as he danced. She liked that too. Gil talked half the time, paying her the most ridiculous compliments. She had to admit she'd been flattered and amused; and every once in a while he'd go into an intricate series of steps quite unexpectedly, and it took her a few seconds to keep in step with him. She thought that often a man's dancing indicated his character. Gil's dancing was graceful, his steps were loose and easy, but they were unpredictable. Adam, on the other hand, danced in a straightforward manner. You had every confidence that he wouldn't go into any odd series of steps. The very way he held her was different from the way Gil held her. He held her loosely; it would have been easy to walk out of his arms at any moment. But Adam held her firmly, and, she hoped, possessively . . . Oh, yes, she hoped that the way he held her meant that he was possessive about her.

She was presently conscious that many eyes were turned towards herself and Adam. Sometimes she could hear a comment as they danced by a table. 'There's Adam Douglas dancing with Lord Oxenham's daughter . . . Pretends to be a gossip writer . . . Wonder if there's anything . . . '

Adam was apparently aware of the comments too. 'We seem to be creating something of a sensation,' he remarked as they stood together applauding for an encore.

She raised her eyes to his. 'Do you mind, Adam?'

Again the faint flush rose up under his tan. 'I don't mind at all. But you, Roxanne?'

'I love it,' she said, and clapped harder.

They must play again. She must dance again with Adam.

For the encore they played the tune which Roxie now called her tune. The crooner was singing:

'Love is like a gambler's heart,
Twisted and troubled from the start.
Love is a thing that two must play the
  same;
Love is a gambler's game.'

She didn't like that verse so much. Her heart wasn't twisted and troubled; it was resolute and full of hope. But the next verse he crooned: 'Love is like a star in the sky,' was far more encouraging.

'I like this tune,' she said to Adam.

'Yes, it's a good tune. One hears it everywhere this season. But like most song lyrics, the words are phoney.'

'You don't think love is a gambler's game?' she questioned.

'I've never thought of it like that.'

She asked breathlessly: 'How do you think of love, Adam?'

'As something very stable and important,' he said quietly. 'Something you go into with your eyes wide open. You've fallen in love with someone and you continue to love them,

112

no matter what happens.'

She was glad he felt like that. But it frightened her too. A vision of Marlene rose up before her eyes as she had last seen her at the Copenhowers' that weekend in Sussex. Thin, almost painfully thin, supremely lovely with her rich auburn hair and her attractive heart-shaped face. He had been in love with Marlene then. Was he still in love with her, even though she was so ill in the Glink Memorial Hospital? Was he thinking of Marlene when he said when you fall in love with someone you continued to love them?

She would fight any woman for Adam. But how could she with all her health and vitality fight a girl who was at death's door? It gave her the advantage. You couldn't deliberately fight anyone as ill as all that. It wouldn't be fair. And yet — she couldn't give up Adam. She'd no intention of giving Adam up. Had Marlene been well she would have fought her with the last ounce of her strength.

The shining cloak of her former happiness fell from her. Her heart was twisted and troubled . . . as the words of the song.

'Shall we have supper together?' Adam asked.

'Yes, please,' Roxie murmured.

'I'll arrange for a table directly this dance is over.'

She nodded, forgetting completely that she had promised to have supper with Gil and Liz Hamilton, with Martin as a fourth.

But Gil hadn't forgotten. He bore down upon them at the end of the dance. 'Hello, Adam! Sorry if I'm butting in, but Roxie has promised to have supper with us. We're waiting for her.'

'That's odd,' Adam said. 'She's just promised to have supper with me.'

'I think I have the prior claim.'

'Isn't that up to the lady to decide?'

The two men stood facing one another. The cordiality they usually showed each other was gone completely. Perhaps it had never existed except as the typical good sportsman's attitude. They were both very complimentary about each other's racing achievements in public. They were always hail-fellow-well-met when they encountered each other. But now a deep-rooted antagonism, which must have been there all along, was showing.

Roxie was very conscious of it and she was a little scared of it, even at the very beginning. She gave a small nervous laugh. 'I'm sorry, Gil, but I did promise to have supper with Adam. I'd forgotten . . . ' Her voice died away.

'Then it's a good thing I have a better memory than you have,' Gil said, almost roughly. His good-looking aquiline features were flushed and angry. 'I certainly remember when I brought you here we'd arranged to have supper together — all four of us. Will you come, Roxie? The others are waiting.'

She felt desperate and lost. Her sophistication was too new to allow her to cope with the situation gracefully. 'Couldn't we all have supper together?' she blurted out rather hoarsely. She looked pleadingly at Adam.

He stepped forward and took her hand and popped it under his arm. 'I'll be glad to have supper with you, Gil, if you invite me.'

Gil's lips were tight and rather white looking. His eyes looked a little dangerous. But he said suavely, 'Certainly. I shall be delighted to include you in my party, Adam.' He gave a short laugh, and added, 'I suppose it's good publicity — two rivals supping amicably together, apparently the best of friends off the speed track.'

'The best of friends off the speed track,' Adam replied, and he smiled, not with his eyes. His grey-brown eyes were hard and unfriendly.

'They don't like each other at all. They might even hate each other,' Roxie thought, and a little shiver went through her.

Gil tucked his hand under her other arm. 'We'll move along then,' he said, and the three of them left the dance floor together.

Many heads were turned as they passed. Roxie wondered what people were commenting now. 'The two rivals are so friendly' . . . probably something like that, 'And they both seem pretty smitten with Lord Oxenham's daughter.' At least that's what she hoped they were saying. She wasn't by any means a flirt but it's always a girl's dream that several men should be in love with her at the same time, and what girl on this earth, she asked herself, could wish for two more distinguished and exciting cavaliers than the two great contenders for the speedboat record — Adam Douglas and Gilbert Rogers? She was confident now in her power to turn what might have been an unhappy situation into a happy one. Adam and Gil couldn't possibly dislike each other; it would just have been the momentary antagonism when she'd forgotten that she had promised to have supper with Gil.

Liz and Martin were talking intimately together in low subdued voices when they reached the table. Liz's attractive upturned face was flushed and rather angry looking. Martin looked his usual self-complacent cynical self.

'I see you've persuaded Adam Douglas to join our party,' Liz said the obvious.

'I'm afraid I didn't need a great deal of persuading.' Adam smiled down at her pleasantly, showing the network of crinkles under his eyes. 'I'm all on my lonesome tonight. At least,' he amended, with a look at Roxie, 'I was.'

Gil muttered something under his breath. It might have been, 'And you'll be alone again soon, if I have my way.'

'It's quite something to be at the table with the two of you,' Liz said. 'We're lucky girls, aren't we?' She nodded mockingly across to Roxie. 'The two shining attractions of the Casino Gala and both at our table. Now I bet there isn't one woman in the room who isn't envious of us.'

'You needn't be so damned sarcastic, Liz,' Gil said angrily.

'Was I being sarcastic?' She opened her large grey eyes wide. 'I didn't think I was being sarcastic; I merely thought I was stating the truth.'

'You don't count me as an added attraction?' Martin asked lightly.

'Publicity men belong to that mysterious

117

coterie of people whose faces never get into print,' Liz laughed back at him. 'Everyone is probably wondering who the devil you are to be so honoured.'

Martin nodded and looked as though he was in his element, enjoying himself immensely. The whole situation might almost have been tailored to suit him. 'At least you two men should smile occasionally,' he commented. 'Or your public may get the very worst impression.'

'To hell with the public!' Gil said explosively.

'Tut-tut. You're behaving like a naughty boy, Gil,' Martin chided him. 'By your sour look anyone would think you've already lost the speed record. I saw you taking *Virginia II* out for a spin early this morning. How did she go?'

'Perfectly — as always,' Gil replied surlily.

'Tut-tut! We *are* annoyed about something. You're not giving any hints as to what speed you clocked in?'

'Why don't you ask Adam what speed he clocked in yesterday?' Gil countered.

'Oh, I did. I got the same sort of reply, only more politely put, if you don't mind my saying so, Gil old man.' He turned towards Roxie. 'I saw you disappearing into the gaming room. Did you have any luck?'

118

Her eyes shone. 'I had wonderful luck — the most wonderful luck in the world.' Beneath the table her hand sought out Adam's. He appeared to hesitate, then she felt his hard lean fingers close around her small hand. She repeated almost with a sigh, 'Wonderful luck.'

Martin wasn't unaware of her starry-eyed look. He sensed without seeing it that her hand was in Adam's under the table. He tried to feel cynical about it, but instead he felt damned angry. 'You mean you won at the tables?' he said deliberately.

'Oh, yes. Adam and I won. We were playing together.' She added importantly: 'We won quite a lot.'

'Did you have a system?'

She was too happy not to talk about it. 'A system consisting of three and all combinations of three.'

'A system consisting of all combinations of three. *Scotsman III*,' Martin said. 'What do you think of that, Gil?'

'I'm afraid I haven't even been following the conversation. Liz and I were talking,' Gil said, lying. But all he'd said to Liz was, 'If you go on behaving as you are behaving to-night, I'll send you into Geneva on another errand to-morrow.'

'I don't think you'll need to. I don't think

119

it would do any good, Gil,' she flashed back at him.

He gave her a sour look and turned his attention to his plate when Martin addressed him. Roxie was only faintly aware of the undercurrents. And if she had been aware, she wouldn't have cared much; she was far too happy. She didn't realise then that there were dangerous undercurrents, the rumblings beneath the earth's surface before the final volcanic explosion. Adam was still holding her hand. She couldn't eat, but she didn't care. Since it was her right hand he was holding she couldn't even raise the champagne glass to her lips. But she didn't need champagne now.

When a fresh dance tune started, Gil pushed back his chair and got to his feet. 'Come along, Roxie. We'll dance this.'

She could do nothing but draw her hand out of Adam's and rise too. She wound her way through the tables and he followed her on to the dance floor. His finely etched handsome face which you might almost associate with a gigolo, was hard and angry looking. 'I thought I brought you to-night, Roxie. What do you mean by disappearing all that time? And then turning up with Adam Douglas?'

'You brought me and I'm grateful, but you

haven't the exclusive rights over me to-night or any night,' she returned with spirit.

'But I mean to have. You know I mean to have, Roxie.'

'I don't know anything of the kind. Why are you talking in this stupid way? I like you, Gil. I'd like to be friends with you. But that's all,' she repeated and emphasised it — '*Friends*.'

'Is that all you want to be with Adam Douglas — just friends?' he asked sharply.

'That has nothing to do with you.' She found she was getting really annoyed with him.

'It has a great deal to do with me,' he insisted. 'Have you forgotten the way you kissed me the other night?'

She felt the colour rise up her cheekbones to the roots of her soft honey-yellow hair. 'I thought it was you who kissed me.'

'I kissed you, certainly, but there was a time you were kissing me back. Have you forgotten so soon, or is it you don't want to remember any longer?'

'That — that was the champagne,' she said in a faint voice.

'Do you have to find an excuse for kissing me? I'm not very flattered.'

'I'm sorry. I've never done anything like that before.'

They had paused to clap for the encore, but when they started dancing again he said savagely, 'You don't think I'm going to step aside peacefully and leave Adam in possession? If you think that you've got another think coming, Roxie. I'm going to beat Adam's record; I'm going to keep you as my girl. Is that understood?'

'Certainly it isn't understood.'

'I'm a pretty persistent bloke and everything I've set my heart upon, I've got,' he said.

'What will Liz Hamilton have to say?' she flashed at him.

'She has no right to say anything. But if she does say something, I can take care of that. You're not frightened of Liz, are you, princess?'

'I'm not frightened of her, but I'm sorry for her,' she said quietly.

'You mean because she's in my employ?' he said, purposely misunderstanding her.

'No, because she's in love with you, Gil,' she said gently.

She saw the flush rise up to his high cheekbones. He looked angry one moment then ashamed the next. 'It's as obvious as all that?' he asked finally.

She nodded slowly. 'It's pretty obvious.'

'I tried to pretend to myself she wasn't in

122

love with me,' he said wretchedly, looking now more like a boy than a grown man. 'I've tried to think she liked me as a good friend and as my employee was jealous of my interests. I like her so much, but . . . ' he paused and drew a breath, 'I don't love her.'

'Poor Liz,' Roxie said softly. She determined to be much nicer to Liz Hamilton in future, no matter what Liz did or said to her.

The encore was over and they went back to the table. The men stood, and Adam said quickly as Roxie was about to sit down, 'Don't sit down, Roxanne. They've started playing again. I want you to dance with me.' He said it with a proprietory air that secretly delighted her.

Gil raised his eyebrows and resumed his seat without speaking. Martin merely smiled.

Roxie almost ran back to the dance floor as though thankful to escape. She found she had to concentrate on Adam's steps harder than she'd had to do the first time. He was holding himself more stiffly. He looked faintly flushed under his tan.

'I can't say I enjoyed myself much at supper,' he said presently . . . Didn't he remember how their hands had clung together? Hadn't he enjoyed that? . . .

'It was rather awkward,' she murmured.

'Damnably awkward! And Martin grinning all the time like a pleased Cheshire cat didn't help matters. The girl, Miss Hamilton, was sarcastic and furious over something. As for Gilbert Rogers . . . ' But he broke off.

'You don't like Gil, do you?' she said quietly.

'I don't like him,' he agreed. 'And the worst of it is I have to pretend to like him. Rivals on the speed track but good friends off it. You know the sort of thing the public wants and likes and expects. I've an intuition Rogers feels the same way about me. Did he give you any hint at all?'

'Perhaps he doesn't like you very much,' she agreed soberly, 'but then you don't like him — you've just said so.'

'If it wasn't for all this hail-fellow-well-met manner we've got to put on, I'd never speak to the fellow.' His voice was rough and angry. 'How come he seems so sure he's got you where he wants you, Roxanne?'

'He hasn't got me where he wants me — if he wants me at all. Anyhow I don't want him.' She said with defiance.

'I'm glad to hear you say that, but . . . apart from being a famous character he's a very rich young man, Roxie.'

'But I haven't any need of his money. I've

plenty of my own.' She flushed after she'd said it.

'Your father's money, you mean. Everyone knows that Lord Oxenham is a millionaire and you're his only child.'

'I didn't mean the money Dad may leave me,' she insisted. 'I meant I have my own money — my mother's money. And that's considerable. I inherited it on my eighteenth birthday.'

'Little Miss Midas, I'm honoured you're dancing with me.'

'Don't say things like that, please, Adam.' Her voice was ragged suddenly. She was almost in tears.

'I'm sorry, but I wish you weren't so filthily rich.' His own voice grated.

'But why, Adam? It doesn't make me any less nice, does it?'

'No,' he agreed. 'But all the same I wish you weren't so rich. It wouldn't matter with Gil Rogers — he's got a whacking great amount of his own. If we're seen about together people may say that I'm after your money.'

'Let them say it, and if I hear them say it I'll smack their faces,' she retorted with spirit.

'You wouldn't mind them saying that?' he asked with humility in his voice.

'Haven't I just told you I wouldn't mind? And it wouldn't be true, would it, Adam?'

He was silent for so long, she repeated it almost pleadingly: 'Would it, Adam?'

'No, it wouldn't be true,' he said finally. 'But there will be people who will tell you that it is true; that to marry someone as rich as you would enable me to pay off my debts and continue in speedboat racing. Even to be seen about with you will probably help my credit in this town at least. And the rumour is bound to reach London, which will undoubtedly help my credit there. You see, I have a great deal to gain by going about with you, Roxanne. I'm damned if I see what you have to gain.'

They were dancing idly, merely shuffling along, so intent were they on this conversation.

'I've said I don't mind what people say, and I'm happy in our friendship, Adam — if you're happy.' Her slim arm tightened about his shoulders. She moved closer to him. She whispered in his ear, 'Are you happy, Adam?'

'Yes, I'm happy,' he said soberly. 'I must be off my nut because I didn't believe I could be happy in this way again.'

A little sigh broke from her. She almost kissed him on the dance floor. But what were they doing still dancing? The band had stopped.

13

Martin stood beside them. 'Before you both dance into the lake,' he said, 'I'm going to claim Roxie for the next dance.' He tried to speak pleasantly, at least pleasantly for him, but there was an angry bitter undercurrent. He had been feeling damnably angry all evening. Dash it all! He had discovered Roxie first. He'd singled her out for his special attention during this festive season. But instead she seemed to be fought over both by Gilbert Rogers and Adam Douglas. He'd known she had a crush on Adam, but he'd hoped that when she'd discovered how wrapped up Adam was in Marlene, she'd get over it. He hadn't reckoned with Gil busting in upon the scene. Why the heck couldn't he content himself with that secretary of his with the rather flat features and large grey eyes? She was an attractive wench. He wouldn't have minded going for her himself but it was obvious that she was completely wrapped up in Gil. What a heck of a supper party it'd been! He wished he'd been a hundred miles away from it. No, he didn't. If he had been he wouldn't have been at the same table with

Roxie. He wouldn't have had the opportunity to ask her for the next dance.

He spoke to Roxie now. 'There's not much sense in going back to the table. The band is already tuning up for the next number.'

'If you'll excuse me, I see old Mac over there. I want to have a talk with him.' Adam moved away from them.

Roxie watched his well-formed body move away from them into the crowd. His six foot two inches made him taller than most men, and his broad shoulders were formidable. She liked the way his light brownish hair fitted closely to the back of his head. But then she liked everything about Adam. Her heart sang with the feeling that in the short space of that last dance their relationship had definitely progressed.

Martin danced erratically and badly. Obviously he wasn't thinking of his steps at all. She did her best to follow him and when Gil and Liz danced past them she even tried to look as though she were enjoying it. But when she stumbled twice and had prettily apologised although she knew that the fault wasn't her own, he said abruptly, 'Don't bother apologising. I know I'm dancing shockingly. I don't feel in the mood for it. Let's go outside and walk down to the lake. It will give us a breath of fresh air. And who knows, it may even improve my dancing.'

'All right,' she agreed. But she didn't really want to go. She knew he was in a bad mood and even in ordinary mood she was a little afraid of him. He had the habit of saying such disconcerting things, of pricking any bubble of happiness that might be floating around her.

The dance music followed their steps down the path, through the gardens and out the Casino gates.

It was only a very short distance down to the lake.

'I thought I'd made a find — a personal find,' he said abruptly. 'Instead I never see you at all. Gil Rogers is smitten with you and you're hell-bent-for-leather on hurling yourself at Adam's head.'

She flushed angrily in the darkness, bit her lower lip and remained silent.

'And don't try to deny it,' he said. 'It's obvious to everyone.'

'I wasn't intending to deny it. But I'm sorry if it seems so obvious.'

'Well it does,' he said. 'It's bound to be all round town to-morrow — that Adam and you are smitten with each other. He acts kind of goofy too — at least to me he does. You're such a direct, intent person that I suppose if you made a dead set at a man it would rather knock him off his pins.'

She asked eagerly, momentarily forgetting everything else he had said, 'You really think that Adam is keen on me?'

'He's making it seem pretty obvious. Of course, to have his name coupled with yours is bound to assist his financial position.'

'You're hateful, aren't you?' she said in a small tight voice.

'I mean to be hateful. I'm trying to knock some sense into your head,' he said rudely. 'You know that at the moment Adam is absolutely down the drain financially?'

'He told me that himself. I must say you're a very fine friend — if you call yourself his friend.'

'I am his friend. That's why I don't want people talking about him — accusing him of being a fortune-hunter. If you want to get yourself entangled with one of the two who are trying to break the speed record, why don't you pick on Gil? He's obviously willing, and I should say he's got as much money as you have.'

'I don't want to get entangled with him. I like him but as a friend. Besides, don't you think it rather a waste when two people with a lot of money marry each other? I've always thought so. If you've got a fortune of your own, what's the good of marrying someone with another fortune? I'd much rather marry a man who was penniless.'

'You've certainly an original way of thinking,' he grunted.

'I think it only makes sense,' she retorted sharply. 'And I don't really see that it's anything to do with you how Adam and I feel about each other.'

'You must have put in some pretty fast work in the short time you've been here,' was his only comment.

Her eyes filled with tears suddenly. 'You like hurting people, don't you? You like making them feel mean and degraded.'

'Do I?' he said, as though it were a new idea. 'You may even be right. Perhaps because I'm not a very happy person myself, I rather resent seeing others happy. I'd like to be happy with someone, then maybe I'd change. I thought when I met you in the train I might have been happy with you, Roxie. Did you like me at first?'

'I didn't like you when you were cynical,' she temporised.

'But cynicism is as natural to me as breathing.' He added in a rather boyish awkward way, 'I don't mean half of it, you know.'

'Then why do you say things that hurt other people?'

'Sometimes I say things to try to prevent them being hurt,' he told her seriously. 'If you suspect the worst of a person you can't be hurt, can you? Apart from you, Roxie — and I admit I've a crush on you — I'm extremely fond of Adam.'

'But you practically accused him of being a fortune-hunter.'

'I didn't. I was merely telling you what people would say. I am fond of Adam.' He paused a moment and then he said, 'and Marlene.'

They had reached the end of the pier where there was a seat. She sat down abruptly and her heart closed up in sudden fear. Marlene Farrar, the half-dead girl in the Glink Memorial Hospital, the girl who had once been the supremely lovely movie star.

'You mean Marlene Farrar?' she asked, to gain time.

He shrugged. 'Who else? Hasn't Adam told you about her?'

'Only that she needs an operation to save her life. And apparently the only surgeon who can perform it is in New York.'

'I don't agree that the operation is essential,' he said. 'I think she's pulling through as it is. I've been up to see her twice since I arrived here.'

'That was nice of you.'

'Oh, I can be nice, Roxie,' he said, laughing suddenly. 'That surprises you, doesn't it?'

She didn't answer that. 'Tell me more about Marlene Farrar,' she urged him.

'I knew her in England when she was a star. I think she already had the lung trouble. She kept on working a long while after she knew she had it, making pictures feverishly. It was as though she knew she was headed, if not for death, for a long and serious illness, and was working against time. She was always full of courage. She still is full of courage.'

She wet her dry lips. 'It must be awful for her lying up there day after day. Especially since she doesn't seem to be getting any better. I — I wish she would get better.'

He turned and looked at her. 'That's an odd thing for you to say, Roxie.'

'Why should it be an odd thing?' she challenged hoarsely.

'I shouldn't think you'd like to have Marlene as lovely as she was and bursting with health and vigour,' he commented dryly.

'You're being hateful again,' she accused him.

'Why don't you get up and leave me?

133

You want to hear more about Marlene, don't you?'

'Yes,' she admitted.

'Then why not ask Adam about her? He knows her even better than I do.'

'I shall ask Adam about her,' she said determinedly.

'Do you imagine he'll tell you the truth?'

'I'm sure he'll tell me the truth,' she said, hating him again. 'And I wish Marlene was better, no matter what you may think. I wish she was here now, able to join in all the festivities. If she is my rival — as you seem to think she is — I hate to think of her lying up there in the hospital. It makes it all seem unfair. And yet . . . ' She didn't finish the sentence, but she finished it in her mind. 'And yet I wouldn't give up Adam, not now — I couldn't. I'll do anything in this world to get Adam. But I wish Marlene Farrar was well and I could fight her fairly.'

They hadn't spoken for several minutes.

'Do you want to go back to the party?' he asked.

'Yes, please.' She rose to her feet.

'I don't seem to have done myself much good in your eyes this evening,' he commented ruefully.

She didn't answer that either. On their way down the pier she glanced out on to the lake.

It was like a silver carpet to-night but she wished she was looking at it with Adam.

As they left the pier they ran into Gil and Liz walking towards it. 'Hello, you two. Enjoying the beauty of the lake at night?' Gil tried to speak in a friendly way. It wasn't quite successful.

'We've seen the lake. We're going back to the Casino,' Martin commented.

'We'll be back there ourselves presently,' Gil said. 'You'll keep me a dance, Roxie?' His voice was boyish and eager.

'Of course, Gil, if I'm still there,' she added.

'But you can't go home so soon. Besides, don't forget I'm your escort to-night.'

'I may still be there. I don't know. I'm a little tired.' She was wondering if she would be able to dance with Adam again or if he would be off somewhere drinking with his team. She didn't want to turn in too late. She wanted to be fresh for her swimming date with Adam in the morning.

Liz and Gil continued on down the pier. They walked a little apart from each other as though they were not on very friendly terms. They reached the end of the pier and stood looking out over the lake before they resumed their interrupted conversation.

'I'd be awfully sorry to lose you, Liz,' Gil

135

said, and tried to make the statement sound very sincere. But he had to admit to himself that Liz was getting in his hair rather badly recently. She was not only secretary; she was mother, sister, nurse. He guessed she would like to have been sweetheart. They had bickered all the way down from the Casino and he found his genuine affection for her turning into a sharp sense of annoyance.

'So you see it's no use my staying on as your secretary once the race is over,' she said finally and flatly. 'Nice of you to say you'd be sorry to lose me, but you don't sound as though you'd be very sorry.'

'Hang it all!' he said angrily. 'You've been picking on me ever since we left the Casino. How do you expect me to sound? But in the morning I'll say the same thing and sound quite different. Why the heck do you think you can't continue as my secretary?'

'Because I'm too much in love with you, Gil,' she said, and gave a small unamused laugh. 'Pathetic, isn't it, to admit that to any man — especially to you? Oh, I know you're not in love with me in that way, but we've always been very close friends, and I thought that sufficed. I thought I could get along with our friendship. I've tried, Gil, but it's hopeless. I don't blame you if I get on your nerves. I'm not liking myself at all at this moment. I'm quite a deal ashamed of myself but it's something I have to say. I thought I could take it — take anything so long as I was with you. But these past few days I've known I can't.'

'What's changed in the past few days?' he asked uncomfortably.

'You've fallen for the Haldane girl, haven't you? All blue eyes and seeming innocence, though I don't believe it. You make it so painfully obvious whenever she's about, I could scream. You almost eat her with your eyes. I hate her, naturally; I might even forgive her if she was smitten with you. But anyone with half an eye could see she's all out to get Adam Douglas.'

'I don't see that at all,' he said roughly and angrily. 'She is just a nice kid and a bit of a hero-worshipper, and Adam Douglas is a hero in her eyes. But on Saturday week I'll show her just how much of a hero he is.' His voice grated.

'You really think you can beat Adam? And don't forget he may even make a new record at the test.'

'The record is 225.73 miles an hour. I swear I can beat that,' he said with exaggerated confidence.

'My poor Gil,' she said. 'You're not confident at all, or you wouldn't be so

137

dogmatic about it. That isn't like you either. Usually you say 'I may be lucky. I'll do my best anyhow.' Usually it doesn't mean much to you one way or another. But this time it means a great deal to you, doesn't it? Something far more important is at stake than beating Adam Douglas.'

'You bet something more important is at stake. I can't stand the fellow. I'm out to make him look a fool in the eyes of the world.'

'My poor Gil,' she said again with genuine pity in her voice. 'That doesn't sound like you talking. And even if you did beat him, you could never make Adam Douglas look a fool. People would just say it was unfortunate but he'll build a faster boat and regain the record.'

'With the Oxenham fortune behind him, he should be able to build as many boats as he chooses. I should say Lord Oxenham will have something to say about a penniless son-in-law who failed once again to regain the speed record,' Gil said savagely.

'You don't sound like a very good sportsman, Gil,' she commented with that same deep pity in her voice.

'Oh, blast this good sportsman business!' he said angrily. 'I wish you wouldn't keep ramming it down my throat, Liz. I don't suppose Douglas likes me any better than I like him. Do rivals in any sport ever like each other, although the newspapers tell the public they do? It's the same with every sport.'

'You are in a bad mood to-night, Gil. Love doesn't seem to be bringing out the best in your character,' she said in bitter mockery. She added after a very long pause, 'I suppose I always knew you'd fall in love some day, but I fooled myself into believing it might be with me. I suppose I've really been too good to you, Gil. The perfect secretary — the lifelong friend, ready to work my fingers to the bone for you, to scrub floors for you if that should be necessary. A modern doormat — that's what I've been. And what man appreciates a doormat? I should have got myself a few boy friends to keep you guessing. I should have seen to it that some man, any man, was crazy about me. I could still do that. I'm not all that unattractive, you know, Gil. But what would be the use of that now? You'd be glad of the excuse to push me into his arms.'

'You're talking a lot of rot,' he said angrily. But he knew she was speaking the truth, and it increased his sense of guilt and embarrassment.

He got to his feet. 'Let's shelve all this for the moment, shall we? To-morrow's another day, and to-morrow we may be able to talk more sensibly about it. I'll admit I'm feeling on edge to-night and I may have said some stupid things, Liz.'

'I'm afraid I've said some very stupid things too,' she said sadly. 'Let's go back and dance. We can lose ourselves in hot rhythm. Let's hope it has more effect on us than the champagne did. I'm beginning to think that champagne is a depressing drink instead of a reviver.'

'I'm taking Roxie home,' he said aggressively.

'Can't I tag along too? Have a heart, Gil.' She was laughing a little but there were tears behind her laughter.

14

Roxie didn't dance with Adam again that night. She walked home with Gil and Liz. She sensed the strained atmosphere between them and felt genuinely sorry about it. She suspected she was to blame for it. But it hadn't been her fault. She hadn't asked Gil to fall in love with her. And even if she had momentarily returned his kisses that night, what of it? She'd been kissed before; she had kissed back. Not that she'd ever wanted to kiss back really, but she felt that not to do so would have hurt the boys' feelings. Roxie was always very sensitive about other people's feelings.

She was glad to be back at the hotel at a fairly reasonable hour. She would get her sleep in before the morning swim. Not that she needed much sleep. At her age one doesn't. Life is too much of an intoxicating adventure to be wasted in excessive sleep.

This morning, like the morning before, was brilliant and sparkling. The light of the newly-risen sun reflected like golden swords on the still surface of the table.

She got into her bathing suit and with

beating heart went down to the swimming pool. 'He won't be there,' she told herself. 'Probably he was up late last night, though I didn't see him after I got back to the Casino. But he must have been racketing somewhere. He'll be tired or he'll have forgotten all about our date.' But all the same she reached the swimming pool hopefully. But her heart sank — Adam wasn't there!

She swam the length of the pool slowly, telling herself it was wonderful, the water was so fresh and invigorating. She had swum the length of the pool three times before Adam appeared. He had rather a haggard appearance in the bright morning light, as though he hadn't slept a great deal. Her heart turned over in sympathy for him. There was evidently a great deal on his mind besides beating the speed record.

'Hello!' She waved to him from the water.

'Hello, yourself.' He slipped off his patterned sports shirt. 'I'm going to dive right in. It may help to clear my head.'

'Don't tell me you had a heavy party after that show at the Casino?'

'No, but I was up most of the night with telephone calls to England.'

'I hope they were successful?'

He hesitated. 'Moderately so.' And then he dived in.

It was a beautiful dive. She held her breath as he slowly surfaced.

'What about that race? I'll give you a length of the pool start, as I promised.'

'Done!' she said. 'It gives me a good chance of beating you.' And she did manage to beat him, but laughingly she accused him: 'You weren't really trying.'

'Perhaps I have other things on my mind this morning.'

'More important than our race?' she challenged, laughing again.

'Perhaps. But not more important than you, my lovely water-nymph. Do you know that I dreamt about you last night in the short snatch of sleep I had just before dawn? I woke up with a start and remembered I had to meet you down by the pool.'

'Were you pleased with the thought?'

His hand covered one of hers which was clinging to the side of the pool. 'I was pleased,' he said gravely, 'and I cursed myself for oversleeping. I thought you might have been down here and gone.'

She laughed again, a little joyous sound. 'I don't give up so easily, Adam.'

He looked at her straight, and said, 'You're a very curious girl, Roxanne. I don't think I've ever met one like you before. You're not afraid to say what you mean. Most girls are. I'll race you two lengths of the pool once again,' he said, 'and then let's dry off in the sun.'

This time he beat her.

'Should we have another as the deciding factor?' she suggested tentatively.

He shook his head. 'I don't like deciding factors — not between a man and a woman. Let's leave it that we both have won once. We're equals.'

'I like that way best too,' she agreed.

They spread out their large gaily striped beach towels on the surround of the pool. They lay flat on their bellies, their chins resting on bent arms.

'When I was on my way back to the hotel, I saw you returning to the Casino with Martin,' he said presently.

'Yes, we walked down to the pier for a breath of air.'

'What did he tell you?' he asked sharply. 'Martin's tongue can be pretty ruthless.'

'He didn't tell me anything that I didn't know already. But there were some things he told me, I'd like you to explain. Your finances are in a bad way, Adam.'

'I told you that myself,' he said tersely. 'I've never let you think anything else, have I?'

'No,' she agreed quietly, 'and I'm glad it

was you who told me first.' She clenched her hands tightly by her sides and went on: 'He also told me about Marlene Farrar. At least he told me something about her. I want you to tell me much more about her, Adam.'

He moved resentfully. 'I thought I'd told you that she's been very ill with lung trouble for the past two years. That in order to put her on her feet again she needs another operation, and that the only surgeon who can do it for her is in New York.'

'Oh, yes, I know all that. What I want to know is . . . ' She caught her breath and held it for a long moment before she finished: 'What are *your* feelings towards her? Are you still in love with her, Adam?'

He didn't reply at once, and when he did his voice was rough, almost angry. 'You should know I'm not, Roxanne, or else I wouldn't have said some of the things I said to you last night. I love her, yes — very dearly — as I'd love a very dear sister, but as for being in love . . . That's something different, isn't it?'

'I suppose it is,' she said quietly. 'To love someone is a steady, companionable emotion. But to be in love . . . it's all thrills and fireworks — supreme happiness and misery. Something that nags at you

145

continuously. You can scarcely bear to let the other person out of your sight.'

He looked at her curiously. 'You know a lot for someone so young.'

'Maybe I didn't know all that until a few days ago,' she said. 'But I'm learning fast.' And then in another pause she asked: 'Were you very much in love with her?'

'Yes. I was deeply in love with her at one time. In love, you know, as you've just described it.'

'And she reciprocated? But of course,' she said quietly.

He shook his head. 'You're wrong — she didn't. She liked me, I know. She was quite fond of me and rather possessive.' He smiled slightly and humorously. 'But she wasn't in love with me in the way I was with her. You see, there had been someone else in her life before she met me. It had hurt her deeply — too deeply for her to recover quickly. It was too soon for her to fall completely in love with someone else. But we became very good companions. We're still very good companions.'

'Are you still in love with her, Adam?' She had to ask it. 'And don't say,' she suddenly raged, 'it's none of my business because I feel it is my business.'

He reached down to her side and took

one of her hands in his. 'You funny little thing,' he said tenderly. 'I'd be a brute if I didn't tell you the truth, wouldn't I? I'm not still in love with Marlene in that way. She's been ill for so long I can't even imagine her well again. I can't imagine her other than lying in that bed on the sunlit balcony of the Glink Memorial Hospital. I feel a deep tenderness for her, but that is all. I swear it, Roxanne.' His hand tightened about hers.

'But if she were well again?' she insisted hoarsely.

'I don't think I'd feel any differently about her. Too much time has elapsed and one doesn't fall in love all over again, does one?'

'I wouldn't know,' she said quietly.

He gave a short bitter laugh, and said, 'I wouldn't know either. But as I feel at the moment I don't think it possible.' And then he added in a much lower voice, 'Especially now that I've met you, Roxanne.'

'Oh, I do wish I knew that you meant that,' she said.

'I do mean it,' he said, and added in a still lower voice, 'my dear.'

She felt her heart fill almost to bursting. She felt tears sting the backs of her eyes. They both lay silent. It was as though

147

they were both self-conscious lying on the surround of the pool so close together. It was as though too much had been said suddenly; there was so much to digest.

Suddenly he sprang to his feet and took her hand. 'Let's go back to the hotel and breakfast on the porch. I'll put on a sports shirt and slacks. You slip into something. I'd love to breakfast with you.' He squeezed her hand tighter. 'It may be the beginning of many breakfasts together,' and he added in an undertone, 'darling.'

A number of guests in the hotel saw them breakfasting together. There were excited whispers and comments. 'It seems as though Adam Douglas has got off with Lord Oxenham's daughter. His fame and her money — what an excellent match.'

Monsieur Henriot, the manager of the Excelsior Palace, himself took a stroll along the terrace, nodding his satisfaction at what he had observed. There'd been ugly rumours about Adam Douglas's financial position and he'd been a little afraid his hotel might become involved, or even that the race might be called off at the last moment, which would damage the hotel considerably financially. But if it was serious between him and the newspaper baron's daughter, Adam's creditors would probably be induced to wait.

There would be no scandal, no cancellation of the race. He hummed under his breath with renewed satisfaction.

After breakfast Adam went down to the wharf to go into a huddle with his team over some minor adjustments which had to be made to the steering of *Scotsman III*. Roxie went down with him. It was her first sight of *Scotsman III*.

It was a thrilling-looking boat, gleaming metal, of extremely modernistic design, more like some futuristic dream than an actual speed-boat. Adam introduced her to the 'team,' mainly young men and all enthusiastic. McPherson, the chief engineer, known as Mac, had been with him for a considerable time. Others like Tedmaster, the chief electronics engineer, were fairly new recruits. Roxie found meeting them all and being shown some of the intricate mechanism of *Scotsman III* a unique and exciting experience. They were all such nice young men, modest and retiring, but masters in their special fields. She promised to come down and see them again. She felt immediately at home with them.

Afterwards she hired a car and was driven up to the Glink Memorial Hospital. It was a good half-hour's drive through heavenly mountain scenery, but she was too full of the plans in her mind to pay much attention to the landscape.

Once there she asked to see the hospital secretary.

He proved to be an intelligent, pleasant little man with the name of Schmidt. Roxie explained somewhat breathlessly just what she wanted. She wanted the hospital to arrange for Miss Farrar to have the necessary operation. They were to put a phone call through to New York and arrange for the doctor to fly over immediately. She would be responsible for all the expenses. She would cable her London bank — or better, telephone the manager and see that all the financial matters were taken care of in London.

When she told the secretary who she was and who her father was, he didn't doubt but that she'd be able to take care of the expenses easily. She did insist on complete anonymity. Marlene must have no idea who her benefactress was. The hospital authorities were to tell her that an admirer of her screen work of the past had made himself responsible for all the financial business entailed in the operation. There was to be no thought of repayment. The pleasure she had given in the past on the screen was sufficient repayment.

'May I say that you are an exceedingly kind and generous young lady, Miss Haldane,' the secretary said with the deepest sincerity.

'Please don't be too generous with your praise,' Roxie said and flushed painfully.

'Nonsense,' he said brusquely. 'What earthly benefit would it be to yourself to take on so much financial responsibility? I repeat you are an exceedingly kind and generous girl, and nothing you can say will alter my mind. But I wish you wouldn't insist so strongly on anonymity. I know Miss Farrar would like to thank you personally.'

'No, please,' Roxie said quickly. 'It is only on the condition that no one knows who paid the expenses of the operation that I am prepared to do anything at all.'

He bowed his head. 'As you wish. But you don't mind me telling you how much I admire you personally?'

She felt hot with embarrassment again. 'There's no reason why you should admire me. I'll contact my bank manager immediately and ask him to make all the necessary arrangements with you.'

She was anxious to get away now. The little secretary's fervent admiration for what he deemed to be a purely noble and disinterested act made her feel more than uncomfortable.

It made her feel small. But she had had to do it, though it would be impossible to make him understand why she'd done it. It was difficult to understand herself just why she had done it. But there had been a deep feeling in her that she couldn't fight a woman who lay helplessly in hospital, waiting for a reprieve — the reprieve which her money could easily give her. She could take Adam from Marlene now, for Adam had told her he was no longer in love with Marlene in that way. But then Marlene had been sick so long. How would he feel about her once she was cured? And much as she loved him, Roxie knew that she couldn't take Adam from Marlene permanently until she should be cured and she knew he was still in love with her, Roxie.

It was unfortunate that in leaving the hospital she ran into Martin, with a bouquet of flowers, coming to visit Marlene.

'Don't tell me the two rivals for Adam's affections have been getting together in a sweet girlish talk?' he said mockingly.

'I haven't seen Miss Farrar. I came to see someone else,' she said shortly.

'Even if you came to see someone else you mean to say you resisted the impulse to drop in and have a heart-to-heart chat with the one-time glamorous Marlene?'

'I don't think either of us would be interested to see each other,' she said coldly. 'We've only met once — for a short weekend, and that was some time ago.'

'But I should think that now you two should have quite a lot to discuss,' he said, knowing he was hurting her and disliking himself intensely for doing it. But it was the way he was made.

'I don't know what you're talking about,' she said. 'It isn't very interesting, anyhow.'

'You mean Adam isn't interesting?'

'I said nothing of the sort. I've a car waiting. So long, Martin.'

He stood looking after her, wondering what the devil got into him every time he spoke to her lately, and he knew that that devil was jealousy. He'd never realised before what jealousy could do to you — how mean and ungracious it could make you. How it could make you hate and despise yourself, and yet you could do nothing about it.

He turned slowly and walked along the corridor to the reception desk. They rang through to Marlene's room and then asked him to wait a few minutes. The matron and the secretary were in with her.

It was a full twenty minutes before he was finally admitted to Marlene's room. It was white and spotlessly clean, and there were cheerful chintz curtains.

Marlene was propped up on the back-rest. Her white heart-shaped face was flushed. Her eyes were alive and excited. She looked so much more alive than she had during his previous visits that he wondered fleetingly if Roxie had been lying to him. Had they had a girls' talk together which had upset and at the same time excited Marlene? Had the matron been sent for as a result?

Directly they were alone, she cried excitedly: 'Oh, Martin, I've had such wonderful news. Matron has just been in telling me an old admirer of mine — who insists on being anonymous — has put up the money for the operation.'

'Did the old admirer give his name?'

'No. Matron told me that was one of the things he insisted upon most strictly. His name wasn't to be mentioned at all. He didn't want me to feel any gratitude. Isn't that wonderful? It will save poor Adam trying to raise the money somehow. I know the poor darling is terrifically worried about it.'

'You won't mind accepting money from this unknown admirer?' he asked quietly.

She made a brief shrug. 'No. Why should I? Everyone tells me I've given pleasure to so many people in the past. Why shouldn't one of them come across and help me now? It makes it all the easier too that he insists on being anonymous. I won't have to be eternally grateful to him.'

'As you might have had to be to Adam?' he said soberly.

'I wouldn't have cared if I'd had to be grateful to Adam all my life,' she cried, and there was a note of passion in her husky voice. 'I'd want to be grateful to him, but I know the poor darling is doing all he can. He just can't raise the money.'

'Maybe Adam has something to do with this,' Martin suggested.

'You mean he's met some old admirer of mine and induced him to put up the money? Yes,' she frowned and bit her lower lip, 'that might easily be. So many people crowd round Adam because he is famous. He might have found the right person and dropped the hint. But what does it matter? I'm going to have the operation; I'm going to be well — well — well!' Her voice raised to a high-pitched excited note. 'I'm going back on films, or maybe it will be television now. Adam will be proud of me.'

'Will you marry Adam?'

She smiled and said, 'Probably. After all, he's the main one who has stuck by me all through this business. I don't know what I should have done if it hadn't been for him.'

'You still think he's in love with you?' Martin probed cruelly.

'But why shouldn't he be still in love with me?' She opened her large amber eyes wide. 'He's always been in love with me. He was — even at the time when I wasn't in love with him — when I was recovering from that painful affair with Tony Frencham. He was so sweet to me all through that period. And was it my fault I was too stunned with the shock of it all to return his love? And then I got this wretched complaint and had to come out here. But he's always been at the back of me, helping me not only financially but with his friendship. Naturally as things are, with me lying abed all day and being a very sick woman, there couldn't be any talk of love between us. But when I've had this operation, which I believe is miraculous, everything will be entirely different. I regard Adam as my best friend.'

'Is that all?' he asked quietly.

She hesitated. 'No. I did regard him as just that, oh, for a number of years. But lately I've felt differently. If I could be cured I'd be able to give him everything he's been waiting for so loyally, so patiently.'

'I see,' he said quietly. 'You're very sure

156

of Adam, aren't you, Marlene?'

'But of course I'm sure of him!' she cried indignantly. 'I'm as sure of him as I am that I'm lying here in this bed, and that soon, very soon, I am going to be well. The matron is telephoning through to the New York surgeon to-night. In a few weeks I should be completely recovered. Just think of it, Martin! Just think of everything it will mean — I'll be in the limelight again. I'll be famous. And I'll have all the fun that goes along with fame.'

'And love?' he suggested.

'Of course I'll have love,' she said, almost in surprise that he should have asked it. She added warmly, 'I've always had love, Martin. If you're a lovely and successful woman, you do have love — you can command anyone's love.'

'But you failed once before,' he pointed out cruelly.

She looked at him with dislike. 'You are really a horrible person, Martin. You're always remembering the worst. I was young and inexperienced then. I didn't realise that you must reach out and take love, not wait for it to be given you. Tony went off with someone who was selfish and demanding. I was too much in love with him to demand.' And then suddenly she lay very still for a

157

moment, then sat up straight. She asked, almost in a breathless whisper: 'You don't think it's Tony?'

'What do you mean — you don't think it's Tony?'

'I mean . . . ' She sounded flustered. 'You don't think it's Tony who could have paid for this operation. He might have found out my predicament. He might have written asking the secretary what he could do to help me. Despite Diane and her possessive, domineering love for him, I always thought secretly he was in love with me. But he was too weak to resist her. But he's had time to get over that affair even though it did end in marriage. It might be him trying to help me now.'

Martin got up and took his hat off the dressing table. 'It might be. It's a mystery, isn't it, Marlene. Have you told Adam yet?'

'No. He's coming up to see me this afternoon. I'll tell him then. He'll be pleased, I know. But I think he'll be a little hurt in a way that it wasn't he who was able to finance the operation. Dear Adam, he's so sweet, so very generous with what he has. I won't say I think it's Tony who is financing this operation. He wouldn't like that.'

There was a faint smile on Martin's face as he walked back down the corridor to where

158

the car he'd rented for the afternoon was waiting. 'Poor Marlene,' he thought, 'with her dream-hero of a past romance. They never do come up to scratch. A past romance is as dead as a dodo.'

He guessed who was financing this operation. He had also guessed her motive. He was even glad it wasn't pure altruism. It wouldn't matter so much if she herself ended by getting hurt. He wondered how Adam would feel if he knew the truth. There was never any knowing how Adam would feel about anything. Adam didn't wear his heart upon his sleeve. He might seem to, but he didn't.

It was interesting to speculate on what Gil Rogers might think of the whole situation, for it was quite obvious that he had fallen for Roxie. His anger that night at the Casino gala had been ill concealed. He was all out to get Roxie, and it was just too bad about poor Liz Hamilton. She loved Gil and would have made him a capital wife, having been brought up in the same set he had been and knowing him thoroughly from childhood. But his experience of men was that they rarely married the girls they should have married. If they had, the majority of marriages would have been a darned sight happier. The elusive elf of sex attraction steered them off the rightful course. Everyone was capable of making a fool of himself. He knew that at that moment he was quite capable of making a fool of himself over Roxie.

15

A few days later the paragraph appeared in one of the gossip columns. American gossip writers don't live in constant dread of the law of libel. The paragraph read: 'Gossip is rife about the newspaper baron's pretty daughter and the racing speedboat driver Adam Douglas. They are seen together constantly, if that means anything these days. And morning dips in the hotel swimming pool can be very refreshing from more than one point of view. It is rumoured that the Englishman's hated rival has an eye for the young lass too. Who knows? At the moment Vitry-sur-Lac is a hot-bed of gossip — romantic and otherwise.'

As usually happens, the two principals concerned were about the last people to see it. Martin saw it and chuckled grimly, wondering what effect the paragraph would have on all concerned. He felt pretty mad about it too. It might have the effect of throwing Roxie directly into Adam's arms. He might think he'd have to protect her. On the other hand he might think it more advisable to leave her alone entirely. And

Marlene! It would burst her little bubble of happiness and hope. That would be a pity. She needed all her strength and all her courage to get well.

He chuckled grimly over the thought of the effect it would have on Gil Rogers. 'He'll be as mad as ten snakes.' But Liz Hamilton would probably enjoy the paragraph immensely.

But in that he was wrong. Liz didn't enjoy the paragraph. It caused her too much heartache. Gil stormed into her sitting-room the moment he had read it. His hand shook with rage as he thrust the folded paper under her nose. 'Are you responsible for this paragraph, Liz?'

She read the paragraph through slowly, her face turning rather white under its make-up. Then she opened her eyes wide and asked slowly: 'Why do you think I am responsible for the paragraph, Gil?'

'It sounds like you, Liz, when you're in one of your jealous moods. I saw you talking to that American gossip writer Hayworth the other night. Heaven alone knows what you said.'

'You accuse me of instigating this paragraph?' she demanded hotly.

'I don't see who else would want to, coupling Roxie and Adam together and making me look a damn fool to boot — the panting unsuccessful suitor.'

'And you think I would want to do that to you, Gil?' she asked very quietly.

'Who knows what a woman in love will do?' he flung out at her savagely.

'You're very sure I'm in love with you, aren't you, Gil?' Again her voice was dangerously quiet.

Something in her tone of voice pierced through his rage. 'I'm sorry, Liz. I shouldn't have said that.'

'But you think it, don't you?'

'Not really — at least not all the time, if you want me to be frank, Liz. Sometimes I think you may care for me, and at those times I've always felt very humble.'

'But you're not in love with me, Gil?' and she hated herself for asking it, for she knew she was asking for her death warrant.

There was a pause — too long a pause. 'I love you very much, Liz. I always have,' he said finally and gently.

'I suppose that's the kindest way you can let me down, Gil,' she said with a small bitter laugh.

'Thank you for being so nice about it, Liz, my dear.' He stretched out his hand to her impulsively. But she moved away.

'No sympathy, please, Gil. And don't

worry that I'm going to break my heart. I would have broken my heart years ago if I were that sort. I'm tough and a fighter — a fighter for my own self-respect, I mean. I'll hie me back to the States. I think you owe me the passage.'

'The passage is yours any time you want it, Liz. But — I don't want you to go.'

'Dear Gil.' Her voice was faintly mocking. 'You do say the nicest things — even things you don't mean. I'll treasure the memory of them in the long years after we've separated. But honestly I'm not responsible for that paragraph. You'd better look elsewhere.'

Marlene read it lying in her hospital bed. The operation was all arranged. The specialist was flying over. But reading that paragraph all the colour drained out of her face and the pleasure she had in the hope of an almost miraculous recovery vanished. She had made the suggestion to Adam that he should get off with Lord Oxenham's daughter to improve his financial position, but only half jokingly. She knew now that she'd hoped for an indignant denial, which she'd got, and since then she'd been satisfied, even happy in the sure knowledge that Adam still loved her, and her only.

She had persuaded herself that her main wish to get well was because of Adam, to confront him once again with herself in all her former loveliness. He had been such a good friend to her; he deserved to be rewarded, and she would reward him. She had determined to reward him with the gift of herself. Hadn't he always loved her? Even when she had still been pining over Tony. She had treated him badly in those days, treading thoughtlessly on his heart. But now she was not only determined to be different, but she would be different. Tony had become a ghost-figure in her life. She thought only of Adam.

She hated that paragraph but she believed there was possibly little truth in it. She herself had been subject to many scurrilous gossip paragraphs in the old days. What if Adam and this girl Roxanne had been seen bathing together in the early mornings? What did that amount to really? Some spy from the newspaper observed them and turned it into what seemed to her a malicious paragraph.

She decided not to ask Adam about it. It was much the best way to pretend she had never seen it, just give him the good news about her operation.

Roxie read it through slowly and she felt quite pleased about it. A faint smile turned the corners of her pretty lips. She wondered how Adam would react. She hoped he wouldn't react too violently. He wouldn't like it. From her past days of association with him, she knew that he didn't like pressure of any kind. But he couldn't blame her for the paragraph. In fact she was equally victimised.

She was having breakfast out on her balcony when Adam burst in. He was waving the newspaper in extreme agitation, and his blunt good-looking face was hot with colour. 'Roxanne, have you seen this? It came out yesterday in one of those filthy gossip columns, but I didn't see it until a few minutes ago. I was too busy to look at this rag yesterday.'

'I've seen it,' she said.

He came and sat down facing her at the breakfast table. 'My dear, what can I say? I wouldn't have had you connected with anything like this if I could possibly have avoided it. And as it is, it's all a pack of lies.'

'But we have been swimming together every morning, Adam,' she replied demurely.

'I know. I know. But that doesn't warrant them saying I'm after you. My dearest girl, you must be mortified almost to death.'

She looked up at him with her violet-shaded eyes. They were smiling. 'I'm not at all mortified, Adam.'

'But that I should make you the centre of gossip in this wretched little Swiss village! Everyone will have read the paragraph. Everyone always reads paragraphs which reflect on other people. I don't know how we shall combat it, how best to save you further unpleasantness. I suppose I had better keep away from you altogether.' But he said it sadly and without much conviction.

'That would be the worst thing you could do, Adam,' she said quickly. 'It would look as though you cared terribly for what they've said. It wouldn't be kind to me either,' she added more slowly. 'It would look as though I cared too, as though I was ashamed and,' she raised her head slightly, 'I'm not ashamed of our friendship, Adam. I . . . I glory in it.'

'Roxanne.' He stared across the table at her, almost as if he couldn't believe she'd said just that. 'Then my friendship means as much to you as all that?'

'It means more to me than anything in the world, Adam,' she said fiercely and with great determination.

'Roxanne, my dear — my dearest. What can I say? I thought you'd be horrified, blaming me that I'd laid you open to such a scandal.'

'Is it a scandal for two people to be in

love?' she asked quietly.

'No. No, of course not. There's no scandal attached to that. We're both free.'

'Wouldn't it be better if we took it in our stride, so to speak — paid no attention to it?'

'But we'd know others were paying attention to it,' he pointed out. 'We'd see them looking at us, whispering behind our backs.'

There was a short pause. She folded her napkin and placed it beside her coffee-cup. 'But they couldn't talk if it were true, Adam — if we freely admitted it.'

He said with a small gasp, 'You mean if we admitted it was true, that there was something between us?'

'Isn't there, Adam?' She leant forward slightly. 'Isn't there *anything* between us?'

He was plainly confused but at the same time there was a note of defiance in his voice as he said, 'I — I suppose there is, Roxanne. We have been a great deal together and I like to be with you — I like to be with you more than anyone I know. If you want it that we thumb our noses at everyone . . .'

'I don't want just that,' she said quickly. 'I want people to believe it's true. I want to be able to freely admit that it is true.'

'But that would be tantamount to admitting

we were engaged,' he said hoarsely. 'Roxanne, my dear, my very dear, do you know what you're saying? You're Lord Oxenham's daughter, a very rich girl. It wouldn't be fair to you to let such a lie go unchallenged.'

'But if it wasn't a lie, Adam. If I didn't want it to be a lie?' she asked steadily.

He had been looking down at the table. He raised his grey-brown eyes now and looked at her. 'You mean you would be willing to consent to an engagement, Roxanne?'

'I'd throw my bonnet over the moon if there was an engagement between us, Adam,' she said, and laughed.

'You'd become engaged to me — even though it mightn't last?' he said in some wonderment.

Her eyes met his defiantly. 'But why shouldn't it last? You told me you didn't love Marlene. You're free to love me.'

'Yes, I'm free to love you, Roxanne.' His voice was so hoarse that it grated.

'Then that's all right, Adam, isn't it?' She smiled. 'I'm free to love you too.'

'Do you love me?' he asked in bewilderment and wonderment.

She laughed again. This time softly and with deep affection. 'I've loved you ever since I met you at the Copenhowers' week-end party that time in Sussex. You were nice to a raw little girl; you treated her like a lady. I adored you for that. You didn't even pretend to be in love with me. You were too much wrapped up in Marlene. But you always made me feel wanted. Let us get engaged, Adam, and see how it works out. If it doesn't work out there will be no harm done. ('No harm,' she thought, with a twist in her own heart. 'Only I'll be desolate to the end of my days.') When we leave here you'll be perfectly free to break the engagement. I shan't hold it against you if you do, Adam.'

'I don't think I'll break the engagement, Roxanne,' he said roughly. 'But you're giving me everything, not only yourself but all your father's wealth.'

'Not my father's wealth,' she corrected him gently. 'I have almost as much of my own, left me by my mother. I came into it when I was eighteen. And what I have is yours, Adam. I want you to feel that it is equally yours.'

'Oh, my very dear.' He came over and stood beside her and put his hand on her shoulders. 'Can I kiss you here on the balcony in the bright morning sunshine, in full view of all the people who are having breakfast on the terrace?'

'Yes, kiss me, Adam,' she whispered. She chuckled, and added, 'It will give them

170

something to talk about beside all their losses at the Casino the night before.'

'Roxanne!'

Wasn't this what she had dreamt — being held close to him, his arms tight about her, his lips hungrily seeking her lips?

The hot sunshine was as satisfactory as the moonlight. More satisfactory. It made the whole thing seem more permanent. Moonlight has the elusive will-o'-the-wisp quality, but sunshine is different. It seems permanent and lasting. But you can't kiss for ever — not at least in plain view of at least thirty people sitting out on the terrace below.

'What shall we do to celebrate our engagement?' he asked gaily. 'I can't believe it even yet, Roxanne. I wish you'd pinch me — you with all your wealth wanting to marry me; and personally, apart from my racing, I haven't a bean.'

She nearly said, 'But your creditors won't be so pressing now,' but bit back the words in time. That was the sort of thing you just couldn't say to Adam, even in a joke. He would have turned on his heel and left her, and her whole bubble of enchantment would have collapsed.

'Let's go for a ride in one of your patrol launches,' she said. 'I'm longing to feel the wind in my hair and the spray in my face. You haven't taken me out on the lake yet, Adam.'

'Then it shall be this morning. It's a glorious morning for a spin. Have you got a sou'wester hat and mackintosh? You will need both of them.'

'Do I need them? When I went out with Gil I scarcely got wet at all.'

'That must have been a very ladylike ride. I'm going to show you this morning what I can make a little old patrol launch do.'

They left the hotel together and people seeing them together nodded their heads sagely. 'There's never smoke without fire,' was the unoriginal comment. And they added — some of them, 'It's a very good thing for British sport really. Adam Douglas will have the money now to keep on building faster boats. It's interesting to be in a ringside seat for a romance. It must have happened very swiftly, but these days young people do act swiftly. They seem to fall in love and know whom they want practically in a matter of minutes.'

It was a wonderful morning. Roxie had never felt more exhilarated in her life. The wind blew into her face with the force of a fist-blow, the spray leaped up practically drenching her. She was cutting through the water but she felt as though she were floating through air.

Adam stood rigid at the wheel. She wanted to lean across and tuck a hand through his arm. She wanted to touch him, to make him aware of her presence, for he seemed wholly concentrated on guiding the boat. 'A man's work,' she thought, 'and a woman should never interfere.' But how she longed for some gesture from him showing her that he was aware of her presence.

When they'd skirted the lake twice, his foot eased on the accelerator and they were able to make themselves heard. 'Goodness, I never dreamt of going so fast in all my life!'

He laughed. It was excited happy laughter. 'This is nothing compared to driving a jet speedboat. You have to wear special togs, a silk overall suit, windproofed, with a life jacket built in, and a crash helmet. You'll see me all dressed up like a puppet figure on the day of the race. I wish to heaven I knew what speed Gil Rogers has been getting out of *Virginia II.*'

'I can't believe he can ever travel as fast as you can,' she said, wiping the spray out of her eyes and off her face. The sou'wester protected her hair, but only partially.

'Don't you kid yourself about that!

Virginia II has been built with every latest improvement and unlimited expense. Gil has poured his own money as well as that of the sponsors into the boat — money I couldn't possibly afford to spend. I may have the edge on him in racing driving, but he has the better boat. I wish to heaven I could have afforded to lay out more capital and get *Scotsman III* in a really first-rate condition.'

'But Adam, you can afford it now.'

He looked at her and his look hurt her. It almost shrivelled her. 'There wouldn't be time now. And anyhow I didn't agree to marry you to use up your money.'

She touched his arm now. 'I'm sorry, Adam.'

'Don't run away with the idea I got engaged to you because of your money,' he said savagely. 'If I hadn't liked you — loved you, Roxanne, I wouldn't have fallen in with the suggestion.'

'Oh, Adam, I am sorry. It's just that because I love you too, I want to do so much for you. And my money means nothing to me. I've always hated having it.'

'Then you're the first person in this world who has hated having money,' he said, and he laughed rather bitterly.

They went back to the hotel and changed

174

their clothes, and then they lunched at the Casino.

'Since that gossip par we may as well put a bold face on it,' he said. 'If we lunched at some little place — which I'd much prefer — they would think we were trying to run out on the gossip.'

'And anyhow, the sooner they know the truth, the better,' she insisted.

'Yes,' he agreed, and added with a laugh, 'But I've awful cold feet, and you can't imagine the kidding I am going to take from the team, darling.'

'Oh, Adam, say it again — just like that! Say 'darling.''

His arms closed about her again. 'Darling, darling. I seem to be falling more in love with you every minute.'

16

Monsieur Chevalier, the fat little manager of the Casino, beamed with excitement and pleasure when they came in for a table. Yes, of course he had a table. The very best table for Mademoiselle Haldane and Monsieur Douglas. Somewhere not too conspicuous and yet where they could see everything.

As he seated them personally, he said archly, 'I read what a little bird said in a gossip column this morning. But there's no truth in it, surely?' But his smile begged them to admit there was truth in it. To make such an announcement would be excellent publicity for the Casino.

'It's quite true, M. Chevalier,' Adam said easily. 'But we had hoped to keep it a secret until after the race.'

'Ah, yes. You young people always want to keep your engagements a secret,' he sighed. 'But when you are famous as you are, M. Douglas, and you too, Mademoiselle Haldane, it is next to impossible to keep it a secret. The whole world is agog for such a romance. And why not? they will eat it up. It will make their day for them. Have I your permission to make the announcement, M. Douglas? I should deem it the greatest privilege.'

'I don't think,' Adam began, and looked across at Roxanne.

'But yes, why not?' she said with a small excited laugh. 'Adam and I don't want to keep our engagement a secret, do we, my darling?'

His face reddened under its tan. He was acutely embarrassed. 'Whatever you wish, my dear.'

She tilted her chin at a defiant angle. 'I wish the whole world to know that we're engaged.'

M. Chevalier laughed and rubbed his hands together as though that was the best news he'd heard in years. Already he was visualising the publicity that would follow his announcement. Thank heavens the young people had come here for lunch and not gone to the dining room of the Excelsior Palace. He, Monsieur Henri Chevalier, would make the announcement from the band platform of the Casino. It would be at once known that the happy couple had gone there for their first lunch. Other people would flock in just to patronise the same place that M. Douglas and Mademoiselle Haldane had lunched at.

'You will let me make the announcement,

please, please.' He bent expectantly and hopefully from one to the other of them.

'I don't see why not,' said Roxie, and Adam made growling noises in his throat.

M. Chevalier chose a propitious moment when the room was full. The drummer rolled his sticks and stopped a hubbub of conversation.

'Ladies and gentlemen!' the fat Casino manager said in English, clearing his throat. 'It is my privilege and pleasure to make the most sensational announcement, and one which I know with me you will rejoice in your hearts. We all of us here love romance, and I am so happy to tell you that during the last week romance has blossomed in the hearts of Mademoiselle Haldane and M. Douglas. You will most of you have seen a little paragraph that appeared in a gossip column this morning. But that did not precipitate matters. They are deeply in love and this announcement would have been made anyhow. The waiters are already circulating champagne on the Casino, and I ask you to raise your glasses and drink to the health of our speedboat racing hero and his charming fiancée. Now please with me; we will all drink a toast and then with the orchestra you will join me in singing that dear old time-honoured English song, 'For

They Are Jolly Good Fellows.' Ladies and gentlemen, I give you Mademoiselle Haldane and M. Adam Douglas.'

Everyone rose and drank the toast. There was wild applause. Then the drums rumbled again and the orchestra broke out into 'For They Are Jolly Good Fellows,' and everyone joined in.

Adam was scarlet under his tan, but Roxie was enjoying it up to the minute. This was just as she had dreamt her engagement would be announced — and to Adam. Everyone wishing them happiness and good will. Everyone so kind. They all seemed to be as pleased in her good fortune as she was herself. She was going to marry Adam Douglas.

He glanced at his wrist-watch. 'I have an appointment, Roxanne. I'll see you later towards the evening.'

She felt sick with sudden disappointment. She wanted this day to be theirs — all theirs. She was jealous of every minute he spent away from her.

'You're going out for a trial run in *Scotsman III*?' she suggested.

'No,' he said almost curtly. 'I have an appointment elsewhere.'

She didn't press him further, but she guessed with whom the appointment was.

She thought, 'I suppose he feels he has to tell Marlene. After all, he and she are very great friends.' Marlene was very sick and it wasn't even known yet whether the operation would be a success or not. She tried not to feel jealous. But she was — damnably jealous.

Adam got to his feet. 'I'll drop you off at the hotel.' He drove up the mountainside at a wild speed. It helped to relieve the tension he was feeling. For although it was Marlene herself who had suggested he become engaged to Lord Oxenham's daughter, he didn't believe she had meant it. Certainly at the time he had taken it as a joke himself. And he wasn't engaged to Roxie because of her money. He swore to himself that was the last thing that swayed him. She was pretty and sweet and pliant. He was very much in love with her. Why else should he have met her in the mornings for a swim? Why would he have resented Gil Rogers' attention to her. He admitted that newspaper paragraph had rather precipitated the engagement, but he told himself that the engagement would have happened anyhow, in the course of a week or so.

He must make Marlene understand that. And surely it wouldn't be so difficult? At the time he'd been so desperately in love with her, she had never pretended to be equally in love with him. She was always thinking of her busted romance with Tony at the time. He wondered what had happened to him in the interval.

The sister in charge told him that Miss Farrar was as well as could be expected, and the prospect of the immediate operation which might easily effect a permanent cure had raised her spirits enormously. 'She is like a young girl again, full of hope and excitement,' she told him, smiling.

Marlene was wearing her most becoming nightdress and prettiest bedjacket — a tinted golden chiffon with innumerable tucks. She wore a gold ribbon about her hair. Even her face seemed more filled out and healthier looking.

He stood in the doorway and smiled at her. 'You do look different, Marlene; almost your old self.'

'Do I?' She smiled brightly back at him. 'I'm feeling tons better. I feel so confident about this operation, Adam darling. I just know in no time I'm going to be perfectly well again.'

He came and sat beside her bed. 'I believe it too, Marlene. I tried to find the finance for it, as you know. What luck someone else came forward. Do you know who did?'

She shook her head so that her rich auburn hair swung back. 'I haven't the foggiest. It's all most mysterious and romantic, isn't it. One moment there doesn't seem the hope of us finding the money, and the next all the money is there. The surgeon's fees and fares guaranteed, I gather, by one of the best-known London banks. It's a miracle, isn't it? — but such a happy miracle. You're happy about it, aren't you, Adam?'

'Of course I'm happy. It's the most wonderful thing in this world that could have happened,' he said warmly, and added urgently, 'You haven't any idea at all who arranged it all, Marlene?'

'I haven't the slightest idea. Matron's not giving anything away either, and nor is that fat little secretary fellow. They just say that it's someone who has admired my work in the past. That sounds fantastic, doesn't it? It must have been someone I knew personally.' She added more slowly, 'I was thinking it might be Tony. When he married Diana, he told me she might be going to come into one heck of a lot of money one day. Do you think she has and he has found out about me? He would want to help me. I'm sure he's still my friend at heart.' She added quickly, 'You don't mind, do you, Adam?'

He looked at her almost in astonishment.

'Why should I mind? I am delighted, my dearest girl. You know that I've moved heaven and earth to try and get hold of the money, but so far I've failed hopelessly.'

She reached towards the table beside her bed. 'I saw that gossip paragraph linking your name with Roxanne Haldane's. We all know what foolish things gossip writers can write, and that nine times out of ten there's not a breath of truth in them. There's no truth in this talk of you and Miss Haldane, is there, Adam?'

He flushed uncomfortably. It was odd he should find it so difficult to break the news to her because for a long time there had been no talk of love between them. 'Is there any reason why Roxanne and I shouldn't become engaged?' he asked at last, rather desperately.

She lay very still for a moment, her amber eyes narrowed.

'Then you did take my suggestion seriously — that it would be a good idea for you to become engaged to the newspaper baron's daughter?' she said finally.

He said angrily, 'I didn't take it seriously. The very idea shocked me at the time. But lately, since I've come to know Roxanne, I've felt differently.'

'You're not going to tell me you've fallen

in love with her?' she said with a light amused laugh that didn't come off at all.

'I think I have fallen in love with her.' His voice sounded even angrier.

'In the matter of a few days! Don't try and fool me, Adam. I knew you were in a tight spot, but I didn't mean you to take my suggestion in dead earnest. What's the girl like?'

'She's a very sweet kid.' He still sounded angry.

'All dewy-eyed and innocent, I suppose,' she said bitterly. 'That always takes in a man. Diana was the same. But they never have any real character. I don't suppose this girl has any real character worth speaking about?'

'You're wrong there. Roxanne has plenty of character. In fact I've never known a girl of more definite character.' He was thinking of the way she'd engineered their engagement in spite of his scruples over the fact that he had no money.

She looked at him through narrow slits of eyes. 'You are rather smitten, aren't you, Adam? I wish I'd never put the silly idea into your head. It isn't fair to me either. What chance have I to fight against her?'

'But why do you want to fight against her, Marlene?' he asked in bewilderment.

'You goose, Adam. I love you, too. Didn't you know that?'

His face slowly whitened. 'Marlene, my dear.'

'Don't sound so shocked, Adam. Do you think I'd have let you do everything you have for me if I hadn't been in love with you as much as I thought you were in love with me?'

'But there was always Tony,' he objected. 'I never thought you'd ever really get over him.'

She laughed, not humorously. 'But I have got over him, Adam — completely. You've been so sweet to me these past two years. You've taught me to forget him. And you wouldn't have been so sweet to me as you have been if you hadn't loved me, would you?'

'I do love you, Marlene,' he said hoarsely, 'but . . . '

'Oh, I know you've come to think of me as a hopeless invalid and it's hard to be passionately in love with a hopeless invalid, isn't it, Adam? If I thought I wasn't going to get well, I'd wish you joy with Miss Roxanne Haldane. After all, it's all very satisfactory — at least from a financial point of view, isn't it? And she's probably all you say she is — a nice sweet brave girl — pretty too. Oh,

I'll grant you that. Even when we met her at the Copenhowers', she was the prettiest kid. If I should die under this operation — and we have to face that fact, Adam; I've faced it. I want you to face it too — I hope you do marry her. But if I should get well, Adam, which I hope and believe I shall,' her hands tightened under the bedclothes, 'then I shouldn't let her have you easily, my dear. I'd fight her to the last ditch. I'd create hell on earth to get you away from her — you understand that, don't you, Adam?' Her voice had risen sharply. She was laughing a little but mostly crying.

A passing nurse must have heard that excited, almost hysterical note in her laughter. She pushed open the door. 'Please don't excite yourself, Miss Farrar. And I think you've probably talked enough for one day.'

Adam took the hint and rose. For the first time in his life he was glad to leave Marlene. 'I must be pushing on back to Vitry. I have several business engagements.'

'You'll be having dinner with her?' Her voice rose hysterically again.

'Please, please, Miss Farrar, control yourself,' the little nurse begged. 'This is shockingly bad for you.' She gave Adam a reproachful look as though she felt that he were responsible.

'Good-bye, Marlene, my dear. I'll be up

in a few days to see you again,' he said formally.

'To-morrow, Adam,' she pleaded. 'Please come to-morrow. It's only a few days now before the operation.'

'I'll try and come to-morrow,' he promised and felt a heel, but still bewildered. The knowledge that Marlene loved him in that way had come so unexpectedly. But he wished she hadn't said what she had. He wished they were still the same good comfortable friends they had been for so long. And yet at one time he would have given his very soul to have Marlene say she loved him.

17

The first caller Roxanne had that afternoon was Martin Cheswick. She could have wished to see almost anyone else but him. He couldn't break her golden dream-bubble but he might tarnish it. He had a cynical outlook and a scathing tongue.

She was sitting out on the balcony when he was shown into the suite. She was watching a streak that looked like blue steel in the distance, which might have been *Virginia II*. She was wondering what Gil would say about the engagement. She hoped he wouldn't mind too much. She hoped that very sincerely — almost desperately. She liked Gil. He was a good companion. But there's no room for the companionship of another man when one is in love — and she was terribly in love with Adam.

Martin looped his long lean body where the french windows folded back. 'You certainly got yourself one heck of an engagement party at the Casino this noon, I hear,' he said. 'You might have invited me in on it. I feel I have a certain interest in you as a publicity project. The whole of Vitry is agog with the story. It all happens to be true, I suppose?'

'Yes, of course it's true. And why shouldn't it be true?' she said hotly, goaded by the mocking undercurrent in his voice.

He shrugged. 'You were out to get him from the day you arrived in the train. I knew, but somehow I didn't think you'd succeed — at least not so easily.'

'It happens we have both fallen in love,' she said coldly. 'And even you must admit, with all your cynicism, that can happen to any man and any girl.'

'Of course,' he agreed suavely. 'But the time is certainly short. But what of it? You came out here in love with Adam. You'd remembered everything he'd ever said to you at some week-end party you'd been to in Sussex. It's odd that first night he didn't even remember who you were, and now you're engaged to marry him.'

'Such things happen. We've been swimming together these past few mornings.'

'And you'd stake all your future happiness on swimming together a few mornings?' His voice mocked her again.

She said hotly, 'We understand each other.'

'Oh, sure you do. You understand each other though you scarcely know each other. He's been your great hero in the past. That he's a man as well, you don't take into account. You've swept him off his feet with flattery. For the time being he's even forgotten Marlene Farrar.'

'But he's not in love with Marlene,' she flung at him.

'Like heck he isn't. Then why has he been hanging around her — not only before her illness but ever since?'

She said, controlling herself with an effort, 'He told me he was in love with her once, but that was some time ago. He feels friendship for her now. But that is all.'

'I wonder what would happen to you if Marlene was up and about again,' he said.

'I'd welcome that,' she took up the challenge.

He looked at her curiously. 'I believe you would. You're a good sport, Roxie. By the way, what were you really doing hanging round the hospital the other morning?'

'I went to enquire how Miss Farrar was if you want the truth. I didn't see her as I told you.'

'It's all very interesting. It would make quite a story. Some day I may even get round to writing the story.'

'I don't know what you're talking about.' She'd flushed.

'Don't worry that I'll give anything away,'

he said. 'I also happen to be Marlene's friend. I want the very best for her, no matter what the circumstances.'

'And for me too, I hope,' she said quietly.

'Perhaps,' he said. 'Perhaps again I'm too much annoyed with you at the moment to wish you all sorts of happiness. You see, I found you first. I happen to like you rather well myself.'

'I'd like you for a friend, Martin,' she said in all sincerity.

He straightened his tall lean frame. 'I don't know whether I'm going to be your friend or not. I'll let you know. I'm not thinking very clearly at the moment.'

Adam hadn't returned, so later in the afternoon she went down on to the porch for tea. The slanting sunlight gilded the lake. The tables were full of attractively-dressed women and men in shorts and gaily coloured shirts. She knew that many eyes were turned towards her. They were curious to have another look at her after that sensational announcement at the Casino.

She wished someone would come and join her at the table, but although she had interviewed quite a number of the rich international society set and got gossip paragraphs from them, she did not know them intimately.

It was a relief to see Gil approach her table, but she was also afraid. His thin good-looking features were set in what could only be described as a murderous expression. There was nothing of the gigolo about him now; his walk was full of purpose.

He stood over her table. 'Have you finished tea? You've had enough anyhow. You can leave the rest. I'm not going to talk to you before this packed auditorium. We'll walk down to the wharf and we'll go for a spin in one of the launches.'

She was taken aback by his manner. It was so purposeful, so domineering. 'I — I don't think I can, Gil. I'm waiting for Adam.'

'Then let him wait for you when he comes back. It won't hurt him. It may even do a power of good. You'd better come quietly.' He gave a brief smile that wasn't a smile, and added, 'I'm not in the mood for argument right now.'

'I'll walk down to the wharf with you, but . . . '

'But nothing,' he interrupted rudely. 'You'll come out with me since I want you to. If I said all I want to say to you here, ears would be flapping and you'd never live the scandal down. Come along, let's get going.'

She hesitated, but she decided it would be best to go with him.

'What's all this rot I hear about you being engaged to Adam Douglas?' he asked, once they were out of earshot.

'We've fallen in love with each other.'

'In a brief space of days?' he said caustically. 'Have you forgotten that first night you kissed me? I think I was entitled to be told about it, anyhow.'

'But why?'

'Because I'm also in love with you. I'm quite deeply in love with you, Roxie. I told you as much over lunch the other day.'

'But you haven't known me any longer than Adam has, or as long,' she pointed out to him.

'But I do love you,' he insisted hoarsely, 'and I'm willing to bet my last cent that he doesn't.'

Her cheeks flamed. There was fire in her eyes. 'How dare you say that.'

'I've watched him with you. He's kind and attentive, but he hasn't the look of a lover. I've watched you jealously. Oh, I've known that you were smitten with him. But I thought it was all on your side and that I'd soon knock all that silly nonsense out of your pretty little head, my princess — my princess with the silver hair.' But he said that sarcastically.

'But you can't make someone love you,'

she said seriously. 'It either happens or it doesn't. You can't love someone just because they're in love with you. You should know that, Gil.'

'What are you hinting at now?' he asked angrily.

'I was thinking of Liz Hamilton,' she said quietly.

He looked uncomfortable and dejected. 'I like her immensely, we've been the best of friends since we were kids. But — it isn't what I feel for you, Roxie.'

'But perhaps it's a better and a more sane emotion.'

'Then how do you feel about Adam?' he asked sharply. 'Is that a sane emotion?'

'I don't know,' she said quietly. 'It's something . . . ' She touched her heart slightly under the linen frock, 'in there. You just seem to know that someone is meant for you.'

'It might be wishful thinking or even self-delusion.'

She shook her head determinedly. 'Oh, no. I couldn't feel as I do about Adam if I wasn't sure that he felt the same way about me.'

'You want your head putting in a basin of cold water,' he told her rather rudely. 'It's in Douglas's interests to become engaged to you — especially in his interests to marry you.

He's a great sportsman — there's no finer speedboat racing driver — but he hasn't the money to finance his hobby. You'd give him the money and a sense of security. I doubt if there would ever be anyone in this world to beat him then. I say that in all sincerity, although I'm his nearest rival. You're going to give him too much, Roxie. You're riding for a head-on crash.'

'And if I don't think so?'

'Then your intelligence isn't working very well since you arrived here. I love you and there's nothing in this world you can give me, Roxie — I've as much money as you have. You needn't use a cent of your own. I'd prefer you didn't. I can love you on equal terms.' His voice was humbler now. He was almost pleading with her.

'I'm sorry, Gil,' she said gently, 'but my mind is quite made up. I am going to marry Adam. Why don't you think of Liz Hamilton once in a while? She's an awfully nice girl.'

'She's all that and some more,' he agreed instantly. 'Maybe Liz and I know each other too well. Maybe we know too much about each other's foibles. Anyhow, though I like her so very much, I don't happen to be in love with her. Incidentally, she's leaving on the plane for the States almost immediately.'

'She's going back before the race!' she exclaimed in a startled voice.

'It's her own decision. I wanted her to stay on, but she doesn't want to. Call it a woman's whim, if you like.'

They were on the wharf by now, but when he urged her to climb into the launch, she shook her head. 'No, I'm quite definite about this, Gil, not to-day.'

'Then when?' he asked. 'Or are you going to have Adam hanging round you all the time?'

'I'll come,' she promised. 'Some day I'll come, Gil, and you can take me for a spin like you took me on the first morning I was here. Will you walk back with me to the hotel? As I told you, I'm expecting Adam.'

'All right,' he agreed morosely. 'But I'm not going to let him get away with you, Roxie. I am not a man who gives up easily.'

She laughed and said, 'I'm not a girl who gives up easily either, Gil.'

18

Adam was in a subdued mood when they met later that same evening. He kept thinking of what Marlene had said — that she was in love with him, and he wished like anything that she hadn't said it or that she had not been so late in saying it. He couldn't help thinking with a certain bitterness how much he'd have liked to have heard her say that at one time and that now she'd said it, it brought not happiness but pain to him.

Roxie was hurt by his silences. Inside she was bubbling with happiness just to be with him. She couldn't understand why he was silent. Did he already regret their engagement? The announcement that had been made at the Casino that noon? It would seem from his manner that he might. But she wouldn't tolerate the idea.

It was a relief afterwards to escape from the crowded dining-room out on to the terrace.

'I went to see Marlene Farrar this afternoon,' he told her presently. 'I want you to know everything that happenned between us, Roxanne.'

She asked sharply, 'Is that necessary?'

'I think it is,' he said. 'I explained to you the other morning that for a long time I thought I was in love with her. And now some friend has put up the money so that she can have that essential operation with the surgeon flown over from New York. I can't tell you how glad I am, how relieved I feel in my mind. Heaven alone knows who the philanthropist is, but God bless him anyhow. Knowing that Marlene is well and fit again will make all the difference to me.' And when she looked up at him sharply he took her hand and drew it through his arm. 'Don't misunderstand me, my dear — my dearest. I mean, knowing that she is fit and well again will make me free in my mind. I shan't feel responsible for her any longer.'

'Oh, Adam, I am glad you feel that way about it,' she whispered.

'How else did you expect me to feel?' He stopped in the path between some rose bushes. He drew her gently into his arms. 'My dearest girl, I know now definitely that I'm in love with you. It's odd how it all happened, but there's the plain fact — I'm in love with you.'

'Oh, Adam.' She offered him her lips and she had a sensation almost of swooning as he kissed her passionately, ardently.

'Oh, Adam,' she breathed again. 'This is

what I always dreamt would happen.'

'My very dear, I only hope I'm going to be good enough for you,' he said in all sincerity.

It was an hour later before they got back to the hotel. They had walked about amongst the shrubbery, down by the lake, arms entwined, their bodies touching. It was love as Roxanne had always dreamt of it. She could scarcely bear to take her hand out of his. She wanted to be close to him all the time, to keep on touching him. But at the hotel she was told at the desk that Lord Oxenham had been on the telephone, that she was to call him back at his home immediately she returned to the hotel.

'Oh dear!' she breathed. 'Daddy must have heard. I wish I'd telephoned him myself.'

'You don't think he'll like the prospect of me as a son-in-law?' Adam tried to speak humorously.

'I don't know. Daddy's quite unpredictable. Usually I can manage him.'

'But there are times when you can't?'

'There are times when I can't,' she admitted slowly. 'And it's usually when he gets Angela Little to team up with him against me.'

'Who is Angela Little?' he wanted to know as they went up to her suite.

'She's one of the directors of the Oxenham Group of newspapers, and one of Daddy's closest friends. She started with a heart-throb column and now edits the heart-throb pages in all our best-selling magazines. It's all quite ridiculous for she doesn't know anything about love — as I've told Daddy often. She must be quite forty, and she's unmarried.'

He laughed. 'You make forty sound like the prison gates.'

'Well it is old, isn't it?' she insisted.

'I gather you don't like this Miss Little?'

'Oh, I like her very much. I really love her. But she's nosey; because of her column she thinks she knows all about love. She even thinks she can tell me about it. I don't know, of course, that Daddy has ganged up with her this time, but he's done so often in the past. Whenever I got into trouble at boarding school, he always sent her down to fix up matters.'

'Was she a good fixer?'

She grimaced. 'At least I was never expelled.'

'Let's go out on to the balcony,' he suggested. But she shook her head. 'No, let's stay in here. I've seen enough stars for to-night.' She was remembering that her balcony adjoined Gil's. She didn't want him to overhear a love scene between herself and

Adam. Not that he'd eavesdrop — but he might. She believed that Gil was capable of most things when he had set his mind on a project.

'Do you want me to go?' Adam suggested.

She looked fiercely towards the telephone. She had been on tenterhooks for it to ring. 'Perhaps you'd better, Adam. If you don't mind, I'd rather talk to Daddy alone.'

'I hate having a telephone conversation with anyone else in the room,' he agreed. 'Especially when it's a conversation of a personal nature. Good luck, and God bless,' and he put his arms about her and hugged her, 'my sweetheart,' he said. His lips kissed hers. It was a most satisfying kiss.

The call came through about half an hour after Adam had left her.

'What the devil's this I hear about your engagement to Adam Douglas?' Lord Oxenham exploded over the wire.

'It's true, Daddy. Aren't you pleased for me?'

'Pleased? To hell with being pleased! That's what comes of my letting you off on your own; letting you pretend you were a gossip columnist. I never heard so much nonsense in my life.'

'Nonsense?' she caught him up. 'But this is serious, Daddy, I'm desperately in love with

Adam, and he is in love with me.'

'How do you know he's in love with you?' he thundered back at her.

'Oh . . . oh, he is. A girl just knows. I'm sure she knows, Daddy. She couldn't be mistaken about a thing like that. Please believe me. I'm desperately sincere.'

'You may be sincere, but what about him?'

'Why shouldn't he be sincerely in love with me?' she took up the challenge. 'Aren't I pretty enough? Don't you think that some man might want to marry me?'

'I don't say they wouldn't want to marry you. Why wouldn't they want to marry you with a cool million inheritance?'

'But you don't know Adam — he isn't at all like that,' she insisted hoarsely.

'Isn't he? Well, if he isn't, he should be,' he barked back at her. 'It's well known that he's personally in debt, that if he doesn't get the speed-record and beat Rogers too, he'll have his creditors hanging about his neck. When you marry, Roxie, I want you to marry someone of your own financial standing.'

'And have a mausoleum of a home and live in what the world calls 'pompous splendour,' and secretly be wretched and heart-sick. That's what you want for me, isn't it?' she threw back at him bitterly.

'Now, my dear, you know I don't want anything like that for you; I only want your happiness.' His voice had calmed considerably. 'But I want to know more about Adam Douglas. More about him personally, I mean, and not what one reads about him in the press or learns from hearsay. I want to find out everything about him.'

'It doesn't matter what you find out, I am still going to marry him, Daddy.'

He said in a tight, angry voice, 'All right, all right — that is, if everything is satisfactory. But I must know for certain that it *is* satisfactory, that you're not just being taken for a ride, as it were. You're too young, my dear, to decide such matters entirely by yourself. I'd come over if I could, but as it is I've got some political irons in the fire at the moment. It's essential that I stay here. I'm sending Angela Little over to you. I know you'll welcome having her around and that you'll listen to her advice.'

'Oh, Daddy, no!' she cried in frantic dismay.

He chuckled. 'There's no 'no' about it. If anyone should know about a young girl's love affairs, she's surely the person. She'll see your Adam, see if she thinks he's not pulling a fast one in getting engaged to you.'

'Daddy, don't say things like that. I — I

hate you when you do.'

'Calm down. Calm down. We've got to get to the bottom of all this nonsense. You don't get engaged to a man you don't know and be left to get along with it — not if you're my daughter, Roxie, you don't, my dear.' He added: 'Book a suite for Angela. She and that Mint girl who is her secretary, will be arriving to-morrow.'

19

At the last moment Liz Hamilton cancelled her flight back to the States and decided upon staying.

'I'm glad,' Gil said sincerely. 'I never wanted you to go in the first place. But why the sudden change of plans?'

'I've decided to stick it out, Gil. I can't be any more hurt than I am already. I might even be happier. Who knows what's going to happen in the future? Who knew,' she added deliberately, 'that Adam Douglas would actually get engaged to Oxenham's daughter? It was certainly a surprise.' She added very gently, 'Are you very angry about it, Gil?'

'I'm not exactly pleased about it. I'll be frank with you, Liz — it sort of knocked me off my balance.'

'Poor Gil.' She came across the room and thrust her arm through his. 'You're used to having it your own way — everything you want, all served to you on a golden platter, m'lord Rogers.'

'If you're trying to be sarcastic, Liz, I don't want sarcasm,' he said angrily.

'But I'm not,' she said. 'Perhaps I was for a moment, but it was only because I am all strung up too. I am sorry. You really think she loves Douglas?'

He shrugged. 'Why did she get engaged to him?'

'I suppose that's the answer. But as for him, that's interesting, isn't it? I've heard his name coupled with the ex-film star, Marlene Farrar, who's in a sanitorium not far from here. Why should he suddenly fall for the blue-eyed girl, Lord Oxenham's daughter?'

'If they're in love with each other good luck to them.'

'Do you think their love affair is going to be all roses?' she asked caustically. 'What do you think Lord Oxenham's reaction will be? And especially if Douglas doesn't get the speed record. If he doesn't, do you think he will welcome Douglas into the family?'

'I hadn't thought of that,' Gil said quietly.

'Well, think of it, and if you want the girl, go all out to beat him and make a new world record,' she said with a savage little shake of her shoulders. 'The girl isn't of age; she can't marry without her father's consent, and somehow in the event of Douglas losing, I can't see Lord Oxenham giving that.'

'No, I suppose in those circumstances he wouldn't,' Gil said quietly.

★ ★ ★

Angela Little was little — as her name implied — and very feminine. She had a small, attractive face and bright brown hair with no suspicion of grey. Only the faint crinkles under her large brown eyes showed that she might have passed the forty mark. She was very sweet, very efficient, and understanding too. She went personally through all the letters sent to her and was very sympathetic and helpful in her answers. She'd brought a wad of letters with her in a suit-case, and also a young secretary with dark hair and large enquiring grey eyes. It was the girl's first trip abroad and she was very thrilled.

Roxanne met them with no little trepidation. She had just lunched with Adam.

'Sending this woman — what's her name? — Angela Little out here means that your father definitely doesn't approve of our engagement,' Adam had said.

She made that small attractive grimace. 'I don't say he definitely disapproves, Adam, but I suppose it was all rather a shock to him. I wish I'd been able to let him know beforehand.'

Adam had her hand held tightly in both of his. 'Was he pretty fierce over the telephone, darling?'

She nodded. 'A little fierce. But if he'd been very fierce he would have come over here himself, no matter what his political obligations. The fact that he sent Angela here shows that he mainly wants to find out what is going on.'

'What do you think she will think?'

She sighed. 'I suppose she will think what Daddy wants her to think. She's always been extraordinarily weak where he is concerned.'

'You mean she's in love with him?'

'I've thought she might be, once or twice.'

'But your father doesn't take any interest in her?'

'I don't know about that.' She hesitated. 'But he leads such a full life, what with his newspapers, his magazines and his political activity, he doesn't seem to have any time over to think about women — only about me. And that's only when I do something that happens to annoy him. But he's always had a very high admiration for Angela. He says she's very thorough.'

Angela was so friendly and apparently intrigued by the whole affair when Roxanne met her that the girl's suspicions were momentarily lulled.

'I'm going to have a nice hot bath first and then you must come down to my suite and tell me all about it. But everything. It's all very thrilling, isn't it? Adam Douglas is quite a hero.'

'Daddy didn't seem to think him such a hero over the telephone the other night,' Roxie said quietly.

'Fathers will be fathers — even benevolent fathers such as yours,' Angela said with a little fluttering gesture of her pretty hands. 'Naturally he wants to know everything, and I think it very wise of him to send me over to chaperone you. You should never have been allowed to come over here on your own in the first place. But apparently, according to your father, you were intent on doing just that.'

'I'm tired of finishing schools and chaperones. I want to be really independent,' Roxie said.

'Ah, yes,' Angela said with a faint sigh. 'There's nothing like being independent, is there? But often too much independence leads one astray.' She looked steadily at Roxie, and added: 'I'm quite independent, but I don't really enjoy it much, you know.'

There'd been a certain note in her voice

that made Roxie reply, stammering, 'But I ... I always thought you were perfectly happy, Angela. You seem to have everything you want — an important position, great success in your field.'

'Oh, yes, I have all that,' Angela agreed. 'But I should so very much like to be dependent for a change. The sweet little woman hanging on some man's words and commands — the sort of behaviour I urge on every woman in my columns.' She sighed. 'It's very sad I should have to be independent, isn't it? I'm glad you've taken a definite stand, Roxie. It can't have been an easy decision for you to make.'

'Why shouldn't it be easy? What's against my decision?' Roxie challenged. She walked over restlessly to the glass windows that led out on to the balcony of the suite. 'You said Adam was by way of being a hero. He is a hero in every way. I'm tremendously lucky that he is in love with me.'

'You're sure of that?' Angela asked quietly.

Roxie swung towards her angrily. 'I am as sure of it as I am that I am standing here.'

'I'm glad you're sure,' Angela said with another faint sigh. 'It isn't always easy to be sure of anything when one is in love — one rarely sees things in their right perspective. My dear, don't think I don't know. Don't think I don't sympathise. I must talk to your Adam and find out more about him. Your father wants me to give him a very clear account of everything.'

'But I am perfectly clear in my mind about everything,' Roxie protested. 'I don't see what right Daddy has in this affair.'

'My dear, you are not of age. He is not only your father but he has control of the Oxenham fortune.'

'But if I don't care about that? I have sufficient money of my own. You know I came into my mother's money when I was eighteen.'

'That makes it a little more difficult, doesn't it? At least from your father's point of view.'

'You always see everything from Daddy's point of view. You always have,' Roxie said bitterly.

'I've tried to be a friend to you too,' Angela told her gently.

'Yes, you have, Angela. I'm sorry.' Roxie's small lovely face crumpled in dismay. 'I shouldn't have said that. But you must admit you are always on Daddy's side.'

'I wonder if I've been too often on your father's side,' Angela said thoughtfully.

Roxie looked at the older woman curiously. 'I've sometimes wondered that too, Angela.

You've always done what Daddy wanted. You've always agreed with him.'

Angela smiled faintly. 'I suppose I'm made that way. When . . . ' But she broke off and didn't finish the sentence.

'I think it would be a good thing for Daddy if you disagreed with him once in a while,' Roxie said, and added with a small laugh, 'I don't mean you to make an issue of my affair with Adam, but I would like you to look at it all not through Daddy's eyes as he wants you to look at it, but as you really feel about it yourself.'

'I'll try and do that, my dear. I'll try and find out the facts. But please don't think I'm unfriendly towards you and your romance. But your father sent me over here to find out what's cooking, and I have to do my duty by him.'

For the next few days Angela seemed to be working most of the time on the voluminous correspondence which poured in on her from the Oxenham press. She made it her boast that she answered every letter personally, and as a matter of fact she did. She always gave sane and sometimes helpful advice, usually within the accepted moral code, and when she was tempted to stray out of that code, she pulled herself back sharply.

Angela and Adam seemed to like one

another, and the little secretary, Hazel Mint, was always thrilled to be in their company.

Adam and his team took his boat out on the lake for a trial run each day. Gil did the same. Martin raged at the city council to make money a little looser for publicity and advertising. Lord Oxenham raged too, in London. He raged over the telephone to Angela, demanding to know why she hadn't yet broken up this nonsense as he called it.

'But Jim, if I believe they are in love with each other you wouldn't want me then to bust it up, would you?'

'I'll say I would, under any consideration. That's what I sent you out there to do,' he shouted back at her.

'Your voice is too loud. It's giving me a headache, Jim,' she said, and put down the receiver.

Roxie continued collecting her gossip paragraphs. She was determined to show her father that love did not in any way interfere with her literary prowess or her ability for collecting juicy paragraphs. She spent as much time as she could with Adam — at least as much time as he was able to spend with her. But he was away a great deal of time, working on the boat with his team, and when he wasn't with the boat he spent a considerable time up at the Glink Memorial Hospital.

'Marlene's undergoing a great strain. I must help her through this, Roxanne,' he said, and added earnestly, 'You do understand?'

'Of course I understand. Since you're her friend you have to help her.'

'Bless you for understanding, my darling.' He bent and kissed her lips tenderly. But sometimes she wondered how many girls would be as understanding as she was being forced to be.

It was a relief at times when Adam was up at the hospital, to escape the hotel and its environment, to escape the sight of Angela sitting in her suite dictating innumerable letters, and go out on the lake for a quiet spin with Gil. Since that scene they'd had after the announcement of her engagement, he'd been quite different. He'd been friendly, never once alluded to the love he had vowed he had for her, putting himself out in every way to make her life more pleasant.

In these circumstances she could be young and gay and laugh with him. When he didn't make love to her, she found him a delightful companion. She remembered the first night she was standing out on the balcony and he'd called her his princess with the silver hair. But as in every friendship of this nature there

214

were moments that were difficult; moments when the cheerful mask of friendship would slip. He would emerge as someone quite different from a friend — the man who loved her; a hard-faced, dark-featured young man, possessive, demanding. But these were only isolated occasions and at these times, as a girl, she was a little afraid of him, feeling very much alone with him out on that vast expanse of lake, wondering just what he might do. And whatever he did she would have to protest. She would have to make him realise how much she loved Adam.

Occasionally he'd laugh and say, 'I'm behaving like a good little boy, aren't I? I never thought it was in me. I'm quite proud of myself.'

She didn't pretend to misunderstand him. 'But can't you always be like this, Gil? I enjoy myself so much with you when you are like this — just a good friend.'

'My dearest, you won't keep me waiting too long, will you?' he said, and bending swiftly he kissed the back of her neck.

She swung round in sharp protest.

He laughed and said, 'It doesn't matter. The curve of your neck is so very pretty at the back. It tempted me. Please forgive me.'

Once the boat lurched suddenly and she

was thrown against him. Just for a moment one of his arms closed about her, but that need only have been to steady her.

'You all right, Roxie?'

'Of course I'm all right, Gil.'

'Just so long as you're all right . . . always.' He pressed her against his lean chest before he released her.

'Roxie,' he said, with both hands on the steering wheel now, looking straight ahead of him. 'If anything happened between you and Adam, anything serious, I mean, you'd let me know, wouldn't you? It wouldn't matter where I was, in what far-flung corner of the earth, you'd send me a cable something like 'I am heartwhole, Roxie,' or just 'Where are you these days?' I'd understand that. Will you promise me, my dear?'

'I can't promise. I might, Gil.'

'But I would know, anyhow,' he said confidently. 'I'd feel you were somewhere in this world — free, waiting for me. I'd feel it in my bones. I'd feel it in my heart,' he added in a low voice. He added abruptly, 'When are you planning to marry Adam?'

She was flustered. 'I hadn't thought. We haven't got Daddy's consent yet, you know. Then there's this race and what Adam is going to do afterwards. A great deal depends upon this race.'

'You mean you'd hate it if I beat the living daylights out of him?' he said roughly.

'Yes, I suppose I do mean that,' she said quietly. 'If Adam didn't beat you and create a new speed record it would certainly postpone our marriage. But it wouldn't interfere with our love,' she added hoarsely. 'Nothing could do that.'

'But it would interfere with your marriage?' he added, looking at her in rather an odd way.

'Yes, I suppose it would,' she said quietly. 'It would be very hard to get round Daddy if Adam didn't make a good showing. Daddy would say that apart from his racing driving he had nothing to recommend him; he was finished.'

'Do you think Adam would be finished if he doesn't create a new world record?' he asked quietly, looking at the glistening waters straight ahead of him.

'I . . . I don't know,' she whispered, and there was a hint of real despair in her voice. 'He's very much mixed up at the moment. He has so many worries and problems. If he didn't have faith in himself I don't see how he could possibly battle through them. It means so much more to him than it does to you, Gil. You're secure in your future and in your financial status too; you're much more secure in yourself than Adam is. I don't quite know how to explain it, but I feel that Adam has just got to do something big. It means everything in the world, not only to him, to both of us.' Her voice broke sharply.

'You know you're talking to his bitter rival,' he reminded her rather roughly.

'I'm talking to you as a friend, Gil. Perhaps I've said too much already. And of course I wouldn't resent your setting up a new world record . . . I'd try to be happy for you.'

'Thank you.' His voice was tinged with sarcasm.

'Oh, please don't be like this!' she cried, almost wildly. 'I'm so fond of you, Gil. I'd like to wish for your success as well as Adam's. But you must see how terribly important it is to me that Adam should set up a new world record.'

'You think he can set up a new world record in *Scotsman III*? That he's done so much with her already shows that he's a superlative driver.'

'She's a wonderful boat, *Scotsman III*,' she said loyally. 'Maybe she hasn't got all the modern finishing touches that your *Virginia II* has, Gil, but her engine's wonderful.'

'My little old engine is pretty good too,' he said, 'and I'm nearly as experienced a driver as Adam.'

They were back by the wharfside and she was glad. She didn't want to quarrel with Gil and they had come near to quarrelling. At times she was a little afraid to think how much his friendship meant to her. How could you be in love with one man and feel so very friendly towards another? And he his rival! But it seemed the human heart was capable of many odd emotions, and love and friendship for the opposite sex were very curious emotions, easily intertwined.

He tied up the boat and helped her up on to the wharf. She looked lovely in a pale yellow dress standing there in the glittering sunshine. His heart missed several beats. He felt a little sick in the pit of his stomach. He wanted her so much — more than he'd ever dreamt he'd ever want anything in this whole world.

He sprang up on to the wharf beside her. 'Roxie!' he put his hands on both her arms. 'You'll remember your promise, that if at any time you should change your mind you will let me know? You will at least give me the chance to make the grade with you.'

She said quietly, 'I promise, Gil. But don't ask me to give up my happiness, with Adam.'

'It is happiness, Roxie?'

'Such happiness,' she sighed.

His hands dropped from her arms. 'He's a lucky devil that you should feel like that about him. I suppose his luck will carry him through. He'll make another record. Your father will consent to the marriage. You will both be happy for ever and ever. Amen.'

He was about to turn away but she reached out a hand and touched his arm. 'Don't you want that for me, Gil?'

'I wish I didn't want your happiness so much; it would make life much less complicated for me,' he said, and sighed.

It didn't seem like the old Gil speaking with his gay laughing ways. He seemed suddenly a stranger to her.

20

Angela Little was talking with Adam. He had dropped into her suite to see if Roxie was there and had been cornered by Angela. He was rather afraid of her although she was such a very feminine little person. He had wanted to make some excuse and go. But she had said brightly, 'I've been wanting to talk to you ever since I arrived, Adam. And now it seems just the right time, doesn't it? Sit down and do smoke. I always feel so much more at my ease when a man is smoking. And Hazel, dear child, stop fussing with those letters and go and get your bathing suit and have a dip. And why not have tea by the pool? There's always a crowd there at tea-time. You're sure to meet some of the people to whom we've already been introduced, and undoubtedly they'll ask you to join them. There's no reason why we should stick to those old letters all day and every day. Especially when we're in such a beautiful spot as this.'

Hazel Mint rose with alacrity. 'Thank you, Miss Little, I'd love to have a dip. I've been dying to go into the swimming pool ever since we arrived but I've never had the opportunity.'

'Tut-tut! That makes me look like a dreadful taskmaster, doesn't it?' Angela said, crinkling up her eyes and laughing. 'Almost an ogre. We'll shut up shop for the rest of the day, my dear, and you can enjoy yourself.'

Hazel thrust the letters they'd been coping with back into the drawer and put the cover on the small portable typewriter. She looked pleased and her large enquiring eyes were eager. Who knew whom she might meet at the pool? It was greatly preferable to sitting up here and making notes upon the letters she would have to reply to for Angela.

Angela waved Adam to an easy chair and sat down in one opposite him. 'Now tell me all about yourself, Adam Douglas,' she said, smoking the cigarette he had just lighted for her. 'Oh, I don't mean what everyone knows — your racing prowess, your speed records and all that. I mean all about yourself and your feelings, if you care to confide in me. Lord Oxenham may have sent me out here to look the situation over in the nature of a job, but I assure you I'm a long way from being a stern Mama.'

He smiled across at her. 'I could scarcely picture you in that rôle, Miss Little.'

'I'm glad you can't,' she said. 'I like to

be cosy with people. Please call me Angela. And I'm going to call you Adam right from this moment.'

'That's very nice of you,' he said, 'but I don't really feel . . . ' He broke off in embarrassment.

'Don't tell me I'm too old to be called by my first name, please,' she begged prettily. 'Do you think I look old?'

'Far from it,' he said sincerely. 'And please don't think I'm flattering you. You might be thirty — a little older, but no more.'

'You are a very nice young man indeed,' she said. 'I can't blame Roxie for falling for you. But I'll confess to you I'm over forty — though not a great deal. I've always been busy working on the Oxenham Group of papers ever since I was a teenage girl, and I think working keeps you young looking.'

He laughed. 'I've worked at the job I'm doing, trying to put up new speed records, but I feel battered and old — at least,' he amended, 'I did until recently.'

'That's the tension you're continually under,' she agreed, nodding sagely. 'To be under terrific tension a great deal of the time does tend to make one older. You do look older than I suppose you are, Adam. You wouldn't be more than twenty-six, would you?'

'I'm twenty-five,' he told her, flushing slightly.

'And Roxanne is nineteen — a babe compared with you.'

He frowned slightly. 'I never feel she's a great deal younger than I am.'

'That's because she's Jim Oxenham's daughter — a typical Haldane. They're one-purpose people and always so sure of what they want. It tends to make them seem much more mature than they are. They ride rough-shod over obstacles that might deter other people.' She sighed a little. 'It makes for success, but sometimes I think it's rather a pity.'

He crushed out his own cigarette. 'I gather Lord Oxenham doesn't approve of my engagement to Roxanne.'

'No, of course he doesn't approve,' she agreed brightly. 'But would you expect him to? Roxanne is his one own pet lamb, and I doubt if he'd consider one of the crown heads of Europe or even a millionaire suitable for her.'

'But he might consider Gil Rogers. He's not only a millionaire but has as good a reputation as I have as a speedboat racer.' There was a note of jealousy in his voice. Her small ears pricked with interest.

'I knew Roxie was friendly with Gil Rogers.

I didn't know it was at all serious.'

'It isn't serious on her part — I'll vouch for that. But he's madly smitten with her,' he said savagely.

'And you resent that?' She raised lightly plucked eyebrows, 'because you already consider Roxanne a possession, and as a man you're naturally jealous?'

He flushed under his tan. 'I don't think I'm possessive in that way — at least I hope I'm not. But I suppose it's only natural for me to resent a man going all out for Roxanne as Rogers does. The fact that we're engaged doesn't seem to make any difference whatsoever to his attitude.'

'You realise you haven't Lord Oxenham's approval to your engagement yet?' she said quietly.

He lit another cigarette. 'I quite realise that,' he said soberly. 'You wouldn't have come out here otherwise. Might I ask if you're just here to check up on me or are you here to stop all talk of any engagement between us?'

'I'm mainly here to check up. At least, that's what I'm determined to do,' she said quietly. 'That's why I want you to talk to me frankly about yourself and about your feelings for Roxanne, Adam.'

She leant forward a little, clasping her

pretty hands tightly on her knees. 'Forgive me for asking the question, but do you really love her, Adam?'

He hesitated, and she liked him better for that hesitation. It would be so easy for him to have avowed that Roxie meant everything in this world to him. 'I'm pretty sure I do,' he said finally. 'At least at the present moment I can scarcely bear to let her out of my sight. Everything she does and says is new, unexpected and intoxicating. I'd thought for a long while I was in love with someone else and I've always regarded myself as a person who would never change, but since I've met Roxanne, I've felt I have changed. I've felt much younger, much happier. I never thought I'd feel that way again.'

'I suppose Roxie jumped her hurdles in the usual Haldane ruthless manner?' she said with a quiet smile. 'Don't I know them — father and daughter. They're at logger-heads half the time but Roxie usually manages to get round her father. But mainly the issue isn't all that important — not as important as her marriage, for instance.'

'You mean Lord Oxenham doesn't find me suitable as a son-in-law? I don't blame him for that. I won't keep anything from you Miss . . . I mean Angela.' He smiled nicely across at her. 'Apart from the speed records

I've made, there isn't much to recommend me. It's common knowledge that personally I'm badly in debt. But I'd hoped if I beat Rogers and made a new record, my financial affairs would pick up considerably. There're always pickings in our racket — advertising, television, newspaper and magazine articles; even films. I'm hoping to land myself a well paid job with the speedboat racing industry. The matter has been under discussion for some time, but they're always cagey — waiting to see if I will regain the world record.'

'You must admit that having become engaged to Lord Oxenham's only daughter ought to help your financial position considerably.' She sat up straighter to say what she felt she had to say, though she didn't like saying it.

'I appreciate that though I must ask you to believe that at the time I became engaged to Roxie that didn't weigh in my thoughts.' He made another faint wry grimace. 'I wasn't thinking in a particularly practical way. It was all . . . ' he hesitated, 'rather unexpected.'

She gave a small laugh. 'You mean Roxie rushed you into it? That child has her father's drive and all his determination.' But she came back to her former question: 'You do love her, Adam?'

He looked down at the cigarette which was smouldering between his fingers. 'I sincerely believe I love her very deeply,' he said.

She stretched out her hand for another cigarette. He sprang to his feet and lit it for her.

'Forgive me, Adam, but I've heard your name coupled with that of Marlene Farrar,' she said finally.

He didn't try to evade that issue either, and she liked him even more.

'I was in love with Marlene for a long time,' he said, 'and I still love her very dearly. But since she's been so ill, I've felt differently about her. I've loved her more as I'd love a closely cherished sister. It's difficult to remain passionately in love with someone who is lying in a sick-bed, fading away before your very eyes. You feel love and a deep compassionate pity.'

'But if she were restored to health again?' she suggested quietly.

He got up and stood with his back to her, facing the open french windows. 'I wish I could give you a simple and direct answer,' he said finally. 'As I feel about it now, I don't think I would fall in love in that way with Marlene again, I don't think I could love anyone but Roxie in that way again. But Roxie and I have known each other such a very short while. I feel I'm putting it very badly, but believe me I'm honest in my love for her. I'm sure once we get to know each other better, the feeling will deepen. It will become the whole love I've always dreamt of and wanted.'

'But in the meantime you don't know her half as well as you know Marlene Farrar,' she commented quietly. 'And that love has stood the test of time, hasn't it?'

'I've told you how I felt about Marlene,' he said rather curtly. 'I'm not at all the impulsive young man I was when I first fell in love with her at twenty-three. But of course,' he added in another pause, 'if Lord Oxenham refused his consent there can be nothing further said about Roxanne and myself.'

'I shouldn't believe he'd withhold his consent indefinitely if he believes your love for her and Roxanne's love for you is the real thing,' she said finally. 'But that is what you will have to prove to yourselves, isn't it?'

Roxie came in at that moment. She looked from one to the other of them inquiringly. 'Well, what have you two been nattering about? You're not trying to persuade him he isn't in love with me, are you, Angela?'

'I wouldn't persuade either of you to anything. I love you, Roxie — I've loved you ever since you were a child. I'm beginning to have a great affection — even admiration — for Adam.'

He flushed again under his tan. 'That's awfully nice of you, Angela.'

'You've been honest with me, Adam, and one thing in this world I appreciate is honesty. I hate people who make sweeping statements — and you haven't made any. You've considered your replies and I believe you've been truthful.' She raised her small head at a defiant angle. 'I shall tell Jim as much.'

Roxie rushed across the room and threw her arms around Angela. 'Oh, Angela darling! You will tell Daddy you approve of Adam. It will mean so much to us.'

'I'm not sure that my approval will mean such a great deal,' Angela said wryly.

'But it will,' Roxie insisted. 'Daddy relies upon you so much.'

'He may rely on me but he doesn't always take much notice of what I say,' Angela replied dryly.

'But when Daddy has a bee in his bonnet he doesn't take notice of what anyone says,' Roxie cried in an exasperated voice. She added after a slight pause, 'Daddy sent you over here to break the engagement, didn't he?'

'I think he had that thought in his mind,' Angela admitted.

'Well, you can tell him from me, I'm not going to give up Adam for him or for anybody,' Roxie said belligerently. She added with a queer sort of smile: 'I wonder if you will stand up to him, Angela. I think it's your only hope with Daddy. You must make him realise that however much he shouts at you it won't make any difference. You're too soft with him.' She added with a naïve sophistication of youth, 'It doesn't do to be too soft with men.'

Angela made a little half-amused, half-mocking gesture. 'I bow to your superior wisdom, Roxie. You've certainly got what you set out to get.'

Roxie smiled across at Adam and held out her hand. 'Yes, I've certainly got what I set out to get. I've got my Adam.'

Angela tackled Jim Oxenham on the telephone that very night. 'I've talked to Adam Douglas,' she said. 'I think he's an honest straightforward young man. I don't see that Roxie is making such a big mistake in getting engaged to him.'

'You don't mean to say you actually approve of the fellow?' Lord Oxenham thundered over the wires.

'I do, in a way. And he's been quite frank

about his financial obligations.'

'But it's all nonsense anyhow. Roxie isn't old enough to know her own mind.'

'I think since she's a daughter of yours she knows her own mind pretty thoroughly, Jim.'

'Don't try to soft-soap me!' he shouted back at her. 'You know I sent you over there to break off the engagement — to have all this nonsense finished and done with once and for ever.'

'But I don't agree with you, Jim, that it is a lot of nonsense. I think they are both quite sincere young people. I think they are entitled to every consideration.'

'You mean you don't agree with my point of view, Angela?' He was almost stammering in indignation and amazement.

'No, I don't agree, Jim. I love Roxie, and I like Adam, as I told you. I'm going to help them as much as I can.'

'What the devil are you talking about?' Lord Oxenham barked at her. 'Do you realise that you're letting me down shockingly, Angela.'

'Perhaps I'm going against you for the first time in my life, Jim. It's quite an exciting experience.'

'Angela, I've always relied upon you so much.' His voice was almost a gasp.

'Rely upon me, Jim. But you mustn't take my opinions and decisions for granted. I think I'm a little tired of being your 'Yes' woman.'

'Angela!' he exploded again. 'Do you know what you're saying?'

'Quite well, Jim. And I'm quite prepared to resign from all your papers, if you want me to resign.'

'Look here, don't do anything of the kind,' he said urgently. 'I'm coming over there to talk some sense into your head. I don't know when I'll be able to get free, but I should be free within a few days or so. I'll let you know when to expect me. But I'm coming. You seem to have gone off your head, my dear.' And he added — even though the operators were warning him that the time had already been extended three times — 'My dear, my very dear Angela, you've really shocked me.'

21

Martin was visiting Marlene. He had left Vitry in a bad mood and he arrived at the hospital in a bad mood. He was having considerable difficulty with the council. Their purse-strings were very tight, and a brief glimpse of Adam and Roxie wandering down the High Street and past the Casino, hand-in-hand, hadn't helped his ill-humour.

Marlene greeted him pleasantly and with affection. But she frowned when she saw his glum lowering expression. 'Don't you know I'm supposed to be kept cheered up before this operation? No one who isn't excessively cheerful and encouraging is allowed to come near me.'

'You feel cheerful and confident about this operation, Marlene?'

'I have every confidence in the world. I not only feel sure but I know the operation is going to be a success. I'm going to get well and strong again. I'm going back on the stage or into films. I'm going to be the big star I was two years ago. I may do some television programmes, too, since I'll probably need the money. Oh, I'm going places, Martin. You don't know how thrilling that is after I've been lying here for nearly two years.'

'Your career means a great deal to you — almost everything — doesn't it, Marlene?'

'It certainly means a great deal,' she admitted. 'But not everything, Martin.'

'I could wish it meant everything to you, Marlene,' he said with great sincerity.

'What do you mean, Martin?'

'I'm thinking of your friendship with Adam,' he said quietly.

'But there's nothing wrong with our friendship. He comes up here nearly every day. We're still the greatest of friends. Maybe once I've had this operation and I'm cured, we shall be more than that.'

'You've heard, I presume, about his recent entanglement with Roxie Haldane?'

She shrugged slightly. Her lovely pale face tightened. 'I've heard something, of course. Publicity rushed them into some sort of an engagement. Adam doesn't talk about it much. Poor darling, I think he's pretty embarrassed and ashamed of the whole affair. That wretched paragraph appeared in the gossip column, and for the sake of the girl's reputation he had to play up.' She moved restlessly, and added, 'Even she can't take the whole affair seriously unless she's a nitwit.'

'I think she does take it seriously,' he said.

She frowned and nibbled her lower lip. 'She was inclined to take Adam seriously at the Copenhowers' week-end party. He played up to her then. I don't consider this affair any more important. I brought him easily to heel. I shall do the same again.'

He leant forward and put his fists on his knees. 'I'm not sure you'll be so successful, Marlene. I should say that the present Roxanne Haldane is a very different girl from the one you met two years ago. She's a most determined young woman, and she's got a huge crush upon Adam. She's lovely and attractive. He'd be a fool if he didn't reciprocate.'

She asked very quietly, 'You think he does reciprocate?'

'I think she's swept him off his feet,' he said bluntly.

She moved restlessly, angrily. 'It's my fault for being sick so long. However devoted a man is to a girl, you can't expect him to be tied to a sick-bed. But directly I've had this operation everything will be completely different. I've wanted to talk to you about that, Martin — about the operation, I mean. I know the operation is going to be successful. But if by any means it wasn't . . . You've always been a very good friend to me. You were a good friend when Tony and I were going about together before he met Diana. Have you kept in touch with Tony?'

He nodded. 'From time to time we've seen each other. I dined with him and Diana the last time I was in London. They had a very Ritzy apartment off Park Lane. You know she recently came into a very considerable sum of money. Tony's bought himself a new sports car. He seems to have plenty of money to fling around.'

'Ah,' she drew a long tight breath, 'I thought that was what had happened.' She added, 'Love never completely dies, does it, Martin? There are always cherished memories, and I believe as well a deep sense of responsibility. Tony and Diana are happy together?'

'So-so,' he said. 'I suppose she's happy because she never sees anything but her own point of view. And Tony's as happy as any tame pet could be on a chain. He drew me aside to ask after you. I told him just where you were and what was happening. He seemed deeply concerned. He said he'd try to get in touch with you somehow.'

Marlene was listening avidly. It was all just as she'd imagined it, and was now firmly convinced of the truth of it.

'But of course he wouldn't get in touch with me personally. He would feel embarrassed. He wouldn't want to. He might even be afraid that Diana would get to hear about it. No, he's obviously got in touch with the hospital authorities. He would write to them and ask them if there's anything he could do for me, and they must have told him about this operation which is essential. He would arrange to have the necessary money put at my disposal at once. The secretary told me it had all been done through a London bank. But of course I knew all the time that it's owing to Tony's generosity that I have any hope of recovery.' She raised herself on her elbow and then leaned forward intently. 'That's what I want you to do for me, Martin — I want you to get in touch with Tony and thank him for me. At once, so that if anything should happen to me, he would at least have known I was grateful and realised that all this time he'd never forgotten me; he was thinking of me. Will you do that for me at once, Martin? Will you promise to do that for me?'

Martin felt sick. He was thinking of Tony as he'd last seen him — completely pleased with himself and the luxury toys that Diana's newly gained wealth was able to give him. He had given one thought to Marlene over

238

a champagne cocktail the two of them had had together at a small bar. But it had only been a passing thought. And Tony owed so much more to Marlene than that. It was she who had given him a start in film publicity. But for her, he would still be a minor cog in an office wheel.

His anger rose. 'Why should you be so sure that Tony Frencham is responsible for your being able to have this operation?'

'But who else could it be? Adam, poor darling, hasn't got the money. He was worried sick about it until this offer came through. And you, Martin, my poor dear, would never be able to think in terms of so much money. You're in with a pretty scratchy little publicity organisation, aren't you? It may be solvent to-day, but I shouldn't bank on what is going to happen to it in the next few years.'

The slighting way she said it increased his sense of anger.

'Pretty good little outfit,' he said. 'We're getting more contacts all the time.'

'I'm sorry, I didn't mean to be beastly. But you will get in touch with Tony and thank him for me?'

'Why should I? If you want to know the truth, I think it is someone quite different.' He was still angry enough to say that.

'But who?' She looked bewildered. 'Who could it possibly be? Who else could have heard of my plight?'

'But how could Tony have heard of the situation?' he argued. 'The whole prospect of this operation has only blown up in a very short while. Only people here on the spot would know about it.'

'But who could possibly be rich enough? Who would care enough?'

'Someone might think it a sporting gesture to give you a chance to get better, Marlene.'

She raised herself on her elbow again. 'Who are you talking about, Martin?' she asked in desperate earnestness. 'Don't you see, I must know?'

'I don't see why you must know. I don't see how that could help you. I don't see that it matters anyhow.' He got to his feet. 'I've said too much already. But I couldn't for the life of me stand the thought of you wanting to thank Tony — that little rat! You've nothing to be grateful to him for. You never had, Marlene. He let you down badly. I can never forgive him for that. Though as I said, I have seen him occasionally, at times I have an almost irresistible impulse to punch his face in. And don't worry about the operation, Marlene. Whoever has put up the money — and your guess is as good as mine — is quite able to do so without feeling any pain.'

She didn't say anything. She was white-faced and very tired-looking suddenly. 'Good-bye, Martin. I think I've talked enough for this afternoon. And don't bother giving that message to Tony. I quite understand.'

He felt guilty and furious with himself. 'There's nothing to understand, Marlene. There're a great number of people in this world who would want you to get well again.'

'But there are not a great number of people who can afford for me to get well again,' she said quietly.

The day before she was to be operated upon, Marlene sent a message to Roxie at the Excelsior Palace asking her if she would come up and see her.

Roxie hired a car and was driven up to the hospital. She didn't tell Adam where she was going. She was alarmed at the summons and arrived at the hospital full of apprehension.

The weather had been cloudy for the past few days, but that afternoon there was bright vivid sunshine. Marlene was lying on the balcony, shaded from the bright sunshine by blinds. It was the first time that Roxie had seen her since that week-end at the Copenhowers'. The change shocked her. She had known that Marlene was desperately ill, but she hadn't visualised how gaunt and tired she would look with the skin stretched tightly across her bones. The rich auburn hair was lifeless, but the hazel eyes looked enormous.

Her eyes were regarding the younger girl seriously. She hadn't attempted to smile when Roxie was shown out on to the balcony. 'You were very pretty as a kid. You've grown into a lovely young girl, Miss Haldane,' she said finally.

Roxie blushed. 'That's nice of you to say so, Miss Farrar.'

'I was as lovely as you are once — and not so long ago either. Men were in love with me. Some men have remained in love with me despite my illness. That love and my ambition to reinstate myself in plays and films have been the only things which have kept me alive.'

Roxie moved uncomfortably in the chair. 'There must be a great number of people who remember you with love and great admiration.'

Marlene moved restlessly. 'The number of people doesn't count, does it — not ever? There's always one person who counts — the one person who means more to you than everyone else in the world.'

'Yes, I suppose that's true,' Roxie admitted.

'Do you consider yourself seriously engaged to Adam?' Marlene asked.

'Of course. Adam and I are definitely engaged,' Roxie answered quietly.

'You're in love with him, of course,' Marlene said with a faint sigh. 'You fell in love with him that week-end in Sussex, didn't you? I steered him off you, and I'm afraid I made you look rather much of a fool. I'm sorry. I'm not a very nice person really. I like to keep my men when I can — when I want to keep them. I don't say I'm always successful,' she paused, thinking of Tony, 'but in the main I have been successful. I've had Adam's undivided love for a number of years. I've had it until I made that silly suggestion to him the day after he arrived.'

Roxie felt her body go rigid suddenly. She wet very dry lips. 'What suggestion did you make to him, Miss Farrar?'

'Marlene — call me Marlene, and I'll call you Roxanne. We've rarely seen each other but I feel we're close enough in our personal interests to call each other by our first names. You were a precocious kid when I first met you, but I couldn't help liking you even then. Not, of course, that I would have allowed you to come between myself and

Adam. I was going through a bad time. I needed his undivided love and admiration. And ever since I've been ill I've needed it more and more. But when I thought I was at death's door, I was prepared to give it up for his sake. That's when I made the suggestion that he should get engaged to you, Roxanne.'

Roxie just stared at her. She felt a sickness all through her. She didn't know whether it was hatred or despair or anguished love. She could only repeat, '*You* made the suggestion he should get engaged to me?'

'I did — half as a joke, but not wholly as a joke, and I want to be frank with you, Roxanne. At the time I thought I was going to die, and I wanted Adam to be secure. But I really thought that Adam took it as a joke until the announcement of your engagement. It was so sudden — too sudden.'

Roxie pushed back her chair as she got to her feet. She couldn't bear to go on sitting there any longer. 'Yes, I suppose it was sudden. Too sudden, as you say. But you see, it was something I'd dreamt about for two long years. I'm afraid I've rather a one-track mind, and my one-track mind had been centred on Adam ever since that week-end party in Sussex. But why are you telling me this, Marlene? Do you think I am going to give up Adam? Do you think he would give me up? Don't you think he's in love with me?'

'I think he's bemused by you,' Marlene said. 'I don't know whether he's in love with you or not. I don't suppose he himself knows, if you should ask him frankly. But you're young and glamorous and very much in love with him. I haven't much chance against you, have I? It's a little unfair.'

'But when you get well you'll be the lovely Marlene Farrar all over again.'

'And if I should get well I have you to thank for it, haven't I, Roxanne?' She saw the girl start, and said with a wryly humorous quirk to her lips, 'Oh, don't think that anyone has given your little secret away — not intentionally anyhow. I just happened to put two and two together and guessed. You're giving me a fresh chance of life, aren't you? If I survive this operation as they confidently tell me I shall, and become my old self again, I shall have you to thank for it — you only. I shall have to be grateful to you for the rest of my life. In the circumstances it wouldn't be sporting of me to try and interfere between you and Adam. I've thought about it, Roxanne, and I don't think I want to be grateful to you for the rest of my life. It wouldn't even make my life worth living.'

'Please don't look upon it like that,' Roxie said quickly and earnestly. 'I wanted to help. I couldn't bear to think of you ill and this wonderful chance of an operation denied you. I couldn't take my happiness with Adam unless I could feel I had done something for you.'

'You mean you're paying me off?' Marlene said with a small dry cynical laugh.

Roxie's face was hot with embarrassment. She felt wretched and desperate. 'I don't feel like that about it at all. I wanted you to get well, not for any reason of mine but because I've always admired you so much, Marlene. But as for Adam,' her voice choked a little, 'I didn't know it was you who'd suggested the engagement. I think that perhaps the whole thing has been rather rushed. When you're better, Marlene, we'll see how both of us stand with him.'

'You mean when I have my looks and my career again I'll have a chance to fight you?' Marlene said through tight lips. 'I'll accept your generosity if you'll agree to that. If the operation is successful I swear I'll pay you back every cent. If it isn't, you're welcome to Adam. He needs someone to look after him.'

The nurse came in and said, 'I think you've been here long enough, Miss Haldane. Please forgive me, but the patient must be very calm for her operation in the morning.'

Roxie gathered together her bag and gloves. 'I quite understand.'

She went over to the bed. She stood looking down on the very sick woman. 'Good luck for to-morrow, Marlene — and I mean that.' She turned abruptly away, tears spilling out of her eyes.

She felt no longer a girl but a small old woman as she walked back along the corridor. Blindly she went through the hospital doors out to where the hired car was waiting for her. She sat stiff and straight on the back seat of the car all through the drive back to Vitry.

Marlene had suggested an engagement between herself and Adam. She'd said she had done so half jokingly, and that she believed he'd accepted it in that way. But had he? Hadn't she rather made an exhibition of herself forcing herself upon him at a time when it might have been disastrous to him financially to have turned her down flatly? 'I've behaved like a stupid little fool,' she told herself. 'How do I know that he won't fall in love with Marlene again once she's well? And I've got to know that. If I don't, everything else is sheer nonsense.'

She arrived back at the hotel and went up in the lift to her suite. She opened the door and stood inside, stunned. The tall portly figure of Lord Oxenham rose out of the deepest and most comfortable armchair.

'Daddy! Oh, Daddy!'

She flew across the room and flung herself into his outstretched arms. She laid her head against his ample chest and burst into sobs. 'Oh, Daddy!' she cried. 'Thank heaven for you! You're just in time to break off my engagement!'

22

To say that Lord Oxenham was stunned was putting it mildly.

'But . . . but what's all this, kiddy? Break off your engagement! I've just been talking it over with Angela. She's definitely in favour.'

'It's very sweet of Angela,' Roxie said, gulping and keeping back her tears with difficulty. 'But you'll be pleased to know, Daddy, my mind is quite made up. For the moment there will be no further talk of an engagement between myself and Adam.'

She said it so determinedly he was convinced.

'Not just a lover's tiff, eh?'

'I haven't seen Adam all day,' she said as calmly as she could. 'When did you arrive, Daddy?'

'I came by plane to Geneva and then motored across. I've been here an hour and a half. Angela has just left me to get ready for dinner.' He coughed, and added, 'I'd hoped we'd make it a foursome.'

She looked across at him and gasped audibly, 'What *on earth* has got into you, Daddy? But whatever it is you've got to forbid my engagement to Adam or I'll never forgive you.'

★ ★ ★

Angela Little was taking a bath. She had a shower cap pulled over her ears and was luxuriating in the lukewarm water. She was forty and then a year or two, but her figure was still that of a young girl. She was humming a little tune as she lay relaxed, soaping herself. It had been a hard afternoon but she had enjoyed it. She had never openly fought with Jim before, but now that it was over and she had managed to get her own way, she felt a surge of exhilaration such as she had never experienced before in her whole life. He had telephoned her from Geneva. He had said, 'I'm on my way and I'm on the warpath. We'll fix up all this nonsense to-night for good and all. Wait for me at the hotel.'

'I'm going for a swim, Jim,' she said. 'You'll probably find me down by the pool. You could join me down there for a dip. You will probably need it after the journey.'

'But you know I don't dip, Angela. I'm too corpulent, and conscious of the fact,' he shouted in exasperation.

'Oh, there are plenty of men more

corpulent than you dipping every afternoon, Jim. You won't be out of place at all. 'Bye — I'll see you down there when you arrive.'

She was terrified once she'd put down the receiver. Had she gone too far? She'd come into the firm as a very young girl and ever since Lord Oxenham had been her god. He had singled her out for promotion and friendship, and his friendship had meant more to her than the love of any of the other men willing to offer her marriage and a home. Lord Oxenham had seen that she was kept extraordinarily busy. Her quick promotion had carried rather spectacular rises in salary. Soon she could afford her own flat and her own personal maid. After his wife's death, he had come to rely upon her for many other things. Until Roxie had left boarding school she had been his official hostess whenever he wished to entertain in his own home.

She'd enjoyed these privileges. They'd meant more to her than anything else. She had persuaded herself she was quite content with them, that she would be content to go down through the years as Jim's devoted friend. She would ask or expect nothing more of him. In the humdrum seclusion of her London office nothing else had seemed possible, but in the few days she'd been in Vitry, something had got into her. It may have been the effect of Roxanne's romance, but it seemed to her that love and romance were in the air. She was suddenly furious with herself that she'd allowed herself to pass forty without fully realising how much she needed and wanted love and a secure home life such as every woman has a right to expect.

She knew she should wait for Jim in the hotel suite, but when he'd telephoned her from Geneva, something perverse had got into her. She didn't feel like his employee. She felt gay and independent. And even if she should have to resign, what of it? She had considerable money saved, and besides, her name was so important now in heart-throb correspondence that any newspaper syndicate would snap her up quickly.

But it was difficult for her to get into a one-piece swimsuit that afternoon, to put on a gaily-coloured beachwrap, to give Hazel Mint the afternoon off and make her way down to the swimming pool when she knew that Jim was expected at the hotel at any moment.

The sun was shining hotly, and since it had been dull for a couple of days everyone in the hotel seemed to have turned out to take a dip and enjoy tea around the swimming pool.

Angela saw several people she'd met. She nodded to them but preferred a table on her own. She waited a little while, smoking a cigarette, and then she decided it'd be better and more convincing if she went into the pool. She tucked her short brown hair under a white bathing helmet and let herself down from the surround into the pool.

She was only a very average swimmer but she enjoyed it. She hadn't had much time for swimming in the past years, or for any sport for that matter. She had played tennis quite well when she was a young girl, but she'd given that up too — her work for the Oxenham Group of newspapers hadn't permitted much time for relaxation.

She had swum the length of the pool twice when she suddenly heard a thunderous voice almost in her eardrum shout, 'Angela!' So great was her surprise she floundered and slid under the water. A moment later she emerged, spluttering and wiping the water out of her eyes.

'Angela!' the voice said again, and a large strong hand was stretched down to pull her up to the surround. Lord Oxenham was actually kneeling on the surround although he was wearing impeccable, well-pressed grey slacks and a white sports shirt with long sleeves.

By the time he had hauled her up on to the surround, one of the sleeves was dripping wet.

'Whatever's come over you, Angela?' he demanded. 'You're no more the age for this sort of aquatic sport than I am.'

'Nonsense,' she said sharply, 'I'm only forty-two and the majority of women swimming around here would be pleased if they could say they were forty-two and have anyone believe them. Besides, I don't think I look so bad in this swimsuit, do I, Jim?'

He looked at her, and then he looked away from her as though he were suddenly acutely embarrassed.

'Come on, Jim,' she teased lightly, amazed at herself, 'let me have the verdict.'

'You look very nice,' he said. 'Much better than the rest of them look, anyhow.' He added grumpily, 'Come on and sit down at the table. Don't you want to put on a beach-wrap or something?'

She crinkled her nose at him and laughed. 'Not yet, Jim. I want to dry off in the sun. But when we're having tea I'll put on a beach-wrap if you feel that way about it.' She looked at him and said, 'You need a spot of drying off yourself. I only went under because I was so surprised when you shouted at me, but I would have been all right. Why did you wet your sleeve pulling me up?'

'I don't know,' he said. 'It was stupid, wasn't it? But I had a sudden awful feeling that you might drown.'

'Dear Jim,' she murmured lazily. 'It was kind of you to be so concerned.'

'But of course I'd be concerned,' he barked out at her angrily. 'I didn't want to see you go down to the bottom of the pool in front of my very eyes. But what's all this swimming nonsense anyhow? And why didn't you meet me in the hotel suite when we could have talked sanely and sensibly?'

'But we've always met in offices or in your drawing-room or, on the very rare occasions when I've been abroad, in formal hotel rooms. I thought this might be a better atmosphere to talk in for a change. You're wedded to offices and formal rooms, aren't you? You never go anywhere where you can simply relax.'

'I . . . I don't understand you,' he spluttered. 'You're saying the most outrageous things.' He added with a touch of dignity, 'I feel at home anywhere, Angela.'

She laughed. She felt a little reckless and suddenly she was gaining self-confidence. 'But you don't feel at home here, do you, Jim? You've never allowed yourself to feel at home in surroundings like these, where you can have fun. This is a wonderful place; the air and the gaiety is a stimulant more potent than champagne.'

'It certainly seems to have gone to your head,' he said morosely. 'Now are you dried off sufficiently? Can we have tea?'

Jim Haldane felt a little happier at the tea table. It was years since he'd given himself time for a holiday in a place like this. It was all very unusual. It was especially unusual to be sitting opposite Angela Little in her one-piece swimsuit, which he had to admit suited her perfectly, with a light towelling wrap thrown over her shoulders.

'I like this place and its atmosphere,' she said as she poured the tea. 'I ought to have taken longer holidays and more often. I've stuck too close to the office desk. I've been letting myself get into a rut. You've got into a rut yourself, Jim.'

'I haven't done anything of the sort,' he said indignantly. 'It's only that I'm so busy I haven't had time for such diversions as this. What do they give you anyhow? They can only mean a lot of waste of time and senseless gossip.'

'But fun, Jim, and a lot of glorious sunshine.' She stretched out her arms as though loving it all suddenly.

Jim Haldane was a very handsome man,

and if it hadn't been for the slight paunch, he was extraordinarily young-looking for his age. More than a few women turned their heads to look at him. Some even recognised him from having seen his pictures in one or other of the Oxenham papers.

'Now let's get down to business,' he said. 'What have you done about this crazy engagement?'

She considered for a moment before she replied. 'I've talked to them — both of them. I've made enquiries as you wanted me to, Jim. I think Roxanne is very much in love with Adam, and I believe he's equally in love with her, though I think she was the prime mover in promoting the engagement.' She gave a faint smile and added, 'She's very much your daughter, Jim. She knows what she wants and she goes straight after it. I think Adam Douglas was rather swept off his feet, but I believe that he has or is falling in love with her quite seriously. I think they're well suited and would be very happy together. I think each supplies in a way what the other needs.'

'But the fellow's personally in debt up to his neck,' Lord Oxenham growled out.

'Does that make so much difference if they should be happy together for the rest of their lives? Does money really matter? Aren't other things more important?'

'You're talking like one of your own answers to correspondents,' Lord Oxenham snapped back.

'But I'm sincere in those, and I'm sincere now. I believe that Adam and Roxie are very well suited.'

'Well, I don't want to have any part of the fellow,' Lord Oxenham thundered. 'I've made enquiries, as I told you. And what does Roxie know about love at nineteen years of age?'

'What do you know about love at over fifty, Jim?' she countered quickly.

'What do you mean, I don't know about love?' he retorted indignantly. 'I was in love with my wife — Roxie's mother.'

'But she died a long time ago, and you've never thought of love since.'

'I haven't had time to think of it.'

She gave a small bitter laugh. 'That's the trouble with you, Jim, you never have time to think of the emotional issues of any situation — only the business ones. I've been a very useful business executive for you, and also a helper in your private affairs, but I've never been a woman to you, have I?'

A hot flush rose to his temples. He sat literally staring at her in dismay and consternation. 'But Angela, I don't know what you're talking about,' he stammered again.

'Don't you, Jim?' She looked across at him steadily. 'I think you do, but I don't think you want to face the issue, do you? Let's talk about Roxanne and the romance she's found here.'

They argued back and forth. He seemed surprised that Angela's attitude was so very definite.

'You seem a different person since you left England, Angela. Different in so many ways.' And he added finally, as though the words were forced from him, 'I never knew you'd look so different in a bathing suit, nor act so differently. Forgive me, my dear girl, but you really have a very fine figure.'

She laughed suddenly with sheer happiness. 'That's the nicest thing you've ever said to me, Jim.'

He looked more confused than ever. 'But Angela, my dear, I've often paid you compliments in the past. At least,' he amended ruefully, 'I hope I have. And if I haven't, I should have.' He grunted: 'You're an uncommonly nice-looking young woman.'

'Not so young any longer, Jim,' she said quietly.

'Young enough by my standards. You

know, Angela, all the time we've been talking, I keep thinking of you as the young girl who first came to work on the press.'

She reached out a hand across the tea table and impulsively touched one of his. 'That's nice of you, Jim. Please keep thinking of me in that way. And keep thinking of Roxie too, in that way — as a young girl to whom romance and the man of her heart are all-important. Give them a chance, please, Jim. I ask you this from the bottom of my heart.' Her voice was low-pitched, sweet and persuasive.

He flushed again. It wasn't easy for him to capitulate, but it may have been that some of the air of Vitry had infected him too. 'All right, if you say so, I'll give them a chance so long as they don't rush headlong into marriage.'

Angela felt a thrill of exhilaration. It made her almost dizzy. It was the first time she had beaten Jim in an argument. She had to admit she'd used very feminine methods. But maybe in the past she should have used those same methods more often. It might be that they would both have been a great deal happier if she had.

★ ★ ★

260

She got out of the bath, dressed slowly in an attractive midnight-blue gown and then went up in the elevator to Roxie's suite. She stood still in the doorway, staring from one to the other of them. Then she stormed angrily over to Lord Oxenham. 'What have you been doing to this poor child, Jim?' she demanded furiously. 'If you've gone back on our decision, I'll give in my notice immediately.'

'I'm as bewildered as you are, Angela,' he said.

Roxie said, with tears streaming down her cheeks, 'Don't blame Daddy, please Angela. I've asked him to withhold his consent. The engagement between Adam and myself was silly anyhow. After all, we scarcely know one another. We mightn't even like each other once we were living together. I'll — I'll tell him so to-night.'

23

She asked Adam to meet her after dinner. She said they'd walk in the garden.

They met in the lounge and walked silently into the moonlit grounds which surrounded the Excelsior Palace.

He drew her hand through his. 'You sounded a bit rattled over the telephone, darling. I gather your father, Lord Oxenham, has arrived.'

'Yes, Daddy's arrived, and I'm afraid he won't countenance our engagement.' She turned her head aside as she said it; her lips were trembling.

Adam's good-looking face whitened, but he answered evenly, 'I expected as much. I can't blame him, Roxanne. I always told you there was nothing to recommend me. Don't look so upset, darling. You must have expected it too, but it was wonderful for a time.' He turned suddenly and took her into his arms. 'Darling, say it was wonderful for a time.'

'It was wonderful, Adam.' She closed her eyes to crush the tears back.

'Some day I'll do something to make

myself worthy of you, but in the meantime I understand that your father doesn't want the engagement to go on. You want me to understand that, don't you?' he asked urgently, hoarsely.

She pressed her face against his chest as she managed to say, 'Yes, that is what I want you to understand, Adam.' She drew a tight breath and went on: 'We're not engaged any longer.'

'But that doesn't mean ... That doesn't mean that I don't love you, Roxanne,' he said, and kissed her lips very gently. 'But we rushed things rather, didn't we? I was in no position to ask you or any girl to marry me. It must be the atmosphere of this place. I'm sorry, my dear. I quite understand how your father feels. Perhaps I even agree with him.'

Suddenly she pushed him away from her with both hands. 'Adam, were you in love with me when we became engaged?'

He looked very wretched and very humble. 'I don't know, Roxanne, that I was so much in love with you then. The fact that you loved me was tremendously exciting and not a little bewildering. If you want to know the truth, I would never have asked you to marry me. How could I have possibly?'

'You wouldn't have asked me to marry

you — you're quite sure of that, Adam?'
she said very quietly.

'No, I shouldn't,' he said definitely. 'Not
that I hadn't begun to fall in love with you
— you were so different from anyone I've
ever known. It'd been so long since I'd been
in love in that way. But I know too well how
your father feels and how you have obviously
begun to feel about it all. My darling, please
don't be unhappy. Some day, maybe, things
may be different.'

'Oh, Adam!' She clung closer to him and
wept on his shoulder. 'You won't let me lose
you out of my life?'

'Not if you don't want to, my darling.
I'll be there in the background. Don't cry,
please, sweetheart. Somehow I knew this
had to come. I knew it was all too good
to last. Something you dream about but
which can't possibly be true. We've had
our dream, haven't we? Good-bye for the
present, my dearest.' He put his arms about
her and pressed his lips to hers.

But suddenly it was all too much for her.
She broke away from his embrace. She knew
she would weaken, her resolutions would go
to pieces. She would beg him to forget that
she'd ever said anything about breaking their
engagement. She would tell him the whole
truth, and that would be bitterly unfair to the

girl who was waiting to have this operation — the girl who loved him too.

'Good-bye, Adam.' She managed to control herself. 'You'll be seeing Marlene to-morrow before the operation, won't you?'

'Yes.' He sounded surprised.

'Just tell her our engagement is broken. Tell her it was all too rushed. Neither of us quite knew where we stood.'

'Why do you specially want me to tell her that?' He came towards her again.

'Oh, for no reason. For no special reason. I just want her to know. Good-bye, Adam.' She turned and ran back up the garden path. She was running from something, she didn't know what, for Adam wasn't pursuing her. But it was her own love she was trying to escape from, the love she still had for him — the desperate, despairing love.

In the lobby she ran straight into Gil Rogers.

'I've been looking for you,' he said. 'I hear your father's arrived. I've always wanted to meet Lord Oxenham. We have mutual friends in the States. But,' his voice thickened with sudden concern, 'what's the matter, Roxie. You're flushed and you've been crying. Oh, my dear, is there anything I can do? You know you've only to command me; I'd do anything for you on this earth.'

She hesitated and then said breathlessly: 'Then take me out on the lake, Gil, but don't talk. Please don't talk. Could you do that for me?'

He drew her hand through his arm and patted it possessively. 'I could do that. I could do that easily, my dear one,' he said.

He guided the launch slowly over the still dark surface of the lake which was pierced by moonbeams. He had drawn a chair up beside the steering wheel for her to sit quietly, and for a time he obeyed her instructions and didn't talk. But after a while he said, 'I'm trying to be a good boy, Roxie, and not ask any questions. But it's almost more than human nature can stand. You wouldn't care to tell me what happened to-night?'

'My engagement is off,' she said. 'It must have been one of the shortest engagements on record.' She gave a small mirthless laugh.

'You mean your father's forbidden it?'

She evaded. 'Daddy didn't come out here with the idea of giving his consent.'

He half turned and laid a hand on one of her arms. 'Oh, Roxie, darling, I'm glad. The engagement happened so quickly, it threw me completely out of my stride. It didn't give us other guys much of a chance, did it? But now you're free, and I hope you'll soon be heartwhole. I'll try my best to help you to be heartwhole. You're probably feeling like hell at the moment, but you'll get over that. You'll let me be your friend — your very good friend — through all this, won't you?'

'I — ' she caught her breath sharply, 'would feel awfully lonesome if you weren't my friend, Gil.'

'That's a deal.' His hand tightened on her arm for a moment, then returned to the steering wheel.

He was very solicitous of her that night and very understanding. He in no way forced his attentions upon her, and she was grateful. Finally she went to bed, but she didn't sleep. She could think of nothing but Adam, and the fact that from what Marlene had said, her money might have been the only inducement to his becoming engaged to her. She was sick at heart. She felt even physically sick.

The night hours wore on endlessly. Occasionally she would say his name into the night, whispering it — 'Adam. Adam.'

★ ★ ★

Adam was allowed to see Marlene for a few minutes before the operation. He came over to her bed and put his hand on her shoulder. 'Keep your pecker up, old girl. You're coming through this all right. Then you'll

267

have everything in this world before you.'

She looked steadily up at him, her amber eyes opened wide. 'Shall I have everything to look forward to, Adam?'

'There's no reason why you shouldn't have everything to look forward to.' But he looked away from her self-consciously. He wished he could say something more, but at the moment it wasn't in him to say anything more — emotionally he felt dead. Then he remembered that Roxanne had asked him to let Marlene know of their broken engagement.

'My engagement to Roxanne is off,' he said. He tried to grin humorously but it was a very poor attempt. 'I don't think Lord Oxenham thought a great deal of me as a prospective son-in-law.'

'Was it Lord Oxenham who broke the engagement?'

'I don't know. I suppose it was. But I — ' he hesitated, 'don't know.'

He had been feeling all through that terrible night that there was something more behind Roxanne's refusal to continue the engagement than that her father had refused his consent. He knew her well enough by now to know that she wasn't the type of girl who would submit easily to parental authority. She was a girl who took her future into her own hands, and it was to hell with the consequences.

He was puzzled and hurt, more hurt than he cared to admit. Perhaps even he hadn't realised what a great hold Roxie had had over his love and affections, even in such a short time. He felt lost and wretched.

'The girl's a good sport. Tell her that from me, if I shouldn't recover, will you, my dearest.'

'But you will recover, my dear.' And he added bitterly: 'I doubt if I shall ever see Roxanne again to talk to in private.'

'I think you will,' she said.

The nurse came into the room.

'I must go now,' Adam said. 'But I'll be waiting downstairs until they tell me the result of the operation.'

She touched his hand and clung to it for a moment. 'It will help me to know you are waiting downstairs.'

It was less than two hours but it seemed a lifetime while he waited, pacing the floor of the attractive airy hospital reception room with the big windows that gave such magnificent views of the surrounding mountains.

He went over in his mind his long past close association with Marlene. But always he thought of her with pity, mingled with a sense of deep and genuine friendship. He couldn't recapture even a spark of that passionate love he had once had for her. He remembered how he'd felt but with wonderment. It seemed as though a stranger had had those feelings. He was no longer the young man who'd been in love with Marlene in that crazy, reckless impetuous way. That young man seemed no longer a part of himself.

'Could I ever have felt that way about her?' he wondered, and acknowledged that he had felt that way but could feel it no longer. It depressed him. He felt small and ignoble. How deeply it hurts to admit a change in oneself.

When finally the sister in charge came back to tell him that the operation had been completely successful in every way, the gulp he gave was heartfelt joy and relief. He found he was shaking badly, as though it was he who'd had the shock of the operation.

'I'm glad. I can't tell you how glad. It's wonderful news, isn't it, Sister?'

'We are all very glad. It is a very joyful day for our hospital,' the sister said gently. 'Miss Farrar has become a general favourite with us all. Her unknown benefactor, whoever she or he is, should feel very glad to have been able to bring about this miracle. There seems no doubt now but that Miss Farrar will not only recover from the operation but be as well as she ever was.'

'We are all very deeply indebted to the man or woman who brought this miracle about,' Adam replied. 'I only wish I could have been responsible for it.'

'You have done as much as anyone could do for Miss Farrar with your help and encouragement,' the sister said gently. 'Certainly money was needed for the operation, but money isn't everything in bringing about a complete recovery. The surgeon has done his work — and done it splendidly; now it is up to us others to help make it a complete and truly miraculous recovery.'

Adam's face coloured under its tan. 'I understand what you mean, Sister. I shall certainly do my best.'

'I knew you would,' she said. 'You're a very fine man, Mr. Douglas.' And she smiled at him with sweet sincerity.

24

Roxie was relaxing in a chaise longue on her balcony when Martin was shown in. She asked him if he'd have some tea. But he said he didn't like tea anyhow; it was a cissy drink and the act of tea-drinking a complete waste of time. She smiled faintly, thinking how typical that remark was of him. In other circumstances she would have taken him up with spirit, but she felt too tired and heartsick today to have a fight with anyone.

He stood leaning against the railing, his back to the view, gazing down at her. Pale as she was this day and rather lifeless looking, she was still extraordinarily lovely.

'What's the matter?' he asked abruptly. 'You don't look as happy as you should be looking.'

She opened her violet-shaded eyes wider. 'Should I be looking happy?'

'I don't see why not. You've got a big handsome hero for a fiancé, and you've just brought about a miracle.'

'Adam and I are no longer engaged. Didn't you know?' She added, her voice tinged with bitterness: 'I should have thought you would be one of the first to know, Martin. You have an ear to the Vitry keyhole. This must be the first sensational piece of gossip which has escaped you in years.'

'I didn't know, though gosh darn it! — that I didn't shows that I'm slipping, doesn't it? What's happened? Lord Oxenham won't have Adam as the blue-eyed son-in-law? He's forbidden it?'

'Daddy didn't come out here to approve of Adam, certainly,' Roxie evaded.

'And you're feeling pretty much down in the dumps. You love that boy, don't you?'

'It was all such a rush,' Roxie evaded again. 'Both Adam and I were somehow pitchforked right into our romance. But what do you mean by saying I've achieved a miracle?'

'I've just come down from the Glink Memorial Hospital. That golden egg you laid that took the shape of a surgeon flying over from New York, has paid off. Marlene's all set to make a brilliant recovery.'

She sat up straight. 'She's going to get well! Oh, I'm glad — so very glad. That's quite wonderful news.' She added more slowly, 'But I don't really see why you think I'm in any way responsible.'

He grinned down at her, mocking her, challenging her. 'I should think it has a great deal to do with you, Miss Roxanne Haldane. It was through your generosity Marlene was able to have the operation, wasn't it? You waved the Midas wand and the great specialist flew over from New York, and Marlene has every chance of being a normal healthy girl again. God bless the poor kid. She deserved that break.'

'I told you I was glad, but why should you still think I had anything to do with it?' she insisted a little hoarsely.

'You needn't have had anything to do with it, of course. In fact it was in your own interest that you shouldn't. But I take off my hat to you, Roxie, that you did do it. You're a good sport — if that means anything these days. You see, I saw you up at the hospital that day, remember? Then almost immediately I heard that this miracle operation was to be performed. I'm not a complete dunderhead. Certainly it didn't need a genius to put two and two together, my dear.'

'You've absolutely no proof at all of what you're saying. It's absolutely ridiculous anyhow.' But she had flushed hotly and her hands were clasping and unclasping in her lap.

'Come off it,' he said. 'Fool the rest of the world, if you like, but don't try to fool an old cynic like me. You wanted to give her a chance, didn't you? And that's why I say you're a darned good sport. I can even guess at your motives, and like all of our motives they weren't completely altruistic. All the same, in my humble opinion, you come out on the winning side, Roxie. To-day you've as good as saved a life, which is saying something.'

She didn't answer that. Something moved in her throat. She looked out towards the lake.

Martin was looking down at her, his eyes worshipping her. 'Look here, Roxie, I hope I haven't made an awful ass of myself and put my big foot into it,' he said hoarsely. 'I feel that somewhere along the line I've spoken out of turn, and I may have done more damage than I intended.'

She looked back towards him sharply. 'Was it you who told Marlene I was financing the operation, Martin?'

His thin rather battered-looking face reddened. 'I . . . I didn't tell her, Roxie — I swear that, but she may have got a hint from something I said. You see, she got me in a bad moment. I was mad at the whole world and especially mad at the idea that she thought that conceited imbecile Tony Frencham should be the one who was making this miracle cure possible. But if you do think it was I who spilled the beans — if any beans were spilt — I'm darned sorry. Am I responsible for this present mess-up between you and Adam?'

'No, of course not. And please don't worry,' she said quickly.

'But I do worry!' He almost thundered it out at her. 'I worry because, darn it all, I've discovered your happiness means as much to me as my own does, Roxie. I've never felt this way before. I never thought I'd feel this way about any woman. But I want you to be happy, even though I may not be involved in that happiness. You're honest and direct, you're sweet and challenging. You're everything I've always hoped to find in a girl. Of course I've known all along there wasn't an earthly hope in this world for me. You've not only had Adam, but you've had Gil Rogers dogging your footsteps. They're both swell people — big heroes in their own special field. How could I hope for any crumb from your table? I only hope I'm not responsible for things having gone wrong for you.'

He was deeply agitated. She hadn't believed Martin Cheswick could be so deeply agitated and so absolutely sincere. 'Don't worry, Martin,' she said gently.

276

'Whatever has happened, none of it has been your fault. I like you as a friend. I want to keep you as a friend, if I may.' She stretched up her hand to him.

He took her hand and pressed it between both of his. 'I'm always your friend, Roxie — any place, any time. A cynically-minded battered old friend, but still a friend.'

'Thank you, Martin. I do appreciate that.'

It was a brief moment of communion between two people — the tall, lean, lanky, hard-bitten publicity agent and the young girl who still held on to all her ideals. But it was a sincere moment and there were times in the future when both would remember it.

Gil came in and interrupted them. 'Hello, there, Roxie! I've just been putting in some gruelling time with the team in overhauling the engine. I shouldn't admit this, but the engine was pretty sluggish when we had her out on a trial run at dawn to-day. Don't quote me, please.' He gave a little mocking bow towards Martin. 'As far as the Press and publicity are concerned everything is just superb, we're just raring to go.'

'I'm raring to be the hell out of *this* place,' Martin said, moodily and angrily. He didn't like the way Gil smiled at Roxie — in that easy confident way as though she were already his girl. He'd had his fill of Vitry and all its inhabitants. It was ridiculous to have fallen in love at his age and with all his past experience. But that was just what he had done.

'I've come to take you for a drive round the lake, Roxie,' Gil said. 'It's too good a day for you to sit here on the balcony surveying a scene you've seen at least a hundred times before. Come along, I've got the car downstairs.'

'I gather I'm not asked to go along with you,' Martin said unnecessarily.

Gil laughed and gave him a good-natured thump between the shoulder-blades. 'No, you're not. And make as much or as little out of that as you like, my good friend Martin Cheswick.'

Roxie and Gil didn't talk a great deal, and she liked him for not insisting upon conversation. She liked being with him but she would have hated him if he had tried to make love to her.

They drove round the lake, through the quaint little Swiss villages and the larger towns. As they turned to come home the sunset on the lake made it look like a red hot stone in a deep emerald setting.

'I wanted to take you out this afternoon because I'm afraid I won't be available to-morrow,' Gil said. 'I've promised to take

Liz a picnic right up into the mountains. It's been a date of some days' standing. I don't want to disappoint her.'

'I shouldn't want you to,' Roxie said quickly, and added hesitantly, 'Is Liz any happier?'

'I don't know.' He shook his head soberly as though trying to shake some apprehensions from him. 'She's been very gay this past day or so — almost unnaturally so.'

'Does she know my engagement to Adam is off?'

He grinned wryly. 'My dear girl, who doesn't know it? The whole of Vitry already knows it as far as I can gather.'

'I don't see how they can have possibly found out.'

'One never knows how these things are found out. But, well . . . ' He paused and gave a little quirk to his lips. 'She knows, as I said, and she isn't any too pleased about it. I don't think she expected it.'

Roxie sighed quietly and looked straight ahead at the roadway. 'It isn't what one expects, Gil; it's what one hopes for. But if two people don't hope for the same thing,' she sighed again, 'then there's tragedy.'

★ ★ ★

279

Liz looked very attractive, provocatively so, when Gil knocked on the door of her suite the next morning. The picnic hamper was already installed in the back of the car. She wore a blue linen dress that was low-cut, and a bright patterned scarf tied about her head. Her scarlet toe-nails, which matched her nails and lipstick, showed provocatively through the exciting low-heeled sandals she was wearing.

'My,' Gil gave a little low-drawn breath of admiration. 'You look all dressed up to kill, Liz. I've put on my oldest and dirtiest. I thought we were going to rough it up in the mountains.'

'Sure we're going up into the mountains. I just put this on because it was cool, Gil.'

He grinned and said, 'Women use that excuse too often. Don't think you can take in an old hand by such a remark as that, Liz.'

'Did you take the boat out this morning?' Liz asked.

'Sure did. She put up a fine performance too. If she does as well over the measured kilometre, I'm all set to take that little old trophy back to the States. Everything's in the car,' he added. 'Even to a bottle of white wine in an ice-pack. These hotels over here certainly know how to do things.'

'I'm glad we've got wine, Gil, but just

in case that doesn't stay us, I've a flask of bourbon in the good old handbag.'

The apprehension he'd had recently sprang to life again. Had Liz been drinking too much recently? Did that account for the terrifically, almost depressingly gay show she had been putting up? She was an unpredictable girl, as unpredictable as her father had been. He reminded himself soberly that her father had shot himself.

'Don't think we'll need the bourbon,' he said aloud. 'The high mountain air should give us all the necessary pep. They say it acts on you like champagne.'

'Whew! Shall I welcome it! Let's get going, Gil. It's hot and oppressive down here. I'm longing to get up into the heights.'

They zig-zagged their way through the mountains, climbing steeply all the time. It took most of the morning, but finally around noon they found themselves high on top of a pass. They parked the car off the road and carrying the picnic basket between them, they climbed still higher.

The view was magnificent and breath-taking; the snowclad peaks surrounding them seemed literally to pierce the blue sky. At some little distance from where they sat was what looked like a sheer drop right down into the deep purple valley below.

'This is like lunching in an eagle's nest,' Gil remarked.

She laughed in a brittle mirthless way. 'Isn't it? And how I wish I could take flight! How I wish I could spread my wings and fly off from that crag over there into space — into oblivion. Oh, Gil, wouldn't it be wonderful if one could just take off from that crag over there and drop gently, quietly, softly into oblivion?' There was a high-pitched, excited, almost hysterical note in her voice which alarmed him.

'You're talking like a silly hysterical female,' he said. 'You don't want to fly or even to drop into oblivion. You've got everything you want to live on this earth for, Liz.'

'Have I, Gil?' She laughed again, a trifle hysterically. 'That's a good one coming from you.'

He was beginning to get out of patience with her. 'I don't see why it shouldn't come from me, Liz. I've done my best to make you happy ever since you came into my employ, and long before that as a matter of fact.'

'Of course you have, Gil,' she said quickly, warmly. 'Let's get the glasses out of the picnic basket and have a drink on it.'

'Do you think either of us needs a drink, Liz?' he asked doubtfully.

'Of course we do. Don't be a spoilsport, Gil. You've brought me up here for this day, haven't you? This is *my* day — I want to enjoy myself.'

'All right, Liz, have it your own way.' He got two glasses out of the hamper.

She pulled a half-pint flask of bourbon out of her voluminous handbag and poured the drinks. He noticed her hand was slightly unsteady as she poured. Had she been drinking already? She raised her glass: 'Here's to us to-day, Gil. What does to-morrow matter?'

'It matters one heck of a lot. I'm going to take the world speed record back to the States.' His irritation with her was beginning to show again.

'You and your old speed records. But I wish that was all you thought of, Gil. I wouldn't have to be jealous of a speed record, would I. I wouldn't go through days and nights of torment over a miserly little speed record. Well, here's hoping you get it, anyhow, Gil.' She raised her glass, three-quarters full of neat bourbon, to her lips and drained it.

'Liz! For heaven's sake what do you think you're doing? Do you want to get yourself completely shikkered at this hour of the day?' he cried in exasperation at her.

'Why not? I want anything that will make me forget, Gil, forget that you don't love me. Forget that you're crazily in love with the Haldane girl and that she's just broken her engagement to Adam Douglas. Why did she do that, Gil?'

'I don't see that it had anything to do with me,' he said quietly.

But she merely laughed. 'You're lying, of course! It must have had everything to do with you. Why else would she break her engagement to Adam Douglas? A girl just doesn't break off her engagement for no reason. And everyone in Vitry knows that you are half insane about her. It's common gossip. What do you think it is like for me to have to listen to it? It seems that everyone goes out of their way to talk to me about it. I could scream — scream — scream!' Her voice rose hysterically again. 'Are you going to sit there and tell me you're not going to try to marry Roxie now that she's free?'

'Hold on to yourself, Liz,' he said quietly and dangerously. 'You're asking some pretty impertinent questions, aren't you?'

'Am I? But I think I have the right to know the answers. I've earned that right — earned it by long years of loving you, Gil. Why should I let you put me out of your life? I loved you long before you met

284

her — years before. I love you now. I love you so much that nothing makes sense. If you're going after her, if you're going to marry her, I don't want to live any longer. Are you going to marry her, Gil?'

'I'd marry her to-morrow, if she'd have me,' he said, and that dangerous note in his voice was more pronounced.

She sprang to her feet. 'You say that to *me*, Gil! You dare say that to me after all that's been between us?'

'What has been between us except friendship — what I hope was a deep and genuine friendship?' he countered.

'Friendship!' She flung her hand wildly in the air. 'I don't give a fig for friendship. What girl wants friendship? You have kissed me, Gil. You've told me I'm beautiful. Once, do you remember, one night you even told me you thought you loved me? You did love me then, Gil — I swear you did. You'd love me now, if you'd let yourself love me. It's funny, isn't it?' She was half laughing, half sobbing.

'Pull yourself together, Liz,' he said, speaking as sternly as he could. 'You don't know what you're saying. You can't make anyone love you by just telling them to or by threatening them.'

'I'm not threatening you, Gil,' she threw

back at him. 'I'd die for you — you know that, don't you? I'd die for you gladly. Maybe you'd be happier if I were dead. Maybe I'd be happier myself — much happier. I wouldn't have to continue with this agony of loving you then. No, I should be free, I should be happy. Why not? Why not?' She turned sharply on the word and started to run wildly in the direction of the topmost crag that gave a sheer drop down into the valley below.

'Liz! Come back here. Come back here at once!' he called after her. But she ran on purposefully, and after a second's hesitation, he started out in pursuit.

She had almost reached the top of the crag by now. He shouted with all his might, 'Liz! Liz! What do you think you're doing? Liz!'

She was standing right on the peak. She turned back once to wave and call, 'Good-bye, Gil!'

'Liz! Listen!' he shouted, panting, clambering up the rocks after her. But she shook her head and seemed prepared to leap right down into the abyss.

He caught her just one instant before she jumped. Caught her and held her struggling, quivering body. She fought him wildly and they swayed there together on top of the crag with that awful abyss yawning beneath them.

She was hitting him with her fists, kicking him with her feet. One kick dislodged his foothold and he started to slip; he felt himself slipping. He clutched madly at something, anything. He heard Liz give a long shrill scream. He felt himself falling, and then a feeling as though a ton of stones had descended on top of him. He flung up an arm as though to ward the avalanche of rock off his face. Just after that he lost consciousness.

He regained consciousness to find two strange men bending over him. 'He's coming round now,' he heard one of them say. 'We'll get him down to a hospital.'

At first he couldn't think what had happened, and then he remembered. He had been struggling with Liz on that craggy summit. Somehow he had slipped and fallen. But if he had fallen into that deep cavern, how could he be alive? And the rocks — he remembered those now; he remembered the rocks falling on top of him before he lost consciousness. And Liz! Where was she. Was she all right?

He heard the sound of someone sobbing and turning his head slowly, he saw Liz crouched nearby, weeping unrestrainedly. 'It's all right, Liz,' he heard himself say through stiff lips. 'It seems I'm alive.'

'Darn lucky you are alive,' one of the men said. 'You fell over that steep incline, but luckily you were caught on a rocky ledge, and a shower of rocks descended on top of you. The young lady ran down on to the road and stopped our car. You were lucky in that, too. Not many tourists pass this way in the mountains.'

The man was obviously English, but his companion, dressed in a chauffeur's uniform, looked Swiss.

'Yes, you're lucky to be alive,' the man went on. 'My chauffeur will drive you down to the hospital where they can set your arm. I'll drive the young lady back to Vitry in your car.'

'My arm?' Gil said. 'What's wrong with my arm?'

'Broken, old chap,' the man said almost nonchalantly. 'But that's nothing. As I said, you're darned lucky that you're alive.'

'But it can't be broken! The day after to-morrow's the race,' Gil heard himself say. 'I've got to race *Virginia II* against Adam Douglas's *Scotsman III*.'

The English tourist, a nice, clean-shaven middle-aged man laughed. 'You'll be lucky if you see any race from your hospital bed,' was his only rejoinder.

'But don't be insane — there won't be

a race if I'm not there!' Gil felt himself shouting.

'Then there won't be a race. Come along. Can you walk? If you can't we'll support you. But be careful of that arm of yours.'

They helped him to his feet. Gil was wretchedly conscious that his right arm was hanging useless by his side.

Liz came forward tentatively. 'Oh, Gil! Oh, Gil!'

Gil sensed the curious glances of the others. 'It serves us right for skylarking on these crags,' he said to her as cheerfully as he was able. 'Cheer up, Liz, we're all right — both of us are all right. Get that into your head, my dear — both of us are all right.'

25

The disappointment which hit Vitry like a hard punch in the stomach when it found that the race between Adam and Gil for the Vitry Cup had been cancelled was somewhat softened when it learned later that Adam would try alone for a new world record over the measured kilometre. The flags purchased for the occasion were unfurled from all the chief buildings. There was no mad scramble to leave the town, which the hotel managers and the authorities had at first feared.

There was great sympathy on all sides for Gil, though not a little speculation as to how the accident could possibly have happened. Roxie was curious and apprehensive. She had wanted Adam to win the race but not through an accident to Gil. She knew how much having to withdraw would hurt him, and she knew Adam well enough to know that he too wouldn't be pleased about it. He had wanted to defeat Gil, but not to have him forced to withdraw.

Adam and she ran into each other for a few moments in the hotel lobby that same evening. They stood still and looked at each other and it seemed that both were holding their breath. There was a long awkward pause.

'Hello, Roxanne. How are you?' he asked at last, very gently.

'I'm fine, fine,' she said. 'Isn't this dreadful about Gil?'

He nodded briefly. 'It's all that. I was looking forward to the race. Looking forward to beating him, of course. But I wouldn't have had it happen this way for anything. It takes all the fun out of it; except that I'm determined on making a new world record.'

'You will, Adam. Oh, yes, you will!' she said earnestly.

'Are you very upset about Gil, Roxanne?' he asked in another pause.

'Naturally I am. We are very good friends.'

'You've been seeing a good deal of him?'

She looked away from him. 'Yes, I told you he's a very good friend of mine.'

'I was wondering if it was he and not your father who was the cause of our busted romance,' he said, and his voice grated.

'No.' She shook her head violently. 'Don't think that, Adam. Gil had nothing to do with it.'

He shrugged. 'Then I am stumped. I ran into your father earlier to-day. He was out with Angela Little; they were both very friendly. Well, whatever made you decide to break the engagement good luck to you, Roxanne. Always good luck to you.'

'Good luck to you too, Adam, for to-morrow — all the good luck in the world.'

His lips turned a little sour. 'You can afford to wish me good luck now that Gil is out of it, can't you, my dear?' And he turned and walked away from her.

They didn't keep Gil long in hospital. They set his arm, put it in a sling and let him go back to his suite in the hotel the following morning. But no sooner was he back than he wished he had remained in hospital. Reporters flocked in upon him all eager for news as to how the accident had occurred.

Gil knew exactly what he was going to say. He had rehearsed it with Liz. He had sent for her to come up to his suite directly he had returned.

She came in trepidation. Her attractive gamine features were still swollen with tears. She had lost her pert buoyancy. She looked listless and defeated. 'What can I say, Gil? It's useless saying I'm sorry, isn't it?' she said in a low flat voice.

'It's always useless saying you're sorry. So cheer up. I don't expect it of you,

Liz.' His voice was firm and reassuring. 'I've had moods of depression myself. You don't know what's eating you, do you? You keep on nagging at your own nerves until you do something damn stupid. You nearly did something damn stupid yesterday. Thank heavens you didn't.'

She shook her head in a quick fierce gesture. 'It doesn't matter about me, Gil. It never did matter very much. I suppose I've a great deal of father's temperament — unbalanced and unable to take it. He wasn't a good sport and he didn't help anyone by bumping himself off. I wasn't a good sport, either, yesterday and the awful part of it, I might have killed you, Gil, not my foolish stupid self.'

'This humility pose doesn't suit you, Liz,' Gil said. 'And it's not going to help either of us during the next few days when we'll need all our wits. It was an accident, of course, and we've got to make it sound a very feasible accident. I'll do my bit, but you've got to help too. You've got to snap out of all this morbidity nonsense, be more than a brave little woman — become the perfect secretary again. If you're here constantly, busily taking letters down or typing them to my dictation, people can't suspect other than that it was a genuine accident.'

293

'You're willing to let me keep on working for you, Gil?' she asked very humbly.

'I'm not only willing — you're darned well going to keep on working for me,' he said decisively. 'I couldn't lose you completely out of my life, Liz. That's one thing I realised when I was wrestling with you on top of that wretched crag. I could have slapped you and hit you for being such a little fool, but I didn't want you to die. You've got to help me put a good front on all that happened. You weren't yourself yesterday. You'd worked yourself up into a pretty silly state, and you'd had one or two drinks to help that state on, hadn't you? No more states of mind, Liz. No more shots of bourbon to help what you think is a depression. If anyone needs the bourbon it's me — stuck here like a fool when I ought to be out on the lake giving a final try-out to *Virginia II.*'

'That's all my fault, Gil,' she said passionately. 'Do you hate me very much for that?'

'No, I don't,' he said quietly. 'To tell you the truth, Liz, I am not all that sorry. I want the world speed record for the States and I'll get it — don't worry about that. Not this week perhaps, but this week six months — or even next year. But just at the moment

294

I'm quite resigned that Douglas should have a try for it. I hope he gets it, even if it's only for the pleasure of wresting it off him again. He's a fine sportsman and he's been having more than a few knocks lately.'

'Do you mean in racing or because of his broken engagement?' she asked.

'Maybe I mean both,' he said. 'But we won't talk about the engagement, Liz. Seems to me we've talked enough about that already.'

'I'm . . . I'm sorry, Gil.'

'Smile,' he told her, 'and remember this is what happened: We were picnicking up in the mountains, larking about. You dared me to chase you. You started to run and I set off after you, but just as I reached you, I slipped. I fell some little distance and the rocks fell on top of me. Luckily I fell on to a ledge. You stopped an English business executive and his chauffeur who were touring through the Swiss Alps. They rendered first aid, drove my car back and put me into hospital. I'm eternally grateful to them. I wish they'd stopped behind in Vitry so that I could thank them properly.'

'And that's all,' she said. She made a half attempt at a smile, but it didn't succeed.

'That's all,' he said emphatically. 'That's all I'm going to remember, anyhow, Liz.

That's all I want you to remember.'

He came towards her and put his good arm about her shoulders. 'That's all you've got to remember too, Liz. Promise me?'

'You mean that's all you want me to remember; Gil?'

'That's all you're going to remember — and that's orders, my girl.' He squeezed her shoulders tightly for a moment, drawing her closer to him.

She covered her face with her hands and started to weep, but this time she wept quietly, without any trace of hysteria.

'Good girl,' he said approvingly. 'Now go and wash and powder your face and become again the perfect little secretary.'

When Roxie came in to see Gil, Liz put the letters she'd been typing together and said, 'I'll go down now and take a bath, Gil. You've driven me hard enough for one day with all this rush of correspondence. You are an old slave-driver.' She spoke jokingly as though nothing in the world was amiss between them, and Gil approved her act.

'Go and have your beauty bath. I'll see you later, Liz. I've got to show myself in public some time or other. We may as well meet in the lounge for cocktails.'

She glanced at him sharply, but all she said was, 'That will be fine, Gil. Thanks a

296

lot. I'll be off now. So long, Gil! So long, Miss Haldane!'

Roxie said, 'I went to the hospital but you'd already been discharged. I can't tell you how sorry I am about it, Gil.'

He smiled at her and said, 'Sit down and have a cigarette and relax. You're holding yourself like a tense little marionette figure. Are you really as sorry as all that, Roxie? The race is off for the moment, but Adam can still make a new world record without any interference from *Virginia II.*'

'But Adam would welcome the competition,' she said quickly. 'Has he been to see you yet, Gil?'

'Not yet, but he sent a note of condolence to the hospital. I'm all on his side now, Roxie. I want him to beat Giovanni's world record. That team of his, amateurs mostly, have done a thundering good job on *Scotsman III.* I'm sorry I'm not in the race, but in a way I'm glad. Adam deserves this chance; he's worked and fought so hard for it against what seemed to me incredible odds. Speedboat racing has always been much easier for me — there's been the backing of my father's fortune; I haven't had to care so much about sponsors. And can't they get into your hair? They can be the very devil! You'll let me take you to the speed test, Roxie? I may be able to explain a thing or two to you that you wouldn't otherwise understand.'

She laughed. 'You'll have to do an awful lot of explaining for I don't understand anything about it at all.'

'I'll do my humble best,' he said, grinning. 'At least I know something about the subject.' His voice altered slightly as he added, 'I won't even mind your praying for Adam's success — at least I'll try not to mind. Or rather I'll try not to show that I mind.'

He stepped closer to her and said, 'You wouldn't let the wounded hero kiss you, would you, my sweetheart?'

She turned rather sharply away. 'Not now, Gil, please.'

'I see I mustn't presume on my slight mishap,' he said lightly, but there was an undercurrent of bitterness in his voice.

26

It was perfect weather for the speed test. Under the brilliant blue sky the lake was smooth sapphire blue and sparkling. Vitry had literally closed up shop and downed tools for the time of the test. Everyone was either crowded on the stands as near as possible to the measured kilometre or crowding around the lakeside.

Roxie was in a stand with Gil, who merited a considerable amount of attention from all the spectators. Gil was well aware of this. He smiled at everyone and when he received condolences he waved them aside with a cheerful 'It will be my turn next time.'

Roxie would have admired him immensely if all her thoughts hadn't been concentrated on Adam, what he was doing, how he was feeling. *Scotsman III* was still in her trap at the end of the pier, though the patrol launches were in position along the course with the official observers and timekeepers on board, waiting with their synchronised chronographs by the marking posts at either end of the measured distance. The marking posts were white iron embedded in concrete, and halfway along the course was a launch with doctors and other officials on board.

Roxie dreaded what was commonly referred to as the water barrier, a barrier which has the same effect on speedboats as the sound barrier has on aircraft — a barrier that had broken up more boats than any other obstacle, but an elusive barrier which seems to vary with each individual craft. It could occur at almost any speed. She thought of all the racing drivers who had been killed, and shuddered. Giovanni, the Italian, had been killed in his last effort to break his own record.

She could scarcely listen to what Gil was saying to her. She could scarcely smile at her father and Angela who were standing at some little distance from them, chatting away gaily together and for all the world like two young people out on a spree. If she stopped thinking of Adam at all, Roxie thought of her father, marvelling at the change in him. He was much more kindly and understanding. He only shouted once in a great while, and instead of tearing back to his offices at the Oxenham Press, as he usually did when he went away on even the shortest holiday, he seemed disposed to linger at Vitry-sur-Lac.

It was Roxie who was longing to be back in London. She couldn't bear being so near

Adam and being separated from him. She couldn't bear the thought of Marlene growing stronger and lovelier each day, waiting as soon as she was completely cured to claim Adam as her right.

There was an excited cry when finally *Scotsman III* slid into the water. She looked like a giant sea mammal, her body constructed of light alloy metal which glinted in the sunlight. Adam was just visible in the small cockpit with the two floats on either side like curling wings. One saw a glimpse of his light fawn overall suit, windproofed, with the life-jacket built in and the harness, not unlike that of a fighter pilot's, as well as the crash helmet.

Scotsman III moved slowly out of the trap, was clear of the pier and was seen heading nicely on to the start of the course. Gil was talking excitedly, describing to Roxie all that Adam would be doing and thinking and feeling just as though he himself were in the cockpit of that boat. He pointed out to her the buoy marking the beginning of the measured distance. Even at this distance she could hear the fast acceleration of the engine as the revs mounted.

At last Adam had hit the measured course. *Scotsman III* fled down it like a streak of lightning. She didn't dare look; she was too afraid. She envisioned every sort of accident and hid her face against Gil's shoulder. She held her breath and the watching crowd seemed to be holding their breaths too. So little time, and yet a time which seemed to stretch to eternity. She heard the shouts and that same instant Gil was shaking her: 'You little goose,' he said, 'Why did you hide your face? It was the most thrilling sight. Gosh! I enjoyed every moment of it. My guess is that *Scotsman III* has made a new world record. But of course we'll have to wait for the timekeepers' official report. I'll go down and see if I can find out anything. Want to come?' He added diffidently, awkwardly, 'You'd want to be one of the first to congratulate Adam, if he's brought it off, wouldn't you?'

'No, I — I won't go, Gil. I'll go over and join Daddy and Angela. But you go down and let us know what you can find out. Let us know quickly. Oh, please let us know quickly.' Her voice cracked and broke.

He looked down at her and a shadow passed over his thin good-looking face. 'That's how you feel, is it, Roxie?' he said gently. He made a rather hopeless shrug and said, 'All right, I'll go down. I'll be back as soon as I've found out anything and let you know.'

But the crowd was so dense Gil found it difficult getting back to them. Roxie could see that there was great movement and excitement on the lake. *Scotsman III* was being towed back gently to the pier. She could make out Adam's form now in the peculiar driving uniform. He had been taken off on to the pier in a launch. She saw people wringing his hand, slapping him between the shoulder-blades, and then the shout went up — a shout of triumph which seemed to fill the whole little town of Vitry. It was so deafening she couldn't hear what was being said, but finally her father's shout penetrated: 'Your ex-boy-friend has set up a new world record, kiddy. Gosh, that was a grand show! I take back everything I said against Adam Douglas; he's certainly a great racer and a fine sportsman. You'll be wanting to go down and congratulate him, eh, kiddy?'

She shook her head fiercely, 'No. No, I don't, Daddy. I want to leave here as soon as possible. Please, please can't we get away in a car at once?'

'You mean you want to miss all the celebration parties to-night?' her father said, astounded.

'Yes. I couldn't bear to be in on one, Daddy. I'll go straight back and pack. Please help me.' She looked at Angela, her violet-shaded eyes wide with appeal. 'You will understand. You will help me, Angela?'

'Very well, if you want it that way, Roxie,' Angela said gently. 'Perhaps, Jim, it would be best if we pushed straight on into Geneva to-night.'

Roxie flung her arms about her. 'Oh, thank you, Angela. Thank you for understanding.'

'But aren't you happy about Douglas's new record?' her father asked her wonderingly.

'Happy?' She caught her breath and then she started to sob violently. 'I'm so happy about it. Happy for his sake. I think I'm going off my nut. It's what he's dreamt about, what I've dreamt about for him!'

'Then I can't see why the devil you don't want to congratulate him in person,' her father rumbled.

'I can't, Daddy — you don't understand!'

Angela took charge of her very efficiently. 'Come along, Roxie darling, we'll go back to the hotel and I'll help you pack.'

Gil didn't like the idea of their immediate departure at all. 'I hoped we were going to make whoopee to-night. You're letting me down badly, Roxie,' he accused her.

'I'm sorry, Gil. I mean that too.'

'If you were really sorry you wouldn't go.'

'I want to go. Maybe I'll see you back in London, Gil.'

He took both her hands and pressed them in his. 'It's not maybe — it's a must, Roxie. I'll be there directly I can arrange for the transport of *Virginia II* back to the States. That's where I hope to race Adam in six months' time and take the record from him.'

She returned the pressure of his hands warmly; she was so fond of him. 'I'll be looking for you in London, Gil.'

'A farewell kiss,' he suggested, trying to speak lightly.

She hesitated, then she raised her lips to his, 'A farewell kiss, Gil.'

He pressed her lips to his for a long moment. 'A farewell kiss,' he repeated, and added with a new conviction and belligerence, 'but a farewell only for the moment, Roxie.'

It was several hours before Adam arrived at the Excelsior Palace Hotel. It had been a gruelling few hours, taking almost as much out of him as the test had. But everything had gone unbelievably smoothly. Once he was on shore reporters thronged about him, eager for every little detail he could give them. There was to be a Press Conference up at the Casino with the official observers and timekeepers, and that was where the official announcement would be made first. But everyone knew already that Adam had a new world record.

McPherson was one of the first to wring Adam's hand, the tears showing in his eyes. 'Congratulations! Congratulations, Adam. That was certainly a grand run.'

The rest of the team came up to grip his hand. They carried him shoulder-high into the shed where he would change his clothes before going on to the Press Conference. Adam thanked all members of the team personally as he shook their hands. Presently, surrounded by a surging crowd, they were all walking up to the Casino.

Adam knew that once the official record had been announced there would be speeches and congratulations. How long would it last? He'd had an urgent wish to find Roxanne from the moment he'd first known he'd broken the record. She had been foremost in his thoughts; he wanted to tell her. He wanted her to know that her faith in him had been justified even though they were no longer engaged. He wanted her to know that she could be proud of him, that there was no need for her to be ashamed of having loved him. He didn't for the life of him know what had happened to their engagement; the breaking of it had shocked him. But now he was far more hurt than shocked. Some day he might get to the root of what had happened. And now, having won this record, he thought he was in a stronger position to find that out.

He hurried through the Press Conference as best he could, but when finally he reached the Excelsior Palace Hotel it was only to learn that Roxanne, with her father Lord Oxenham and Angela Little and her secretary Hazel Mint, had already left.

He turned his eyes up to the mountains. He supposed he had better go up to the Glink Memorial Hospital and give Marlene the news personally. She would be pleased, bless her heart, and it might all help towards a quick recovery.

But he didn't want to go up to the mountains that day; he didn't want to see Marlene. He was the hero of the hour, everyone was swarming round him, pressing congratulations upon him, but he didn't want any part of any of them. The little town of Vitry was completely empty now Roxanne had gone.

27

Some six months or so later Roxanne was alone in her father's big Georgian house in Cadogan Square. It was a cold afternoon in late winter. Spring was just around the corner but as yet it had been very nervous in its approach. For the past month Roxanne had intermittently been travelling round the countryside collecting notes, interviewing leading women in all different spheres of life, compressing the interviews into a weekly column called 'Women In The News.' It was interesting work and she enjoyed it. It helped to keep her mind off other things.

This afternoon she had stayed at home to write up the latest column which would appear the following Sunday. Her father had given her a suite of rooms for her own use in the vast house. She was sitting in her mother's boudoir, which had been turned into a study, when the maid came in to tell her that a lady was below and wanting to see her. 'Such an important lady, too, Miss Haldane.' The little maid was almost breathless with excitement. 'The actress and movie star, Miss Marlene Farrar!'

Roxie rose to her feet. 'Oh, Miss Marlene Farrar.' She said more slowly, 'Bring her up here, will you, please.'

'My, doesn't she look lovely!' the little maid enthused. 'More beautiful than I've ever seen her look on the screen or on TV. And it's her opening night to-night in the West End. Did you know, Miss Haldane? She's going to appear in that new play, 'Woman in Searchlight.' Cook let me slip down into the West End at lunch time and already they're queuing up for the opening, Miss Haldane, right along one street and down the side of the next.'

Roxanne smiled faintly. 'Don't chatter so much, Enid. Bring Miss Farrar up here.'

This was the first time Roxanne had met Marlene since that afternoon in the Glink Memorial Hospital — it seemed a lifetime ago.

The little maid hadn't been wrong. Marlene looked ravishing. She could wear the mink coat belted at the waist. She was still thin enough for that. Her rich auburn hair showed under the jewelled velvet beret-styled cap. Her lovely heart-shaped face had filled out since Roxanne had seen it last. She looked younger even than she had looked at that week-end at the Copenhowers' place in Sussex nearly three years ago.

Roxie's heart missed a beat when she saw her and dropped deep into her breast. How could she, a raw young girl, have ever hoped to compete with Marlene? Lovely, seductive, so very feminine, Marlene, who had already made a victorious comeback, who had her own programme each week on TV, was lined up for several films, and tonight was to make her debut in the West End as the heroine of the play which had been highly successful in the United States.

Roxie spoke impulsively and sincerely: 'You look lovely, Marlene. More beautiful than you've ever looked.'

'Thank you, Roxanne,' Marlene made a little half bow. 'I won't pretend I'm not pleased with the compliment, especially coming from you. You don't bear me any ill-will?'

'No,' Roxie answered slowly. 'Why should I? And how could I? We were both in love with the same man — it wasn't either of our faults.'

'But you made me a very sporting gesture in giving me back my health, Roxanne. You were a good sport all through, especially when you broke your engagement to Adam. I admit it helped me considerably at the time. I don't know if I would have pulled through if you hadn't done so. But . . . ' She made a vague little gesture, and let the sentence lie there.

'You're happy, Marlene?' Roxie asked quietly. She had almost said, 'Are you happy with Adam?' but couldn't bring herself to say it.

'Oh, yes, I'm happy. Success means a great deal to me, and I've been very successful since I came back from Switzerland. But I'm keeping my fingers crossed that this play will be a huge success to-night and I will make a hit of it. If so, dream-worlds are open to me — a chance of playing the same part in Broadway, new film contracts, possibly Hollywood.'

'I do hope it's a success,' Roxie said, with deep sincerity. Marlene smiled across at her. 'You're a nice kid, Roxanne. You're a good sport even now . . . Do you still think of Adam?'

Roxie swung sharply away from her. 'Is there any need for you to ask me that question, Marlene?'

'No. I just wondered. Have you heard from him?'

Roxie shook back her silver-blonde hair. 'No, I haven't heard.'

'But you've heard of him, of course?'

Roxie gave a small mirthless laugh. 'Who

doesn't hear of Adam Douglas these days? Since he's won the world speed record he's been constantly in the limelight — newspaper articles, magazine articles, interviewed on TV and on the radio. I understand he's installed a new turbo-jet engine in *Scotsman III* and is taking the boat over to the States.'

'All that is true,' Marlene said. 'But I'm surprised you haven't seen him, Roxanne.'

Roxie said nothing, but once again she turned half away from her visitor.

Marlene came closer to her. 'I did something pretty mean to you once, didn't I? But I was a very sick girl and it seemed I had very little to live for except the love of one man. But now my outlook has changed. I don't say I'm a better woman, but I'm certainly broader minded and I have so many new interests which absorb most of my time. I told you something once which I shouldn't have repeated, didn't I? I told you that I suggested to Adam that he become engaged to you because of your money. I told you at the same time that Adam was furious at the very idea. I should have told you why I made the suggestion. Even then I was jealous of you. I knew he'd been attracted to you at the Copenhowers' week-end party, and I was afraid that since you'd arrived at Vitry-sur-Lac he would really fall in love

312

with you. I thought that by making the suggestion I did, it would keep him off you permanently. And it probably would have but for circumstances that neither you nor he were responsible for. The Press pushed you into that engagement.'

'No.' Roxie shook her head fiercely. 'No one pushed me, Marlene. I went after Adam. I wanted to marry him. I wanted that more than anything else in this world.'

'Then why haven't you seen him since you've been back?'

'I don't know,' she said slowly. 'I promised I'd give you the chance to recover. And then afterwards maybe I thought that Adam would come after me. I've been waiting. He hasn't come.'

'Adam had a deep-rooted pride as well as a great sense of loyalty. While I was recovering I think he thought that I needed his loyalty. Besides, you're still the very rich Miss Roxanne Haldane, and your father is Lord Oxenham, virtually a millionaire. Adam has had one success and is going out after further successes. But he can never hope to make a fortune that will match yours. All the money he can make will go into building better and faster speedboats. But you wouldn't have it other than that, would you?'

'No,' Roxie said, 'I wouldn't have it otherwise.'

'He called to see you at the hotel after the Press Conference, but you'd already left Vitry. He told me that a few days ago,' Marlene said.

'I — I see,' Roxie murmured. Her lips trembled; a quick rush of colour flooded her cheeks, her heart lifted in her breast.

'I want you to do something for me as a personal favour,' Marlene went on rather quickly. 'I want you to take this envelope and make use of the contents.'

Roxie drew away from her slightly. 'You don't need to repay me . . . '

'Oh, this isn't a cheque,' Marlene broke in. 'But I am saving up the money to pay you back, Roxanne. I'm keeping what I can save in a separate account, but this isn't a cheque. Will you promise me on your word of honour you'll make use of it?'

'I promise to do my best,' Roxie said in bewilderment. 'But I don't understand.'

'If you promise me to do this, it may mean a great deal to the happiness of several people,' Marlene said quietly. She picked up her bag and gloves off the chair. 'I'm going now. I don't think we have any more to say to each other. When you broke your engagement to Adam to give me a chance,

314

you acted as a very good sport. I needed the belief in Adam's love and loyalty at that time more than anything. I am grateful and I'm trying in my own humble way to be a good sport too. Good-bye, Roxanne. And please take note of the contents of that letter.'

Roxie saw her out. The interview had left her feeling bewildered and mystified. Marlene had looked ravishingly beautiful but she seemed gentler in manner than Roxie had remembered her. Had Adam done that to her — Adam's love? But what was all this talk about her, Marlene, being a good sport? As yet she hadn't opened the envelope. She was still holding it clutched in her hand. She opened it now slowly.

It contained nothing but a theatre ticket with 'Complimentary' stamped across it. She saw that it was a stall ticket for to-night, the opening night of Marlene Farrar in 'Woman In Searchlight.' That was nice of Marlene. She probably knew the tickets for the opening night were very hard to come by, even if you had influence with the Press. Her father and Angela were going and had asked her if she would like to go along with them. But she had declined. It was the night of Marlene's triumph and Adam would be there. She had wanted to go and yet dreaded going. But now that Marlene had made such a point

315

of it, she had practically made her promise, she supposed that she had better go. But it was curious that Marlene should have been so insistent. Was this merely her way of thanking her for having put up the finance for the operation?

She had thought Gil was over in Paris and was surprised when he was shown into her sitting-room a little later. He had been back to the States twice since that time in Vitry. His arm was better and he was racing again. He had recently won several cups in the States and was now planning an all-out attempt on Adam's record with a newly-built boat which he called *Virginia III*.

She was pleased to see him again. She was always pleased to see Gil after one of his absences. Their friendship had deepened in the months, but when he talked to her of love she wouldn't listen to him.

Sometimes he took her refusal to be made love to light-heartedly. They would both end by laughing and go out and have dinner together and be friends. But at other times he got really mad at her and would storm out of the house. They had had one such session a few days ago just before he flew over to Paris. But always after one of these rows he came back contrite, a good friend again. And Roxanne always accepted his apologies. She was too fond of him not to do so.

He stood before her now, handsome, very slim, looking at her quizzically and a little sadly. 'I made a fool of myself again the other night, didn't I, Roxie? I can carry on for a time in this good palsy-walsy fashion that you insist upon, and then something gets into my hair. I wish I wasn't a fool, loving you as much as I do. I wish you were a little more of a fool, my dear, and could love me in return.'

She was embarrassed and unhappy when he was in one of these moods. 'I like you so much, Gil — so very much,' she said with a desperate sincerity. 'If only you were happy to leave it like that.'

'Happy.' He caught up the word. 'I am not happy, Roxie. Some of the time I'm happy when I'm with you, but most of the time I'm with you I'm always striving to get something from you which I know you're unable to give me. I have a maddening feeling of frustration. Aren't you human, Roxie darling? Can't you love me a little at least?'

'I love you more than a little, but . . .'

'Don't say as a friend,' he broke in with a grin. 'I'm sick of the very word friendship. It means a great deal sometimes but at other times it can mean very little. And especially when someone wants more than friendship it can be damnably maddening. Roxie, my darling.' He came over and tried to take her in his arms. But she slipped away and went over and stood by the mantelshelf, looking down into the hot logs in the fireplace.

'It's no use, Gil. I don't love you in that way,' she said quietly. 'And you'd never be happy in the sort of love I could give you. You're much too virile and masculine — much too demanding. You'd want a woman's wholehearted love or eventually you'd throw her aside. It isn't in your nature always to give love and have so little in return. You couldn't stand it — I don't think anyone could stand it. There's always a time when patience gives out and then sometimes some tragedy happens. You need a woman to love you wholly, Gil. It's in your nature to demand such a love.'

He said in a low voice, 'Sometimes you get that sort of love but you don't always appreciate it.'

She turned to him and said very earnestly, 'I know whom you're thinking of, Gil. I think if you could only get me out of your system once and for all, you'd find you really loved Liz. She's your type, a daredevil with a likable, extravagant nature, always ready to toss her bonnet over the windmill, not caring for the consequences. She was brought up the same as you were, Gil, with the same friends and with the same traditions. She understands you better than anyone. I think she'd die for you.'

He half turned away from her and thrust his hands into his pockets. 'You don't need to tell me about Liz. I know what a good friend she is to me. We've been through quite a lot together but she still stands ace-high in my regard. You say she understands me. I think I understand her too — what makes her tick, if you know what I mean. I'd do anything for Liz.' There was an odd, rather cracked note in his voice.

'Then keep away from me, Gil. It's only going to hurt both of us eventually. I think you might find, underneath everything, you've been half in love with her for a very long while. You've known her so well — almost too well for that madly delirious *in love* feeling. But you haven't seen her for some time, have you? Once you go back to the States you may find you've changed and that you see her differently.'

'I don't know that I shall see her. She wrote to me the other day she was thinking of getting married.' He sounded so angry that she laughed.

'And you don't like that at all, Gil?'

'Why should I want to lose a perfectly good secretary?'

'Then if you don't want to lose a perfectly good secretary you'd better get back to the States pretty fast, Gil,' she said and grinned at him knowledgeably.

It took him some time to return the grin, but finally he managed it, though only in a half-hearted manner. 'I'm intending to fly back to the States anyhow, within a few days. I want to supervise the final stages of the building of *Virginia III*. The team have been looking after her for me, but they're anxious for me to get back. No, you're right, Roxie, I wouldn't want to lose Liz as my secretary.'

'Then I'd fly back to-morrow, if you can, not wait a few days.'

'I might at that,' he said moodily. 'But you'll come out with me to-night for dinner, Roxie?'

She shook her head. She had switched on the candelabra and the lamplight glinted upon the blonde fairness of her hair. 'I'm sorry, I can't to-night, Gil. I have a very important prior engagement.'

'But if I'm to fly back to-morrow you must come out to dinner with me to-night,' he insisted.

She shook her head. 'No, it's a promise I've given. I must keep this date with someone to-night.'

'You won't tell me who it is?'

She merely laughed and said, 'You'd be surprised if you knew to whom I've given my promise.'

He might have tried to wear down her resistance but Lord Oxenham came up the stairs shouting, 'Roxie! Roxie! Where are you?' He sounded in a great state of excitement, and excitement always made him shout louder than usual.

She flung open the door and called, 'I'm here, Daddy!'

She welcomed his interruption. The things she and Gil had said to each other hadn't been said easily, but they had been said sincerely. And as always after you have been utterly sincere, an embarrassment follows.

Lord Oxenham went straight up to Roxie and took her into his arms. 'Kiddy, Kiddy, you're the first to congratulate me. Something wonderful has happened. I've finally persuaded Angela to be my wife.'

She laughed and hugged him back, congratulating him, thinking, 'But Daddy darling, why didn't you ask her that ten years ago? I've a notion you could have persuaded her then.' She linked her arm through his. 'Looks as though I'll be flat-hunting, doesn't it, Daddy?'

Lord Oxenham looked shocked. 'My home will always be your home, my darling child.'

She shook her head. 'I'm too modern for that sort of nonsense, Daddy. This will be Angela's and your home, and I'll have a little snuggery of my own somewhere.'

'You could always come over to the States on an extended visit,' Gil said eagerly, after he in his turn had finished congratulating Lord Oxenham.

She smiled at him. 'I may come. But it's all too new for me to decide just what I'm going to do at the moment.' She glanced at her watch. 'I'm going to the show too to-night, Daddy. I'll have to get dressed. You should be starting getting dressed too. You're taking Angela, aren't you?'

'You bet I'm taking Angela.' His voice rose belligerently.

Roxie laughed at him. She threw her arms about him again and kissed him on the cheek. 'You ought to have shouted it out in that aggressive manner ten years ago, Daddy. But I'm glad for you both. I can't tell you how glad.'

28

On a first night the tense excitement runs right through the theatre from the star and the other players to the meanest odd-job man backstage. Those members of the audience who had waited in the queue for the pit or the gallery had long since caught the excitement. The dress circle and orchestra stalls captured it the moment they arrived in the theatre. Until the bell for the final curtain the whole auditorium, backstage and front is alive with chatter and eager nervous laughter. 'Well, what do you think Marlene Farrar will be like in this? This is her first big West End part, isn't it? They say she's going to be terrific. She is divine on TV. I always watch her programme.'

Martin Cheswick was sitting in his ill-fitting dinner suit towards the end of the fifth row. He had been on several publicity assignments since Vitry, the last one a job organising a super charity carnival on the Riviera. He was bronzed and felt as fit as he was ever able to feel. He didn't set much store by fitness anyhow. He usually felt pretty mouldy in the mornings, but it never stopped him being on the job. He looked cynically about the theatre and thought how few had actually paid for their seats, barring the pit and the gallery, and of the few who had paid, how many had paid to come and see the play or were paying to be seen?

A few rows back he saw Tony Frencham and his wife Diana, and he wondered who had persuaded whom to come, or whether neither of them cared much any longer. It was just the thing to do — to be seen at an important first night opening. Tony, he thought, looked pale and flabby, not at all the up-and-coming young publicist with whom Marlene had once fallen so desperately in love. Was he still working or had he become a mere playboy since Diana had inherited her money?

She was beautifully gowned in green chiffon and taffeta, and every dark hair of her head was immaculately in place. But Martin thought there was a new hardness about her face. Tony wasn't going to find it easy living on Diana's money.

His glance strayed from them to where he saw Lord Oxenham in tails, sitting with Angela Little. There was a rumour — and Martin heard all the rumours — that they were about to be married. 'Good luck to both of them,' he thought. 'If he can only pitch his voice on a lower key he'll probably make an ideal husband. Anyhow, isn't this what she's been waiting for? But why the heck should a sane, sensible woman have waited for so long? Emotionally she must be as goofy as those love letters she answers. She ought to have taken the millionaire press Baron by the ears and made him propose years ago. She's probably a romantic, that's why she's such a success at her job. I bet you she's sincere in that. You can't fake sincerity. If you do, the public gets on to it at once.'

From them his gaze wandered back to the stalls, towards where at the end of the third row he saw Adam.

Adam looked as handsome as ever, though his sun-tan had faded. It might have been the theatre lights but Martin thought he looked older than when he had seen him last. Despite the fact that he held the world speed record and business and society were crowding in upon him, he didn't look happy.

Martin saw there was a vacant seat beside him. He thought he'd step over and have a few words with Adam when the third bell rang. The lights were dimmed but as his eyes grew accustomed to the darkness he saw the slight figure of a girl slip into the vacant seat beside Adam just before the curtain rose.

The taxi bringing Roxie had been held up

in a traffic jam. She had been afraid she wouldn't make it in time. She had delayed her departure until almost the last moment; for some reason she was afraid. But she had dressed with much more care than she had dressed for some months now, putting on her newest and prettiest evening gown of golden taffeta with a gold lace bodice and innumerable tucks, a present from her father, 'Just to cheer you up, kiddy,' he had said. It bore the label of one of the most famous dress houses in the world.

Except when Gil was in town, she had been going out very little socially, and this was the first time she had worn the dress. She railed at herself while she put it on. 'It's just another first night. It was decent of Marlene to get a seat for me. But why the secrecy? Why couldn't she just have handed me the ticket in the normal way? Why go through all that act of trying to make me solemnly promise to come?' But the act had heightened her excitement, and with the excitement had come tension.

She had refused the offer to drive to the theatre with her father and Angela in the chauffeur-driven limousine. She knew her father always liked to arrive early and despite his own importance he took a great joy in watching all the other celebrities piling into the theatre. 'There's old so-and-so. Wonder if he's solvent by now? By gad, there's Lord What-not, and what a pretty bit of goods he's got with him to-night!' he would exclaim excitedly and loudly.

Angela enjoyed the game of spotting celebrities with him. She enjoyed most things with Jim. She knew she indulged him shockingly but she was determined after they were married to go on indulging him. There was so much of the boy in him it was impossible for her to resist playing his little games with him. And she was rewarded by his great tenderness and consideration of her.

Panic descended on Roxie again directly she had paid off the taxi and entered the foyer. 'Don't be a fool,' she told herself angrily. 'There's nothing to this. Just a seat to the show.' But she noticed to her annoyance that her hand was trembling as she gave up her ticket.

The theatre was heated but she felt very cold. She pulled her white ermine cape more closely about her shoulders as the usherette showed her to her seat.

She slipped down into the seat just as the lights were lowered. She wasn't immediately aware that Adam was sitting beside her, not for the first few moments. She slipped off her fur jacket, opened her programme, although it was too dark to read it. She half turned and then she saw Adam, and almost instantaneously he saw her.

'Roxanne!' His voice was low-pitched and hoarse.

'Adam.' She breathed the name and again she started to tremble.

'I didn't expect . . . I didn't have any idea . . . ' He was stammering, and Adam didn't usually stammer, his speech was easy and forthright.

'I didn't know either, Adam,' she murmured. 'Marlene brought me the ticket this afternoon.'

'She gave me my ticket this morning, but she was very cagey about whom I was to sit with. It was,' he drew a deep breath, 'jolly decent of her.'

'It was very decent of her,' Roxie agreed.

'She must have known how very much I wanted to meet you again, Roxanne.' His voice was still low-pitched, but hoarser.

She swallowed something in her throat. 'I've wanted to meet you too, Adam. I — I couldn't understand why you didn't come round to see me.'

'But I thought when you left Vitry as you did without even waiting to congratulate me, it was all off between us for ever, and that you wanted it that way.'

'I was trying to do what I thought best.' Her voice was unsteady. 'But it was stupid now that I look back upon it. I suppose I was all mixed up and muddled. I wasn't thinking straight.'

'It was an awful blow to me when I found you'd gone,' he said in a very low voice. 'Nothing seemed to matter — not even that I'd just beaten the world speedboat record. No triumph is worthwhile if you have no one to share it with,' he added in a much lower voice.

'But you had lots of people, Adam — all your team; Marlene . . . '

Someone said, 'Shush!' They hadn't been aware that the curtain had already risen.

Roxie found it extremely difficult, almost impossible to concentrate on the opening of the play. Her whole being felt suspended, waiting until the next interval. So much had been said, and yet not enough — not nearly enough.

The house rang with applause at Marlene's entrance. She was very lovely in a clinging white gown. The part of the famous woman illicitly in love with the world's searchlights upon her was eminently suited to her, and she carried it through superbly.

Roxie watched Adam anxiously. Had he re-fallen in love with Marlene? She was so beautiful on the stage; there was so much glamour surrounding her, she couldn't believe that he hadn't. But she couldn't tell from his face what he was feeling. She hated to admit it but she watched Adam's face more than she watched the stage. As the curtain fell to loud applause after the first act, 'Good old Marlene! I think she really put it across,' he said excitedly.

'Good old Marlene?' It wasn't exactly the expression you'd expect from a lover. Roxie's heart lifted.

They talked briefly of the play and Marlene's obvious success in it. Then they reverted to the much more enthralling subject — themselves.

'I knew you'd broken our engagement, but I still didn't expect you to run out on me like that.' Suddenly he accused her harshly.

'I've tried to explain.' She wrung her hands together in her lap. 'The moment I left Vitry, I wished I hadn't gone. But I couldn't turn back. But I wanted and hoped, as I said, that you'd come and see me in London.'

'If you'd sent me even one word of congratulation, I would have come like a shot,' he said.

'Oh, Adam, you don't know how glad I was, how much your success meant to me.

I thought of it all day and every night,' her voice broke again.

'And yet you couldn't write one little line?'

The people on either side of them had gone out into the foyer, the stalls were three-quarters empty, but neither Adam nor Roxie made an attempt to move.

'I'm not trying to excuse myself, but when you feel something very deeply it's often difficult to write,' she said humbly. 'I thought of dozens of letters to write to you, Adam, but I could never get them down on paper.'

'I suppose I should have come to you, but even though I'm holding my own now and have paid off my debts and have as many sponsors as I need for the new boat I'm going to build, I still didn't feel I had the right to chase you, if you didn't want me,' his voice was almost savage.

'Oh, Adam.' Tears came into her eyes and trickled slowly down her cheeks. 'How very stupid of you.'

His hand reached out and closed over hers suddenly, pressing it almost hurtingly tight. 'Was that stupid of me, Roxanne? Should I have come? Would you have welcomed me?'

'Oh, my darling, you don't know how I

would have welcomed you!' The endearment slipped out. She blushed furiously afterwards.

His pressure on her hand tightened. 'You meant that, didn't you, Roxanne, when you said 'my darling'?' And then when she didn't reply he shook her hand sharply, half angrily, 'Answer me, please.'

'Yes, I meant it, Adam,' she whispered.

'Oh, my dearest . . . Curse all these people. Let's get away somewhere by ourselves.'

'But Marlene has asked us here as her special guests. She would want you to stay and join in her final triumph, Adam.'

'Yes, she might.'

'You're . . . you're not in love with her, Adam?' Her voice was tentative and very small.

He almost threw her hand out of his. 'How can you ask that, Roxanne? Would I be talking to you as I have been if I were in love with Marlene? I did all I could to help her get her health and strength back, and I think in a small way I helped to renew her confidence in herself. But we're friends — just friends. Ever since I first met you in Vitry we've been no more than just friends. I think she's your friend too, Roxanne. For some reason she seems to have a great affection for you. And it was she who arranged our meeting to-night, obviously.'

'That was very sporting of her,' Roxie said. She added with a faint smile. 'She and I have both tried to be good sports, but I don't see that it's made either of us any the happier.'

'Roxanne, my darling.' He took her hand again, holding it this time more gently. 'Can't we be happy now that we've met again, now that we seem to understand each other?'

'Hello, you two! I've been looking for you all through the bar lounge and the foyer. I wanted to buy you both a drink. But I guess it's too late now. The curtain is about to go up again.'

They had both started when he spoke to them, as though his presence and his words were pulling them out of a dream-world of their own.

'Martin, how nice to see you again!' Roxie exclaimed with pleasure.

'You old so-and-so! Fancy running into you here,' Adam said with equal affection.

'Then let's forgather in the bar at the next interval,' Martin suggested. 'I haven't seen you both in ages. I want to hear all your news.'

'We want to hear your news too, Martin.' But she used the 'we' unconsciously. She flushed again after she'd said it.

Martin's cynically amused eyes looked

from one to the other of them. He hadn't missed that 'we.' 'There's nothing much about me,' he said. 'The outfit I'm with is gathering strength each day. In no time I think we'll find ourselves the international publicity outfit in Europe. But I'll tell you all about it over a grog in the bar later on. I'd best be getting back to my seat. The curtain's about to go up again.'

They crowded with the others into Marlene's dressing-room after the final curtain. The enthusiasm for the show and especially for Marlene was overwhelming. She had had to take at least ten curtain calls. Her speech at the end had been so simple and charming, thanking the producer and the cast. But she'd also said she wished to thank some very good friends of hers who had stood with her through her long illness. 'Some of these are out in front,' she said, 'and I wish to say from the bottom of my heart that I hope they'll be as happy as their efforts on my behalf have made me happy to-night.'

Roxie thought she'd looked directly down into the stalls where Adam and she were sitting. She seemed to smile at both of them.

Marlene's dressing-room was full of flowers and friends and well-wishers. There was no doubt that it had been a triumphant first night, and the whisper was current that the Press reports would be favourable too. She kissed Adam on both cheeks and said, 'How much I have to thank you for.' She squeezed Roxie's hand and smiled. 'My dear, have I repaid the debt or haven't I?' And then other friends swept them away from her side and they were left alone in a corner.

'Supper together?' he suggested.

She smiled up at him. 'But of course.'

He laughed happily. 'That's the girl I first fell in love with — no pretended excuses, no subterfuge. We'll have a wonderful night out, just you and I. It's something I've been dreaming about and planning for ever since Vitry.'

She laughed tremulously, happily. 'Then what are we waiting for?'

'Nothing. Let's get going,' he said.

They walked round the corner to a night club he knew that was just starting to be fashionable. They ordered supper, which wasn't necessary; they were too much wrapped up in themselves to eat. They didn't even dance at first, they just sat there, hands clasped under the table, gazing at one another as though they'd never seen each other in this whole world before.

Then for an encore the band changed its

tune and started playing a song that was still high up on the hit parade.

Roxie gave a little gasp as she remembered it and all its associations:

'Love is not an endless romance
Or a crown to be worn for a day,
Nor a kiss that may follow a dance;
Love is a gambler's game.'

She laughed and said, 'Let's dance this, Adam. I was mad on this tune in Vitry. I don't think but for it I would have had the courage to practically force our engagement upon you.'

'You didn't,' he interjected determinedly. 'It was the other way about.'

'Oh, I did,' she insisted. 'I took advantage of that little publicity paragraph.'

'Do you think I didn't want to become engaged to you too?' he demanded hoarsely. 'Do you think I hadn't then already fallen in love with you?'

'Oh, thank you, Adam — thank you, my darling.'

They started to dance. The crooner was singing:

'Love's like a star in the sky
To shine in your heart or to die,

336

The feeling is great but it's one you
    can't tame;
Love is a gambler's game.'

'That's the verse I like best,' she said.

As they danced smoothly by the orchestra,
she smiled at the crooner: 'Please sing that
verse again.'

Adam's arms tightened about her. He was
holding her so tightly she could scarcely
breathe. 'When are you going to marry me,
Roxanne, my dear — my very, very dear?
Don't keep me waiting too long.'

She laughed with throbbing happiness
underlying her laughter. 'Don't hold me
so tight, Adam; I want to speak and I have
quite a lot to say to you. You'll be shocked,
but I'm not going to keep you waiting at all.
We'll be married as soon as you can get a
special licence. You see, I've got to clear
out of my home. Daddy is marrying Angela
almost at once, and I'm not going to be a
spoil-sport and live with them. I was going
flat-hunting to-morrow. Will you come with
me, my darling? We'll choose the ideal flat
for both of us.'

'Of course. Oh, Roxanne!' He smiled down
at her. 'My head is just dizzy with happiness.
Lord only knows what my feet are doing.'

'I don't know how mine are behaving

either,' she laughed tremulously. 'I feel like a jelly. Oh, Adam, the dance is over! Everyone is staring at us. We've just kept on dancing.'

'Let them stare harder, my precious darling,' he said. He bent and kissed her lips tenderly and urgently there on the dance floor.

THE END

McLEAN AT THE GOLDEN OWL
George Goodchild

Inspector McLean has resigned from Scotland Yard's CID and has opened an office in Wimpole Street. With the help of his able assistant, Tiny, he solves many crimes, including those of kidnapping, murder and poisoning.

KATE WEATHERBY
Anne Goring

Derbyshire, 1849: The Hunter family are the arrogant, powerful masters of Clough Grange. Their feuds are sparked by a generation of guilt, despair and ill-fortune. But their passions are awakened by the arrival of nineteen-year-old Kate Weatherby.

A VENETIAN RECKONING
Donna Leon

When the body of a prominent inter-national lawyer is found in the carriage of an intercity train, Commissario Guido Brunetti begins to dig deeper into the secret lives of the once great and good.

A TASTE FOR DEATH
Peter O'Donnell

Modesty Blaise and Willie Garvin take on impossible odds in the shape of Simon Delicata, the man with a taste for death, and Swordmaster, Wenczel, in a terrifying duel. Finally, in the Sahara desert, the intrepid pair must summon every killing skill to survive.

SEVEN DAYS FROM MIDNIGHT
Rona Randall

In the Comet Theatre, London, seven people have good reason for wanting beautiful Maxine Culver out of the way. Each one has reason to fear her blackmail. But whose shadow is it that lurks in the wings, waiting to silence her once and for all?

QUEEN OF THE ELEPHANTS
Mark Shand

Mark Shand knows about the ways of elephants, but he is no match for the tiny Parbati Barua, the daughter of India's greatest expert on the Asian elephant, the late Prince of Gauripur, who taught her everything. Shand sought out Parbati to take part in a film about the plight of the wild herds today in north-east India.

THE DARKENING LEAF
Caroline Stickland

On storm-tossed Chesil Bank in 1847, the young lovers, Philobeth and Frederick, prevent wreckers mutilating the apparent corpse of a young woman. Discovering she is still alive, Frederick takes her to his grandmother's home. But the rescue is to have violent and far-reaching effects . . .

A WOMAN'S TOUCH
Emma Stirling

When Fenn went to stay on her uncle's farm in Africa, the lovely Helena Starr seemed to resent her — especially when Dr Jason Kemp agreed to Fenn helping in his bush hospital. Though it seemed Jason saw Fenn as little more than a child, her feelings for him were those of a woman.

A DEAD GIVEAWAY
Various Authors

This book offers the perfect opportunity to sample the skills of five of the finest writers of crime fiction — Clare Curzon, Gillian Linscott, Peter Lovesey, Dorothy Simpson and Margaret Yorke.

DOUBLE INDEMNITY — MURDER FOR INSURANCE
Jad Adams

This is a collection of true cases of murderers who insured their victims then killed them — or attempted to. Each tense, compelling account tells a story of cold-blooded plotting and elaborate deception.

THE PEARLS OF COROMANDEL
By Keron Bhattacharya

John Sugden, an ambitious young Oxford graduate, joins the Indian Civil Service in the early 1920s and goes to uphold the British Raj. But he falls in love with a young Hindu girl and finds his loyalties tragically divided.

WHITE HARVEST
Louis Charbonneau

Kathy McNeely, a marine biologist, sets out for Alaska to carry out important research. But when she stumbles upon an illegal ivory poaching operation that is threatening the world's walrus population, she soon realises that she will have to survive more than the harsh elements . . .

TO THE GARDEN ALONE
Eve Ebbett
Widow Frances Morley's short, happy marriage was childless, and in a succession of borders she attempts to build a substitute relationship for the husband and family she does not have. Over all hovers the shadow of the man who terrorized her childhood.

CONTRASTS
Rowan Edwards
Julia had her life beautifully planned — she was building a thriving pottery business as well as sharing her home with her friend Pippa, and having fun owning a goat. But the goat's problems brought the new local vet, Sebastian Trent, into their lives.

MY OLD MAN AND THE SEA
David and Daniel Hays
Some fathers and sons go fishing together. David and Daniel Hays decided to sail a tiny boat seventeen thousand miles to the bottom of the world and back. Together, they weave a story of travel, adventure, and difficult, sometimes terrifying, sailing.

1	28	121	192	250	308	351	386	417
2	35	123	193	251	310	352	388	418
3	39	124	195	252	311	353	390	419
4	40	132	198	257	312	354	392	421
5	41	136	203	258	317	355	393	422
6	42	148	208	259	318	357	394	423
7	54	149	212	262	320	359	395	425
8	55	154	216	263	321	360	396	427
9	61	157	220	268	322	361	397	428
10	64	160	224	269	324	362	399	429
11	68	164	227	272	326	363	400	431
12	69	166	232	273	327	364	401	432
13	78	167	233	274	328	366	403	433
14	79	168	234	279	331	368	404	435
15	80	169	237	285	333	372	405	436
16	84	172	238	288	336	373	406	437
17	85	174	240	295	337	374	407	438
18	90	175	241	297	338	375	408	440
19	99	180	242	299	341	376	409	441
20	100	182	243	301	344	377	410	442
21	101	183	244	303	347	379	411	443
23	110	188	247	304	348	380	413	444
24	119	189	249	307	350	383	416	445

447	470	493	516	539	562	585	608
448	471	494	517	540	563	586	609
449	472	495	518	541	564	587	610
450	473	496	519	542	565	588	611
451	474	497	520	543	566	589	612
452	475	498	521	544	567	590	613
453	476	499	522	545	568	591	614
454	477	500	523	546	569	592	615
455	478	501	524	547	570	593	616
456	479	502	525	548	571	594	617
457	480	503	526	549	572	595	618
458	481	504	527	550	573	596	619
459	482	505	528	551	574	597	620
460	483	506	529	552	575	598	621
461	484	507	530	553	576	599	622
462	485	508	531	554	577	600	623
463	486	509	532	555	578	601	624
464	487	510	533	556	579	602	625
465	488	511	534	557	580	603	626
466	489	512	535	558	581	604	627
467	490	513	536	559	582	605	628
468	491	514	537	560	583	606	629
469	492	515	538	561	584	607	630